Murder in Highgate

A Redmond and Haze Mystery

Book 9

By Irina Shapiro

Copyright

Table of Contents

Prologue

The morning was misty and cool, the leaves dripping tears of dew onto the weathered gravestones. The cemetery was quiet. Even the birds dared not sing as the cortege moved down the lane, led by a hearse pulled by two magnificent horses decked out in ebony plumes. The black hearse was decorated with a gold and silver pattern that gave it a regal appearance. The mahogany casket, visible through the glass windows, was smothered in white lilies that gave off a sickening miasma that wafted over the mourners. Two undertakers, their top hats trailing black ribbons, walked behind the hearse, closely followed by the weeping widow and her son, Neville Ashford, the new viscount.

The late viscount's daughters walked behind their mother and brother, followed by at least forty mourners, the few ladies present swathed in yards of black satin and lace, the men wearing their most somber suits, black armbands encircling their sleeves. A train of carriages stood by the main gates, ready to collect the mourners after the entombment, the drivers waiting silently out of respect for the departed instead of chatting and dicing as they normally would to pass the time.

The procession finally reached the family vault. It was fairly new, compared to some of the other vaults in Highgate, and extravagantly large, built of pink granite with two columns flanking the entrance and a peaked roof, reminiscent of a Greek temple. Only three generations of Ashfords were buried in the vault thus far. Those who had come before rested in Scotland, where they had been born and wished to be buried, the family tombs there less ostentatious and more in keeping with the landscape.

The hearse came to a dignified stop before the vault, and Gregory Fielding, the director of Fielding and Sons Undertakers, broke away from the procession and went to unlock the doors. The funeral service had been performed at St. Paul's Cathedral, no less, so now the only thing left was to transfer the coffin to the vault and wait for the mourners to depart.

Gregory Fielding took out the key the new viscount had given him and unlocked the double doors. Sullen morning light penetrated the interior of the vault as the panels swung open. Fielding's breath caught in his throat, his heart pounding with shock at the sight that greeted him. There, hung from a noose suspended from a hook in the ceiling, swung the body of a young man, his face white, the blue eyes staring in death. Gregory Fielding had seen many a dead body since joining his father in the family business at the age of ten and knew right away that the man had been a victim of murder, but just then, the cause of death wasn't the issue.

The funeral procession had stopped just outside the vault, the family ready to see the late Viscount Ashford laid to rest in the family mausoleum. They would be shocked and distressed, and possibly refuse to pay the balance of the fee, blaming the undertakers for this unprecedented fiasco, but there was nothing Gregory Fielding could do. The police had to be summoned and the body taken away before he could proceed with the entombment. He only hoped the family wouldn't publicly blame him for this grotesque display and spread the word to their social circle, therefore putting a kibosh on new and lucrative business.

Gregory Fielding backed away and quickly shut the door to protect the ladies' sensibilities before requesting a quiet word with the viscount, who turned as white as the corpse inside when informed of the problem. Fielding sighed heavily and dispatched one of his sons to fetch a constable. This was going to be a very long morning.

Chapter 1

Tuesday, September 15, 1868

Jason Redmond hurried up the steps of Scotland Yard and made his way directly to Inspector Haze's office, where he found Daniel looking broodily into space, his black notebook open on the desk and an empty pewter mug before him. Daniel was dressed in his usual manner, in a dark gray tweed suit, a white shirt, and a black tie, his round spectacles perched on his nose and his short beard neatly trimmed. The only concession to mourning was the black armband, which he'd been wearing since the unexpected death of his wife three months before.

"Ah, Jason, I'm glad you're here," Daniel said when Jason entered the room.

Jason removed his hat, set down his Gladstone bag, and settled into the guest chair. "What exactly happened?"

The only thing he'd been told by Constable Napier, who'd come to fetch him at St. George's Hospital, where Jason had just come out of the operating theater after removing a gall bladder, was that he was needed urgently at Scotland Yard. As the young constable had so eloquently put it, uncharacteristically slipping into his native Cockney in a moment of great excitement was that, "Some daft cove 'ad the temerity to 'ang 'is foolish self in a viscount's tomb, and lucky for 'im, 'e's dead or the Viscount Ashford would 'a murdered 'im with 'is bare 'ands, and make no mistake 'bout that, yer lordship."

Jason preferred to go simply by Dr. Redmond when volunteering his services as a pathologist at Scotland Yard, but everyone was aware of his noble rank and still used the proper address, out of respect as well as habit.

"What a debacle this morning," Daniel said with an exasperated sigh. "One would think the poor undertakers had hung a body in the Ashford vault for their own amusement. Neville Ashford, the new viscount, was livid, blaming everyone from the London Cemetery Company to the Commissioner of Police for allowing such an unseemly display to disrupt his father's funeral. Of course, his rage was more than justified," Daniel said with a shake of his head.

"The undertaker sent for a constable, who, when he finally appeared, immediately took off for Division N to alert the desk sergeant. The desk sergeant wisely decided that this was a matter for Scotland Yard, given the exalted rank of the family involved. He sent a runner here, who had to wait at least a quarter of an hour to be seen by Superintendent Ransome, who was in a meeting with the commissioner and didn't realize the severity of the situation until Commissioner Hawkins went puce in the face upon hearing the news and advised him to send an inspector, crime scene photographer, and several constables to Highgate forthwith or Ransome would be speaking in falsetto because the commissioner would have his bollocks if he so much as put a foot wrong."

"Sounds like an eventful morning," Jason said with a smile. "Where is the body? I assume you had no choice but to move it, given the *exalted* rank of the family."

"It took more than three hours for the late viscount to finally assume his final resting place, so yes, we had no choice but to move the body as soon as the photographs were taken and the victim was cut down. He awaits your pleasure in the mortuary."

"Were you able to examine the crime scene properly?"

"I was given about ten minutes, since the Viscount Ashford wasn't about to delay the proceedings by a minute longer than he had to. Had it been just him, he might have been persuaded, but when the body was carried out, the widow burst into hysterics all over again, and the two young ladies, the viscount's sisters, got the vapors and had to be taken back to the carriage to recover. I was ordered to leave and take 'that damned nuisance of a corpse' with me," Daniel said.

"Tell me about the victim," Jason invited. He liked to know as much as possible about the crime before beginning the postmortem.

"The body is that of a young male. Early twenties, I'd say. There are no signs of violence that I could see."

"Are you sure this wasn't a suicide?" Jason asked.

"Quite," Daniel replied. "I've seen a number of individuals who had died by hanging, and they presented very differently from our man."

"How so?"

"Unless their hands were tied behind their back, there are usually scratch marks and bruising to the neck, and their facial expression is nothing like the almost peaceful countenance of our victim. Likewise, there was nothing the man could have stood on as he placed the noose around his neck, and the noose was fairly high up. The vault was locked from the outside, so unless he had help, he couldn't have done it to himself."

"Is he in any way related to the Ashfords?" Jason asked. "It was well known that the viscount would be laid to rest this morning, so this display may have been intentional."

"None of the mourners knew who he was, and believe me, I checked. I had the two constables carry the body past the funeral attendees, his face exposed, to see if anyone might recognize him, but no one knew who the man was, and I noticed nothing that would lead me to suspect that someone was hiding anything beyond the natural unpleasantness of being faced with a dead body. I also interviewed as many of the mourners as would speak to me after the viscount was finally entombed."

"And did many of them agree to speak to you?"

"None of the women would stop, but most of the men paused long enough on their way back to their carriages to assure me that they hadn't recognized the man and were deeply shocked by what had taken place."

"How difficult is it to get into the vault?" Jason asked.

"One would need a key. There were no signs of forced entry, and no evidence of a struggle inside. Whoever this person was, he walked right in. You can examine the crime scene once the photographs have been developed. Norm Gillespie promised to bring them by in an hour or two."

"Did you notice anything else when examining the vault? Anything that stood out?"

Daniel shook his head. "The only thing I noticed was that the hinges were well oiled, and the interior of the vault was cleaner than I would expect. The floor in particular surprised me, as it looked as if it might have been recently washed. However, this is the viscount's family vault, so I expect the undertaker had made it his business to prepare it for the interment. No widow wants to see her husband laid to rest in a vault thick with cobwebs and swirling with dust motes."

"Well, let's see what the postmortem tells us," Jason said, pushing to his feet. He was ready to begin.

Daniel pulled out his watch and checked the time. "Would three hours be enough? Superintendent Ransome wants a report as soon as possible. Given that the commissioner is now involved, there's pressure from above to see this case solved quickly and efficiently."

"I'll do my best to have the results in a few hours," Jason promised. "Would you like to attend the postmortem?"

Daniel gave him an incredulous look. He never attended postmortems, having discovered early on that he didn't have the stomach for them. "Let's reconvene here once you're finished," Daniel said.

"Very well," Jason replied, and headed to the mortuary, located on the basement level, just down the corridor from the holding cells.

Chapter 2

Jason hung his coat and hat on a coatrack, set down his bag, and donned the leather apron and linen cap he wore during autopsies. The corpse was laid out on a granite slab, still fully dressed. Jason had expressly requested in the past that the victims be left exactly as they had been found, since there could be telltale stains or secretions on their clothes that might help him narrow down the cause of death as well as identify the method of murder if it wasn't immediately obvious.

Standing back, Jason began by studying the deceased. At first glance, he appeared to be in his early twenties, with longer-than-fashionable fair wavy hair, a neat goatee, and unblemished skin. No one had bothered to close the eyes, and they appeared to be staring at the ceiling, the blue irises still as bright as they must have been in life. The young man must have shaved shortly before he was killed, since there was no stubble on his cheeks or jawline.

His hands were clean and surprisingly soft with neatly trimmed and buffed nails. Jason reached for a magnifying glass and examined each finger carefully, peering beneath the nails to determine if there might be skin cells or traces of blood. He found none, so he moved on to the clothes. The garments were of good quality, the shoes almost new, and the hat that had been set aside when the body was brought in was neatly brushed. The cravat that was wrinkled and soiled with what looked like dried dirt must have been pristine before coming in contact with the rope, which lay coiled on a nearby chair in case Jason needed to examine it. He would take a look at it after he was finished with the postmortem.

The clothes were clean, the cuffs of the shirt crisp and white, with expensive-looking onyx cufflinks still in place. The soles of the shoes bore stains consistent with walking through the streets of London as well as a cemetery, where the paths were graveled, with bits of grass sprouting between the stones, but there were no traces of blood or any other organic matter besides that which one might step into while out about town. On a table in the corner stood a small cardboard box containing the deceased's pitifully few belongings. Jason decided to examine them before beginning the autopsy in the hope that they might tell him something of the man he was about to eviscerate.

There was a leather purse of good quality containing nearly five quid in coins of various denominations, a brass key that was probably to the man's front door or rooms in a lodging house, and a clean handkerchief. There was also a pocket watch. Jason reached for the magnifying glass again and examined the watch carefully for an inscription not visible to the naked eye or some sort of identifying mark. There was nothing distinctive about the watch, nor did Jason think it was particularly expensive. He was no expert, but based on experience, he decided that this was the sort of timepiece any clerk could afford, so it wouldn't be readily identified as having been crafted by a watchmaker of distinction.

He then checked all the pockets before undressing the corpse, in case something had been overlooked, but there was nothing. Ready to begin, Jason removed the shoes and socks and was surprised by how dainty the man's feet were, the nails as carefully buffed as those on the hands. There was a faint smell of lavender soap as well as a hint of expensive cologne. This was a man who had paid attention to detail and taken personal hygiene seriously, unlike many of the corpses and patients Jason had had to deal with in the past, who made him grateful for the linen mask he usually wore during surgeries and postmortems to minimize the smell.

Setting aside the shoes and socks, Jason untied the cravat and examined the neck thoroughly before removing the coat and trousers, leaving the man in just his shirt and underclothes. Jason gently touched the face, looking down at the body.

"Who were you? And what happened to you?" he asked the silent corpse, a wave of pity for the young man washing over him.

Then, bracing himself for what lay ahead, he went to remove the rest of the clothes and begin the more invasive part of the process.

Chapter 3

It was nearly three in the afternoon by the time Jason finished the postmortem. He covered the remains with a sheet, leaving only the face exposed, then cleaned up the mortuary, thoroughly washed his hands with carbolic, and removed the apron and cap. Grabbing his things, Jason left the mortuary and headed to Daniel's office on the ground floor. He hoped the deceased would be identified and receive a proper burial rather than be dumped into a pauper's grave with not even a wooden cross to mark the victim's final resting place.

"Well?" Daniel asked when he spotted Jason in the doorway. "Was it murder?"

"Without a doubt," Jason replied. "Let's speak to Ransome."

Superintendent Ransome looked up eagerly from the paperwork he'd been perusing, his eyes glinting with something akin to derision. "You seem to get all the best cases, Haze," he said as the two men settled before him after shutting the door on the busy station. Daniel had been the only detective on hand when the runner from Division N had arrived that morning, and Ransome, who hadn't looked nearly as calm then as he did now, had dispatched Daniel to Highgate Cemetery with all due haste.

"If you mean the most complicated, then I suppose I do, sir," Daniel replied acerbically.

Daniel admired and respected the superintendent, but he also resented his lack of support and the naked ambition Ransome never bothered to conceal from those working beneath him. John Ransome meant to be commissioner one day, and he would be, not through luck or useful social connections, but through the dogged pursuit of his goals. Ransome liked to be kept abreast of every intriguing case that came into Scotland Yard and made sure to give a statement to the press in person, getting his photograph in the papers with irritating frequency. This tactic ensured that he received credit when the case was solved.

If the case hit a dead end, as they sometimes did, he was quick to lay blame at the investigating detective's door, therefore absolving himself of any responsibility and reassuring the public that their safety was his number one priority and always would be. Ransome was not only driven but good-looking, which made him popular with the ladies who saw his photograph in their husbands' newspapers, and with the men who were drawn to ambitious, smooth-talking officials in whom they could place their trust.

Ransome chuckled. "Complicated, yes, but also career-making," he said. "No one remembers the copper who cuffed a thief or a smuggler, but they remember the man who cracked a puzzling murder case with few clues to go on. And speaking of clues, what have you got for us, Lord Redmond? Is it safe to say the victim died by hanging?"

"No, sir," Jason replied.

"Sorry?" Ransome asked, looking disappointed.

"The victim died by asphyxiation, but there are no signs of strangulation and no extensive bruising to the neck, the sort you would get if the individual were alive at the time of the hanging and was bucking and jerking as the breath was choked from the body. There are no scratches on the neck, and the nails are not broken or chipped as they would be if the victim had clawed at the rope. Likewise, there's no bulging of the eyes or pallor localized to the areas of compression. Neither urine nor feces had been evacuated at the time of death, and the hyoid bone is still intact. Also, there are no defensive wounds that I can see, so there doesn't appear to have been a struggle."

"How would you explain that?" Ransome asked.

"Aconite poisoning presents as asphyxiation but leaves no discernable traces in the body. When the victim ingests a small amount, they might experience stomach pains, nausea, vomiting, diarrhea, and irregular heartbeat. If a large dose is taken, death is almost instantaneous. The poison causes paralysis of the heart and the respiratory system. The victim suffered none of the physical symptoms before death occurred, so it had to have been a considerable dose."

"How can you tell?" Daniel asked.

"The stomach still contained the remains of the last meal, which would no longer be there had the victim vomited. And there were no traces of either vomit or excrement on the victim's clothing, hands, mouth, or rectum. However, the victim did ingest strong spirits shortly before death. Brandy, most likely," Jason said. "It was difficult to tell, since the alcohol had almost certainly been infused with the poison."

Jason paused briefly and continued. "If the root of aconite had been soaked in the contents, the concentration of poison would be extremely high. Death would have been quick and virtually painless. Since there are no witnesses, I have no way of knowing what symptoms occurred just before death, but the few facts I possess support the theory that the victim had ingested aconite or some other highly toxic poison."

"So, he was poisoned, then strung up to make his death look like a hanging?" Ransome asked.

"Yes, I believe so. But there's more," Jason added, his gaze fixed on Superintendent Ransome so as not to miss his reaction. "He is a she."

"What?" Ransome and Daniel cried in unison.

"The victim was a woman."

"But he wore a goatee," Daniel protested.

"Attached with some sort of adhesive, probably the kind used in theatrical productions."

"Are you quite certain?" Ransome asked, still unable to accept Jason's pronouncement.

"I think I can tell the difference between a man and a woman, sir," Jason replied, enjoying Ransome's reaction more than he should.

"Good God! How was she able to pull it off?"

"As you already know, she wore a fake goatee, her breasts were tightly bound, and she had inserted a balled-up wad of cloth into her drawers to simulate the male organ, should someone look too closely at her groin. She also wore no corset, so her waist wasn't cinched in, allowing the clothes to hang more naturally off her frame. She wasn't tall or broad for a man, but she was of slightly more than average height for a woman, and her arms and legs were firm, which leads me to believe that she had spent a considerable amount of time on her feet and had probably worked with her hands in some capacity, although it wasn't manual labor because her hands were neither calloused nor reddened."

"Why was she dressed as a man?" Ransome exclaimed.

"The better question is, what was she doing in Highgate Cemetery in the middle of the night, and who murdered her and locked her in a vault?" Jason asked.

"Could she have been murdered elsewhere?" Daniel asked.

"It's possible," Jason replied, having considered the possibility. "She'd been dead for twelve to fifteen hours at the start of the postmortem. Had she been killed elsewhere, the body could have been transported to the cemetery and taken to the vault. No one would have been there to witness the final act, given that it would have been in the dead of night. However, neither the clothes nor the shoes show any signs of the victim being dragged or dropped."

"Extraordinary," Ransome muttered, shaking his head. "And utterly pointless."

"How do you mean, sir?" Daniel asked.

"Well, what's the point of this charade? If someone wished to kill this woman, they could have simply done so. A poison could be administered anywhere, even in the middle of a crowded restaurant. If it can't be traced definitively during a postmortem, then the poisoner is safe in pretending their companion simply became ill and died. Why go to all the trouble of either transporting the body to the cemetery or luring the victim there and then making it look like a hanging? The gates would be locked, so the murderer would have to get in somehow, drag the body all the way to the Ashford vault, then prepare the noose and suspend the body. That's a lot of physical effort, and as you have pointed out, Lord Redmond, there's no evidence the body had been dragged. And if they meant to make it look like a suicide, why lock the door from the outside?"

"Even if the door had been left unlocked, no surgeon would mistake this death for a suicide. The victim was dead by the time she was hanged. She couldn't have done it herself."

"She might have had an accomplice," Ransome pointed out.

"Yes, she could have, but that still doesn't explain the need to hang the body once it was already dead."

"Perhaps the display was meant to implicate someone," Ransome mused. "Someone connected to the viscount's family, or the viscount himself."

"None of the mourners were able to identify the deceased," Daniel said. "I watched them carefully as the body was carried past, and I didn't notice even a spark of recognition. The victim was a stranger to them all."

"Some people are good at hiding their emotions," Ransome said, "and if someone knew the body was in the vault, they would hardly be surprised, so perhaps you shouldn't be so quick to discount an Ashford connection, Inspector Haze," he added, taunting Daniel.

"I intend to question the family, sir," Daniel replied, his tone controlled, "but I could hardly insist on an extensive interview during the funeral beyond the obvious question of whether anyone could identify the deceased."

John Ransome inclined his head in an uncharacteristic show of acknowledgement. "No, you couldn't," he said. "It wouldn't do to behave in an insensitive manner. We don't want any complaints made to the commissioner. Talk to the family as soon as it's seemly."

"Yes, sir," Daniel replied.

"Well, I for one would dearly like to know what the purpose of this morning's display was," John Ransome said, turning to Jason.

"Whatever it was, it was a terrible waste of a young life," Jason replied. "Did you find anything in the vault or just outside?" he asked, turning to Daniel. "A vial, a cup, or even a flask?"

"No," Daniel said. "We found nothing out of the ordinary except several cheroot stubs, but those were still fresh and belonged to the mourners, who were smoking to pass the time."

"Lord Redmond, had the woman been sexually interfered with?" Ransome asked.

"There were no signs of assault or sexual activity."

"Was she a virgin, then?" Ransome asked.

"The victim's hymen had been broken, but the hymen is not always a reliable proof of virginity."

"Last I heard, it was," Ransome countered.

Jason didn't reply. He had no way of knowing if the woman had been sexually active without visible proof, so he wasn't willing to commit himself either way.

"Might she have been sodomized?" Ransome persisted.

"I found no evidence of anal penetration or any semen in the rectum."

"And was she in good health prior to death?" Daniel asked, clearly uncomfortable with the images Jason's reply had conjured up.

"She was in excellent health. She did have a slight curvature of the spine, but it wasn't enough to be noticeable or cause her any real discomfort. And the forefinger and thumb of her right hand were a bit calloused. It could be from holding an instrument of some sort."

"So, you believe she did some form of physical work?" Daniel asked.

"She might have been a devoted letter writer, for all I know," Jason replied. "Without knowing something of her life, I can't really tell."

"What sort of profession would account for such callouses?" Ransome asked.

"Someone who wields a knife, like a cook, or a paintbrush."

"Was there anything beneath her fingernails, like traces of food or paint?" Daniel asked.

Jason shook his head. "No. Her hands had been scrubbed clean."

"And we have nothing that would help us to identify her?" Ransome asked, turning to Daniel.

"Not at the moment, sir. There was nothing distinctive about the watch or the cufflinks."

"Lord Redmond, did the young woman have any distinguishing marks?" Ransome asked.

"She had a birthmark on her neck, just here," Jason pointed to the left side of his own neck, "and a small scar on the palm of her left hand, right below the thumb. I left the woman's face uncovered and made sure no scars from the postmortem are visible. I think you should ask Mr. Gillespie to take some photographs of her face for the purpose of identification."

Ransome nodded. "Excellent idea, my lord. In fact, if we don't have any leads by tomorrow, I think we should appeal to the public and have the photographs of her face, both as a man and a woman, printed in the papers. Someone is bound to recognize her."

"Yes, that would probably yield results," Jason agreed.

Seeing photographs of a deceased person wasn't pleasant, but most people wouldn't find it shocking or gruesome. Many families invited photographers into their homes to take photographs of their dead so they could remember them once they were buried. Some even went as far as to ask the photographer to pose the departed with the family, as if they were still alive. Jason found the practice morbid in the extreme, but he could understand the need to have one last memory of a loved one, especially when the deceased was a child, or a baby whose face would be forever lost to time without that one piece of tangible proof that they had existed at all.

The woman on the slab was someone's child, and it was very possible that her parents were still alive and hoping for word of her.

"I will check with the other stations in case anyone fitting the victim's description has been reported missing," Daniel said. "Although it's probably too soon for her loved ones to realize she's gone. If she was seen yesterday, they might not report her disappearance for several days yet. Still, it's worth a try."

"Do that," Ransome replied, his tone indicating that the meeting was at an end. "Thank you for your assistance, your lordship," he added, smiling at Jason in an ingratiating way before turning his attention to a stack of papers on his desk, effectively dismissing them.

Jason and Daniel walked out of Ransome's office together. "I'm giving a lecture at the Royal College of Surgeons from four to six, but I can come by after, if you'll be at home," Jason offered.

"Given that I have virtually nothing to go on in this case, I think it's safe to assume I'll be there," Daniel replied sourly. "I'll see you this evening."

Chapter 4

Having said goodbye to Jason, Daniel dispatched Constables Napier and Collins to check with other divisions for a possible missing persons connection, then returned to the office he shared with Inspector Lang and sat at his desk, a notepad open before him. He'd call on Viscount Ashford tomorrow, but since the man had just buried his father, Daniel thought it best not to intrude on the family's grief just yet. Instead, he needed to come up with at least three lines of inquiry he could pursue regardless of the constables' findings. Daniel reached for the pen, dipped it in ink, and began to write. His list wasn't overly inspiring, but it was a start.

1. Interview the undertaker.
2. Question the gravediggers.
3. Attempt to trace the victim's tailor.

That was a satisfactory enough starting point, Daniel decided, so he pushed his spectacles up his nose, grabbed his hat, and walked out of the office.

The offices of Fielding and Sons Undertakers were in Holborn, a stone's throw from both Newgate and Fleet prisons. As Daniel approached the less-than-elegant shopfront, he wondered why the family of a viscount would use them in lieu of a firm with a reputation for catering to the upper echelons of society. Perhaps money was tight. Or perhaps the late viscount hadn't been well loved by his family, although he had to admit that the undertakers had put on a good show. Daniel couldn't imagine a more elaborate display of grief than the one he'd witnessed this morning when he'd arrived at the scene. Perhaps Fielding and Sons was moving up in the world.

The two younger Fieldings had been dispatched to collect the earthly remains of a new client's loved one, but Gregory Fielding, funeral director and patriarch, was in his office, poring over a ledger and enjoying a cup of milky tea. He was a tall, thin man in his forties, his pale face long and pockmarked. He had deep-set black eyes offset by thick brows and receding dark hair. Despite his morbid occupation, Daniel sensed that the undertaker didn't lack for a sense of humor, a trait that probably served him well in his profession. Mr. Fielding seemed surprised to see Daniel, but then his face took on an expression of bland servitude, the sort he probably used for the bereaved and the hysterical.

"Inspector Haze. I didn't expect to see you again so soon. How may I be of service?" Gregory Fielding asked.

"I have a few more questions of a confidential nature to ask you, Mr. Fielding, which is why I decided to wait until we could speak privately," Daniel said, accepting the proffered seat.

"Oh?"

"It's nothing to be alarmed about," Daniel assured him.

"Please, go ahead," Mr. Fielding said, his expression changing to one of resignation. The sooner he answered Daniel's questions, the sooner he would be rid of him.

"Was this the first time you took a funeral for the Ashford family?" Daniel asked.

"Yes, it was. They'd used Simpson and Quinn in the past."

"Do you know why they decided against using them this time?"

Mr. Fielding allowed himself an eyeroll of irritation. "There's only one reason, Inspector. The cost. The new viscount wanted to keep the expenses to a minimum."

Daniel considered this response. "I can't imagine this morning's funeral came cheap," he said at last.

"It didn't, but we were able to offer a more reasonable package than Simpson and Quinn. In fact, we did not make any profit on this morning's funeral."

"So why did you take it?"

Mr. Fielding looked at Daniel as if he were a complete idiot. "For the cachet, of course. If the Viscount Ashford contracted us to bury his father, then other noble families might consider using our services as well, especially once they hear how opulent the funeral procession was."

"It was that," Daniel agreed. "And who had the key to the vault prior to the entombment?"

"I did. The viscount gave it to me after the contract was signed and the deposit received. I visited the vault two days ago to make sure all was in order."

"And did you see anything out of the ordinary?"

"I did not." Gregory Fielding looked thoughtful. "Actually…" His voice trailed off as he considered something.

"Actually what?" Daniel prompted.

"The inside of the vault was surprisingly clean. The last Ashford to be entombed in the family vault was Verity Ashford, the Viscount Ashford's unmarried sister. That was more than three years ago. There were no cobwebs and a minimal amount of dust. Usually it looks like something out of a gothic novel," Fielding joked. "And there was a hook in the ceiling."

"The hook from which the body was suspended this morning?" Daniel asked.

"Yes, the very one. I thought it might have been installed by the builders to hang a lantern."

"Is that unusual?"

Fielding shrugged. "I've never seen that before, but then I haven't taken many funerals for the wealthy and titled," he added. "Perhaps it's a standard feature in these newfangled vaults. The Ashford mausoleum is bigger than some people's homes."

"Where's the key now?" Daniel asked.

"I returned the key to the viscount after locking the vault."

"How many keys are there?"

"I don't know. I only needed the one," Gregory Fielding replied.

"Would there normally be more than one key?" Daniel inquired.

Gregory Fielding shrugged again. "Our burials are usually in the ground, so there are no keys involved. We've had several vault interments, but the vaults were old and kept unlocked. I can't imagine anyone would enter them willingly, especially in the dead of night."

"Do you bury many people in Highgate?" Daniel asked.

"A fair number."

"Do you know the gravediggers personally?"

"I do. There are four full-time gravediggers, and they are honest."

"And by honest, you mean…?" Daniel asked, surprised by Mr. Fielding's description.

"I mean they don't work with the body snatchers. They value their jobs and will run off anyone who's trying to desecrate a grave."

"And if they weren't honest? How would that go?"

"They would turn a blind eye and allow the graverobbers to do their job. The families of the missing cadavers would be none the wiser, since the graves look recently filled in for days after a burial and the body snatchers want corpses that are still fresh."

Daniel tried not to imagine men working by moonlight as they dug up newly buried bodies, wrapped them in sacking, and carried them off to be sold to private anatomists and medical schools. "A terrible business, that," Daniel said, involuntarily wondering if Sarah's remains were still in their rightful place.

"There's an easy way to put an end to the graverobbing, in my opinion," Mr. Fielding said.

"And how's that?"

"All the dead from the prisons should be sold to the surgeons. Most of them wind up in unmarked graves anyhow. Why not use them to further the study of medicine and use the profits generated by the sale of the corpses to improve the prison system? The way I see it, everyone would benefit."

"Except the deceased and their families," Daniel pointed out.

"The families of the inmates don't benefit anyhow, and many of them can ill afford the cost of a funeral, so they're happy to have their dead buried by the prison authorities. It won't matter much to them."

"Still, it's a callous thing to do."

"Maybe. Or maybe it's a courageous thing to do. A sacrifice for the greater good."

Daniel could see that the disposal of cadavers was a topic close to Mr. Fielding's heart, but he wasn't there to discuss the merits of an arrangement with the prisons.

"Mr. Fielding, can you give me the names of the gravediggers at Highgate?"

"Certainly. You'll find that they're all members of the same family. The Ludlows. Harry, Barry, Gary, and—"

"Larry?" Daniel supplied.

"No. Rob," Mr. Fielding said with an amused smile. "Bring them a bottle or two of gin, and they'll tell you everything you need to know and everything you never thought to ask."

"Thank you, Mr. Fielding."

"It's my pleasure, Inspector Haze. I would greatly appreciate it if you would mention our humble firm to anyone who might be in need of reasonably priced and compassionate undertakers."

"Of course," Daniel said, knowing he'd do no such thing.

Chapter 5

Daniel found the Ludlows in a shed on the cemetery grounds. There were spades, buckets, ladders, rope, and numerous lanterns, all items needed for their work. The four men sat around a small table, playing cards, an unmarked bottle of spirits in the center. The alcoholic fumes inside the shed were a dead giveaway, but one of the brothers snatched the bottle as soon as Daniel entered and hid it beneath the table, probably fearful that Daniel would inform their employer. Daniel couldn't imagine that drinking on the job would be condoned but had no desire to report the men. It was none of his business what they did, and he'd probably need to remain numb to do the job they were paid to do— although, at times, his own job wasn't any better.

Leaving the door open to air out the cramped space, Daniel introduced himself and stated the reason for his visit. "Were you present when the body was discovered?" he asked.

"It were funny, that," one of the men said. Daniel had no idea which one he was. They all looked similar and about the same age.

"Funny?" Daniel asked.

"Never 'appened afore," the man replied. "Odd place to top yerself."

"Which one are you?"

"I'm Rob. This 'ere is 'Arry, Barry, and Gary," Rob said, pointing to each brother in turn.

"Right. So, did any of you see anything last night? Hear anything?" All four men shrugged.

"What time did you go home last night?" Daniel tried again.

"Six," Harry said. "We 'ave lodgings nearby," he added.

"Is there a night watchman?"

"Nah," Barry said. "The gates are padlocked at night."

"But what about the graverobbers?" Daniel asked.

"They usually come in pairs, or if they're in a 'urry, they bring more men. Ye'd need more than one watchman in a place like this, guv. 'Sides, a watchman can always be bribed, or knocked over the 'ead with a shovel." The men laughed at that.

"Who employs you?" Daniel asked, frustrated by their childish antics.

"The London Cemetery Company," Harry said importantly. "It owns the cemetery and pays us to dig the graves and maintain the grounds."

"Well, you seem to be doing a very fine job," Daniel said sarcastically. His rebuke was lost on the brothers, who nodded in appreciation of the compliment.

"Why, thank ye, guv," Barry said. "Kind of ye to say."

"Are you missing any rope?" Daniel asked, taking in the coils of rope piled in the corner.

Another shrug. "Hard to say. We don't measure it or nothin'."

"Do you keep keys to the vaults?" Daniel asked, but he thought he already knew the answer. He wouldn't trust these four as far as he could throw them, and certainly not with a key to a family vault, given that some individuals were buried with valuables that could be stolen if someone gained access.

"Nah. The keys are held by the families," Rob said.

"Did you have to do anything to prepare the vault for the interment?" Daniel tried again.

"Not our job, guv. The undertakers see to that. Saw that Fielding fellow 'ere the other day. 'E went inside. Maybe 'e did it." Harry's laugh sounded phlegmy. "Good way to get rid of the competition." The brothers sniggered, then fell silent. "Anyroad, we saw nothin'. All was quiet and dignified," Harry concluded.

Daniel sighed. He wasn't sure what he'd been expecting, but he found these dimwitted brothers irritating all the same. "Let me know if you remember something. I can be found at Scotland Yard."

"Sure will, guv," Barry promised. "Must do our bit to aid the law."

Daniel left the shed and headed toward the main exit. The cemetery was beautiful, in a hushed, watchful sort of way, the park more like a nature preserve than a burial ground. There were hundreds of graves, some with crosses and simple gravestones, others with elaborate statues, mostly of weeping angels, and stone urns. There were avenues of tombs, a grim necropolis erected in the middle of a bustling city to remind its inhabitants that even in life, they were always in the midst of death.

Daniel thought of Sarah's grave. She had been buried in the graveyard in Birch Hill, next to their son Felix. Once the ground had settled, he'd have to order a gravestone, but he couldn't begin to imagine what he'd want the epitaph to read. *Here lies a loving mother? Devoted wife? Dutiful daughter?* How about, *Here lies a woman who chose death over her husband and child?* And left them to deal with their loss and grief without so much as a note to explain her actions or a letter to the heartbroken daughter who'd never know her mother.

Perhaps he should order a cross or a simple stone with just Sarah's name and her birth and death dates. That would serve her right, Daniel thought angrily. No loving words. No eternal grief etched into the stone. Just nothingness, like the emptiness he felt when he thought of her. But it wasn't nothingness, he admitted to himself as he hurried along the deserted avenue of the cemetery. It was anger, grief, bone-deep loneliness, and disbelief. Some part of him still couldn't accept that Sarah had taken her own life, choosing to rot beneath the soil rather than remain with the people who loved her, indifferent to their suffering. Sarah's mother, Harriet, had aged ten years in the past few months, and who could blame her?

Once, she'd had a full house with her husband and daughter, and then with Daniel and Charlotte filling the empty rooms, but now she was left to live out the rest of her life in bitter solitude. Harriet would love to have Charlotte with her, but Daniel wouldn't be parted from his daughter. Charlotte had already lost one parent; she wouldn't lose both if he had anything to say on the subject. She clung to him and their servant Grace in those first weeks with a fear born of suddenly losing her mother and Daniel would not do anything to disrupt her fragile sense of security, even if her life would probably be more peaceful and well-ordered in Birch Hill.

The Reverend Talbot had advised Daniel to remarry, a callous statement made by a cold and unfeeling man immediately after Sarah's funeral, but that was the way of it, wasn't it? When a spouse died, those left behind often remarried, some sooner rather than later. The way he felt now, Daniel couldn't imagine loving someone enough to tie his life to them forever. But grief ebbed, feelings changed, and hope inevitably floated to the surface, because such anger and sorrow wasn't sustainable, not if one hoped to snatch some happiness from the jaws of bereavement. Unfortunately, Sarah had not been able to bear the weight of her grief once they lost their boy. It was as if the two of them had been in a shipwreck, and where Daniel had chosen to kick and stay afloat in the hope of being rescued, Sarah had just given up and sacrificed herself to the sea, sinking below the waves and allowing her waterlogged skirts to drag her down to the bottom, choosing oblivion over struggle.

Daniel mourned Felix every day of his life, but he'd be damned if he continued to mourn the woman who had willingly left him alone with a small child to raise. Sarah didn't deserve any more misery from him. He'd suffered enough in the four years since they'd lost their son, forced to deal with Sarah's endless grief and guilt. He'd done his best to understand, to support, and to uplift, but there was only so much a person could do to heal someone who had no wish to recover. It was him and Charlotte now, and Miss Grainger, who was paid for by his mother-in-law and who was an absolute treasure.

Daniel had allowed Harriet Elderman to interview potential nursemaids, but the final decision had been his, and he'd chosen Miss Grainger. She was practical but warm, competent but not overbearing. She was also lovely, Daniel had decided during one of his sleepless nights. She was very different from Sarah in looks. Miss Grainger—Rebecca—had naturally curly blond hair, dark blue eyes, and a pert nose that gave her a slightly impertinent air. She was quick to smile and had an infectious laugh. Sarah had had a charming laugh once, but Daniel honestly couldn't recall the last time he'd heard it. Charlotte adored Miss Grainger, and Daniel was overcome with gratitude to the woman who made his daughter feel safe and loved.

Daniel shook his head, angry with himself for allowing his thoughts to stray to Sarah yet again. He'd deal with his feelings in time, but today, he had a job to do and a child to care for, and he wanted to get home to her at a reasonable hour so that he had more than a few minutes with her before it was time for her to go to bed.

Once through the gates and out on Swains Lane, Daniel checked the time and considered his options. It was past four, so most of the tailors would be closing for the night soon, and he'd have to visit a few if he hoped to locate the right one. Perhaps once the photographs appeared in the papers, he wouldn't need to waste his time on tailors and cobblers. Daniel sighed and headed for home. It had been a long and frustrating day, and he looked forward to spending an hour with his baby girl followed by a hot meal and a drink with Jason, whose company always helped him to feel human again.

Charlotte smiled joyfully and ran to Daniel when he walked through the nursery door. She had been playing with her wooden blocks but left them behind in favor of her father.

"Story," she said as Daniel swung her up into his arms and kissed her velvety cheek. He couldn't help smiling, the joy of seeing Charlotte erasing all his earlier anxiety.

"Good evening, Inspector Haze," Miss Grainger said. "Did you have a good day?"

"Not really," Daniel confessed. "But it's better now."

"Story," Charlotte demanded again.

"Of course, my darling," Daniel said, smiling at her. "Which one would you like?" He set Charlotte down, and she toddled over to the bookshelf, where she pulled out her favorite book and held it out to him.

"I'll leave you to it, then," Miss Grainger said, turning toward the door.

"Miss Grainger, Lord Redmond will be stopping by shortly. If you would…"

"Yes, of course. I'll just sit in the garden for a little while and come upstairs as soon as Lord Redmond arrives."

"Thank you."

"Don't mention it, sir. I know how you enjoy his lordship's visits." Miss Grainger smiled at him and left, closing the door softly behind her.

Daniel sat down and lifted Charlotte onto his lap, opening the book to the title page. "Ready?"

The little girl nodded. Charlotte liked it when Daniel got into character, and he made sure not to disappoint and endowed everyone in the story with their own voice and personality.

Charlotte snuggled closer to him as he began to read and Daniel lost himself in the story, glad of a few moments' respite from real life.

Chapter 6

Jason arrived just before seven and settled into his favorite chair. Daniel handed him a whisky, poured one for himself, and sat across from Jason, eager to discuss the case.

"How was your lecture?" Daniel asked politely.

"Good. I won't bore you with the details. I'm sure your mind is buzzing after today."

"It is. I haven't had much luck with either the undertaker or the gravediggers. No one saw anything out of the ordinary leading up to the funeral."

"Not surprising," Jason replied. "The murder would have taken place after the cemetery closed for the night."

"I will call on the viscount tomorrow morning, although I don't imagine he'll be too pleased to see me."

"What do you plan to ask him?" Jason inquired.

"Well, for one, I'd like to know how many keys there are to the vault and who has access to them. The door hadn't been forced, and the victim had been locked in, so whoever had been there had a key. Also, I'd like to show him a photograph of the woman's face. When I asked him if he knew the deceased, he was looking at what he believed to be a man. Maybe if he sees her face, he'll know who she is."

"Do you think it might have been a prank gone wrong?" Jason asked.

"How do you mean?"

"A young woman dresses in her brother's clothes and goes out carousing, just to see what life is like for the other half. Someone she knows or meets during the evening brings her to the cemetery, claiming it's just a lark, then murders her and hides her body."

"But why?" Daniel asked. "There are those individuals who get pleasure from killing. They might rape their victim first, then maybe strangle her to watch the light go out of her eyes. Someone might torture their victim for the sheer pleasure of watching them suffer, but if this woman's death had been swift and without agony, what joy would the killer have derived from it?"

"That's what we have to find out. Was it a random killing or a planned execution? Did the killer and the victim know one another? Did she come willingly, or had she been forced into accompanying the killer to Highgate, assuming she was still alive at that point? Did they trick her into taking the poison, or did she know she was about to die?"

"Would she have tasted the poison?" Daniel asked.

"Probably, but by the time she realized something was wrong, it would have been too late, especially if the concentration was high."

"And how would one go about obtaining aconite?" Daniel asked. "Is it readily available?"

"Aconite has been used in medicine for centuries. In small doses, it can reduce fever, act as an anti-inflammatory, and slow down a person's heartrate if they're in danger of suffering a cardiac event. It can also be used as a sedative. I've no doubt it can be purchased at any pharmacy in London, but it can also be obtained organically."

"How?"

"It's a plant with distinctive purple flowers. I believe it's more commonly known as wolfbane or monkshood. If the killer is knowledgeable about poisons, they could simply have picked it somewhere or had an infusion ready for when they needed it. The roots are the deadliest part of the plant, so steeping them would turn the liquid highly toxic."

Daniel nodded as he considered this information. They had no tangible proof that the poison had been purchased, so to visit the pharmacies would be a colossal waste of time, given how many there were in London.

"Given that the gates are locked at closing time, it would have been difficult for the killer to bring in a dead body. Perhaps the woman was still alive when she arrived at the cemetery," Daniel speculated.

"Perhaps, but there's no way to know for sure."

"Her clothes and shoes were clean. Had someone dragged the body, the clothes might have become wrinkled and stained, and the shoes would be scuffed."

"Yes, that's true," Jason agreed. "But what if the killer dressed her up in men's clothes after she was already dead and disposed of her usual attire? Since they obviously had the key, they might have stored whatever they needed inside the vault so they wouldn't have to bring it with them on the night of the murder."

"Mr. Fielding, the undertaker, did mention that the inside of the vault was surprisingly clean. Perhaps someone had been there recently."

"We won't know the answers to any of our questions until we identify her," Jason replied. "Has anyone reported a young woman or man missing over the last few days?"

"I'll find out tomorrow morning. I sent out two constables to check with the other divisions before leaving the Yard, but there's no guarantee that someone would report their loved one missing so quickly. It might take them several days to either realize that she's gone or to work up the courage to walk into a police station. Many people distrust the police and would rather work out their family difficulties privately."

"This woman did not come from the lower orders," Jason replied. "She was well nourished, clean, and expensively dressed. Her hands were white and soft, except for the small calluses on her fingers, and her feet are those of someone who's always had good shoes and has never walked around barefoot."

"Which in itself doesn't prove she couldn't have been a prostitute," Daniel replied. "Some brothels take good care of their girls in an effort to appeal to a more persnickety clientele who like their whores to look like fine ladies."

"She wasn't a prostitute, Daniel," Jason protested. "There were no signs of sexual activity, previous pregnancy, or any sexually transmitted diseases. This woman came from a good home."

"I'm sure you're right," Daniel conceded. "I'll stop by the Yard tomorrow morning to collect the photographs before calling on Viscount Ashford and to check the missing persons reports. If the photographs were developed and delivered to the press in time for the morning edition, then hopefully we'll have our victim identified by end of day tomorrow."

Jason finished his drink and set the glass on the occasional table at his elbow. "I must get going.."

"Would you be able to come with me to speak to the Ashfords tomorrow?" Daniel asked. One titled man speaking to another would yield better results than Daniel questioning the viscount and his family on his own. The upper classes had a healthy disdain for the police and showed it as plainly as the lower orders.

"I have a surgery scheduled for eight. An amputation of a gangrenous foot. The auditorium is bound to be full. Nothing brings in the students like an amputation," Jason replied.

"I'm glad my father never encouraged me to become a surgeon," Daniel said. "I don't have the stomach for it."

"I think you found exactly the right occupation for your talents," Jason replied with a smile. "I should be free by noon. Stop by the hospital if you can."

"I will," Daniel promised.

"And now I really must get home. Katherine will be expecting me for dinner," Jason said and pushed to his feet. "I'll see you tomorrow, Daniel."

Daniel walked Jason to the door and bid him a good night.

Chapter 7

As was their nightly custom, Jason told Katherine about his day after she told him about hers. Katherine's days were rarely as interesting, but Jason always listened patiently and took her woes seriously, not that there were many. With their ward, Micah, back at school, Lily thriving, and the household running smoothly under the competent leadership of the Dodsons, there wasn't much for Katherine to fret about except for her lack of usefulness.

Before they'd married, Katherine had kept house for her father, the Reverend Talbot, and had taken on the duties of a vicar's wife, since her mother had passed away years before. She'd visited the sick and the old, arranged flowers in St. Catherine's, and planned annual events, like the autumn bake sale and the summer fête. Now that she was Lady Redmond and resided in a rather upscale area of London, all she could do was join charitable organizations and socialize with her newfound friends, who sometimes came to call on Katherine and tried desperately to introduce their husbands to Jason. Jason didn't mind attending the occasional supper party or musical evening, but he hadn't forged a bond with any of the men and preferred to spend time with Daniel, with whom he'd felt a kinship from almost the first day they'd met.

When Sarah had been alive, the two couples had occasionally invited each other to dinner or met up for a walk in the park or a visit to the zoological gardens with the children, but with Sarah gone, Katherine no longer saw Daniel as frequently, leaving Jason to comfort him in his bereavement and pass on useful advice regarding Charlotte.

"The woman was dressed in men's clothes?" Katherine asked after Jason told her about the morning's discovery, her eyes sparkling with curiosity. "How daring."

"You think it was her choice?" Jason asked. He was always eager to hear his wife's opinions, since, as a woman, she had a unique perspective on the motivations of those involved.

"Were the clothes in disarray?"

"No."

"Then I think she dressed herself."

"You think a man wouldn't be able to dress her without betraying his clumsiness?" Jason asked with a chuckle.

He was sure his valet, Henley, who was something of a ladies' man, would be able to do a competent job if the situation called for it, especially if he were stone-cold sober. He decided not to point that out, given that Henley was not one of Katherine's favorite people and was only tolerated by her because he was the nephew of the Dodsons, whom she liked and respected.

"Not unless the man was a valet or an experienced manservant, but even then, I think there are certain aspects that might present a challenge for them," Katherine replied. "I think she was in disguise."

"I agree with you, given that her breasts were bound, and she'd stuffed balled-up fabric in her drawers. I can't see anyone going to such lengths if all they meant to do was leave her body for someone to find."

"Exactly!" Katherine exclaimed, clearly pleased that they were in agreement. "And if she were wearing women's pantaloons, the wadded fabric would fall right through the opening, so she had to be wearing men's drawers to start with or the killer had thought of everything."

Jason hadn't considered that and was glad Katherine had pointed it out. Unlike men's undergarments, women's bloomers were split to make them more functional when the lady was in need of the toilet. They also allowed for easier access for amorous husbands and paying customers, if the woman in question was a prostitute.

"And what do you think the purpose of her disguise was?" Jason asked as he finished his soup and set down the spoon. Rumor had it that Mrs. Dodson had made beef Wellington for the main course, and Jason looked forward to sampling this new culinary delight. If nothing else, he liked the name.

"Perhaps she needed to gain admittance somewhere," Katherine said as she continued to eat her soup.

Jason considered this interesting suggestion. "Such as where?"

"Perhaps she was looking for someone and dressed as a man in order to enter a gentleman's club or a school, for instance."

"And what do you think happened after that?"

"I think that perhaps someone told her they knew where to find the person she was looking for and lured her to the cemetery, where they killed her."

"But what would be their motive?" Jason inquired, intrigued by Katherine's theory.

"Perhaps the person she was searching for didn't care to be found."

"You mean she was a threat, and the killing wasn't random?"

"Precisely."

Katherine looked like she was about to say something else but went quiet when Fanny came in to collect the soup plates. Fanny's departure was followed by the arrival of Dodson, who carefully set the platter of beef Wellington on the table. Fanny reappeared moments later, bringing dishes of potatoes and buttered peas.

"Dodson, that is gorgeous," Katherine said. "Please tell Mrs. Dodson she's outdone herself. I will come down later to thank her in person."

"I hope you both enjoy it, my lady," Dodson said, but he was looking at Jason. He was too old-fashioned and set in his ways to give Katherine the same respect as the master of the house. He sliced the beef and departed, leaving them to their meal.

"Do you have any thoughts on how to identify the victim, assuming no one comes forward to claim her as their own?" Jason asked once he'd sampled the dish and found it to his liking.

"That's a tough one," Katherine said. "With nothing to go on, where do you even begin? She could be anyone, from anywhere. She might not even be from London. Or English. Did she look foreign?"

"Not really. A typical English rose," Jason said, having heard the expression from one of his colleagues at the hospital.

"So, she's fair in coloring?" Katherine asked.

"Blond, blue-eyed, fair-skinned."

"That doesn't mean she couldn't be from one of the Eastern European countries. Poland or Russia, or even Germany."

"It would be impossible to tell without hearing her speak."

"Not all foreigners have an accent," Katherine replied.

"No, I don't suppose they do," Jason agreed. "That would depend on the age that they came to their new country. The older they were, the stronger the accent. Just look at me," he joked. "I couldn't sound like a born Englishman if my life depended on it."

"You also have no desire to sound like a born Englishman," Katherine pointed out, smiling at him in that knowing way. "You like your Americanness. It sets you apart and lets everyone know that you are bold and open-minded, and sometimes a little bit dangerous."

"Am I?" Jason asked, both surprised and flattered by Katherine's words.

Katherine cocked a dark eyebrow at him. "Jason, you're the most open-minded, courageous person I know, and to some people, that makes you dangerous."

"As long as you don't find me dangerous or frightening, I really don't care," Jason replied.

"Don't be silly," Katherine said. "Tell me about her hands."

"Clean, soft, the nails neatly trimmed."

"Hmm," Katherine said as she speared a piece of potato and popped it into her mouth. "Not a servant, then."

"Where would a servant get such fine clothes?" Jason asked, going along with Katherine's suggestion that the woman was in disguise for the sheer pleasure of watching the gears shifting in her brain.

"Her master, obviously," Katherine replied.

"That's only if her employer happened to be exactly the same size as she is, and she was slender and not very tall for a man. Also, she had rather dainty feet, and the shoes were made for her. They fit perfectly."

"You think the clothes were made specifically for her as well?"

"Either for her or someone who's of almost exactly the same build."

"Are the clothes fashionable?" Katherine asked.

"I'm the wrong person to ask, Katie. I know they're of reasonably good quality and well cared for, but I'm not familiar with the latest styles. I leave fashion to Mr. Reynolds."

Katherine clapped her hands together in delight. "You must show the clothes to Mr. Reynolds. He's an experienced tailor, and he'll be able to tell you something about the victim."

Jason grinned. "That's an excellent idea, my love. You always make such clever suggestions."

"Don't patronize me, Yank," Katherine admonished him with a warm smile. "Just because I'm a woman doesn't mean I can't have clever ideas."

"Have I ever intimated such a thing?" Jason asked, genuinely hurt that Katherine would even joke about something like that.

"No, you haven't, and I'm sorry. It's just that I run into that sort of thinking so often."

Jason studied her across the table. "You've had a letter from your father, haven't you?"

"Yes. Is it that obvious?"

"He's the only person I know who chastises you routinely, even from a distance."

"Yes, he had quite a lot to say on several domestic matters, but I won't bore you with the details."

"Please don't," Jason said. "The man infuriates me."

"I know," Katherine said, smiling guiltily. "I didn't mean to take out my pique on you."

"All is forgiven." Jason glanced at the clock on the mantel. "Katie, it's a lovely evening, and I've barely stepped outside today. What do you say we sit in the garden for a little while?"

"You Americans have the most outlandish ideas," Katherine intoned, mimicking the esteemed Reverend Talbot, who would benefit greatly from having the rod removed from his backside.

Jason laughed. "We do. That's what makes us such firebrands."

"You're on. But not before dessert. Mrs. Dodson will suffer an apoplexy if you don't sample her apple marmalade tart."

"Is Mrs. Dodson in love with some young, handsome footman she's spotted on her outings to the market?" Jason asked, a smile tugging at his lips.

"Why would you ask that?"

"She's trying out all these new recipes. I hear that's a byproduct of falling in love and a desire to express one's feelings through sudden bursts of creativity."

Katherine laughed joyously. "She's met our neighbor's cook, who's regaled her with tales of the dinners she prepares for Lord and Lady Sutton's guests. I think Mrs. Dodson is feeling a bit insecure about her culinary skills and hopes to amaze us with her newfound exuberance in the kitchen."

"Well, in that case, I hope Lord and Lady Sutton continue to entertain lavishly," Jason said, looking forward to the tart despite being full to bursting.

Chapter 8

Wednesday, September 16

Jason took his place at the operating table, making sure all his instruments were clean and laid out in proper order and the ether was ready to be administered to the patient. Nurse Clemson stood by his side, ready to assist. She was a woman of middle years who'd trained with Florence Nightingale herself during the Crimean War and was as tough as any old general. Jason trusted her implicitly and was glad she had been assigned to assist him during this particular surgery, since nothing ever distracted or distressed her, not even the teeth of the handsaw biting into the patient's bone or the rivulets of blood streaming from the incision and dripping into the box of sawdust placed beneath the operating table to absorb the overflow. Nurse Clemson was efficiency itself, handing Jason the proper instruments, mopping his brow, and keeping an eye on the patient should he or she start to wake up during the procedure.

The surgery was due to start in a few minutes, once the patient was transferred from the ward by an orderly, and most of the seats in the auditorium were already full of medical students, eager to watch the amputation. Most of the students were young, but there were several older men, who were either interested in the more modern techniques or there to criticize the "upstart American," as Jason was known in certain circles. The moniker didn't bother him. His goal was to help as many people as he could, and if there were those who found fault with his methods or attitude, then it was something they had to find a way to deal with. It had nothing to do with him.

And neither did the criticism he routinely had to endure for helping the police with their inquiries. Jason could understand his colleagues' confusion, since the police were generally looked down upon until someone required their services. People expected Jason to act like a nobleman and adopt the customs of his new homeland, but as Katie had so aptly pointed out, Jason didn't care to change his ways. He was proud to be an American and intended to return home someday, with his family in tow. There was no reason to hurry back at the moment, but he did miss New York and the friends he'd left behind.

Jason pushed aside thoughts of New York and focused on the students. There was the usual hum of conversation, the open notebooks and bottles of ink standing at the ready. Many of the faces in the auditorium were familiar, even if Jason didn't know them by name. There were several medical schools in London, and the students attended whichever procedures interested them. The nature and time of the surgeries were posted at the Royal College of Surgeons as well as at the teaching hospitals, of which there were several. Jason assumed that nothing interesting was happening at Guy's Hospital, since most of the students seemed to have flocked to his surgery this morning. Or perhaps because it was an amputation, and they liked the barbarous necessity of the procedure and fervently hoped that they would never, ever find themselves on that table as a patient rather than a spectator.

Jason had performed many an amputation during his years as an army surgeon during the American Civil War, but teaching was different from operating. He had to not only remain focused on the patient but simultaneously narrate what he was doing and why. At times, he became so engrossed that he forgot to speak, and his assistant had to quietly remind him that the students were awaiting his commentary and instruction. He was becoming better at it, though, having been teaching for nearly six months now, and he was gratified to learn that the students found him efficient, approachable, and sympathetic.

Some of the other surgeons had been given cruel nicknames that had stuck, even though the students who'd thought them up had already qualified and were practicing medicine, sometimes alongside the surgeons they'd ridiculed. Jason studied the eager faces, wishing the orderly would hurry up and deliver the patient. He was ready to begin, and the students were growing restless.

A fair-haired young man in the third row turned to his neighbor and asked rather loudly, "George, have you seen Alex?"

"No. Don't you two usually arrive together?"

"We do, but he was already gone by the time I came down this morning."

Another young man leaned forward from the row behind them. "You mean Alex Gray?"

"Yes. Have you seen him?" the fair-haired man asked.

"No, but I have some notes I must return to him. He always takes such excellent notes, I borrowed his last week. He even drew some diagrams of the kidney removal. Immensely helpful."

"You can give them to me. I'm bound to see him later."

The man handed over a notebook and opened his own in preparation for the surgery. Jason didn't mind being watched or asked questions during a procedure. Rather than distract him, it helped him to focus on what needed to be done. He'd performed countless amputations during the war and was grateful he didn't have to saw through the bone of a conscious patient. Ether really was a godsend, for both the patients and the doctors.

Even though English surgeons were addressed as Mister rather than Doctor, on account of being apprenticed rather than university educated, Jason was known to the medical students as Dr. Redmond, since he'd attended both a university and a medical school in New York. He preferred the title to plain Mister and was glad the students didn't refer to him as Lord Redmond. His title sounded pompous in a hospital setting and had no bearing on his skills as a surgeon. The title was handy from time to time, he had to admit, especially when dealing with other nobles.

Jason was distracted from his thoughts by the arrival of the patient, who was wheeled into the theater by a middle-aged porter and helped onto the operating table. The patient was a thin, balding man of thirty-two. He looked terrified, his eyes rolling wildly like those of a spooked horse. Jason put his hand on the man's shoulder and looked at him steadily.

"It will be all right, Mr. Wilkins," he said softly. "You will not feel any pain."

"I don't care about the pain, Doctor. It's my foot that troubles me. I don't want to lose it," the man moaned. "How will I live with only the one foot?"

"You will learn to adjust," Jason promised him. "You will be able to walk again once the stump heals and you're able to tolerate putting pressure on it. You will be fitted with a wooden prosthetic. That will help."

The man seemed to calm down a little, resigned to his fate.

"Nurse Clemson, are we ready?" Jason asked as the nurse prepared the ether mask that would go over the patient's face.

"Ready, Doctor."

"Let's proceed, then."

Jason tuned out the hum of conversation from the auditorium and focused on the task at hand. For the next few hours, all his attention would remain on Mr. Wilkins.

Chapter 9

Daniel arrived at Scotland Yard at nine o'clock, by which time he was already aware that the photographs had not made it into today's edition, since he'd passed several boys selling the dailies on his way in. This would delay the identification process, but hopefully, he'd be able to discover something useful before then.

A slim file holding two photographs waited on his desk, and Daniel studied the images, amazed that he hadn't immediately noticed that the man was indeed a woman. He supposed people saw what they expected to see if there was nothing to alert them to the fact that they were being deceived, but now that he knew the truth, he could see the telltale signs—the lack of an Adam's apple, for one. But the woman had been found wearing a cravat that cleverly disguised her neck, and he doubted too many people got close enough to notice the lack of stubble on the smooth cheeks and jaw, the eye immediately drawn to the false goatee. She wasn't very tall for a man, but she was of a good height for a woman and, without a corset, not so narrow of waist that one would immediately think her feminine.

Setting the photographs aside, Daniel went in search of Constable Napier, whom he found in the back room, making tea using the potbellied stove in the corner.

"Shall I make you a cup, Inspector?" Constable Napier asked.

"No, thank you. Were you able to discover anything last night?" Daniel asked, thinking that the constable should have reported his findings before making tea.

"More than a dozen people were reported missing yesterday, but none of them match the description of the victim. Several were older, several much younger, and a few had distinctive facial features and marks and the like."

"Thank you, Constable," Daniel said. He'd expected as much, so he wasn't overly disappointed.

Ten o'clock was too early to set off for the viscount's residence in Belgravia, since he would no doubt be turned away at such a socially inappropriate hour, so Daniel decided to visit several tailors in the hope that someone would recognize their work or that of their competitor. Taking the bundle of clothes with him, Daniel found a hansom and directed the driver to take him to the West End. There were several upscale establishments in Saville Row, but he didn't believe the clothes he carried had been tailored by any of them. These were not the garments of a nobleman, nor were they the second-hand or hand-stitched clothes of someone who was poor. Daniel alighted at the corner of Oxford and Bond Streets and set off, walking into any establishment that might provide him with clues as to the victim's identity.

Three hours later, Daniel gave up. The proprietors were willing to look at the garments he showed them, but each one told him virtually the same thing. The broadcloth was of good quality, the stitching was exquisite, and the shoes were well made, but no one could identify the tailor who'd made the clothes or the shoemaker who was responsible for the shoes. Nor could the jewelry shops he'd stopped at comment on the cufflinks the victim had been wearing. They weren't cheap, but there was nothing distinctive about them, like the owner's initials or a jeweler's mark.

It was a dead end, and Daniel felt frustrated with his lack of progress. It had been more than twenty-four hours since the woman's death, and he had no inkling of who she was or why someone had felt the need to kill her in such a dramatic way.

Oxford Street was humming, the sidewalks packed with shoppers and the road congested with midday traffic. Daniel felt an irrational stab of irritation at all these people who had nothing better to do than stroll from one shop to another searching for the perfect hat or just the right pair of gloves. He couldn't recall the last time he'd bought himself anything new. Since he now had to maintain his own household, he had to be careful with his money, and his detective's salary only stretched so far.

Leaving the main thoroughfare, Daniel found a street vendor and bought an eel pie, which he wolfed down in two bites before making his way to Belgravia. It was past one o'clock. The viscount was sure to be up and receiving callers.

Chapter 10

The viscount's butler was less than welcoming but didn't ask Daniel to call at the tradesmen's entrance, nor did he refuse him entry, which was a promising start. Usually Daniel had to get past dragon-like gatekeepers to see their masters, but evidently the viscount had been hoping Daniel would call.

The new Viscount Ashford was a tall, dark-haired man of twenty-seven. He was lean and graceful, and Daniel suspected that he frequented a boxing gymnasium or an exclusive fencing establishment to keep fit. His hooded dark eyes, aquiline nose, and thin lips gave him a somewhat intimidating appearance, but he was pleasant and eager to help, at least more so than he was yesterday, when he was livid and bordering on unreasonable in the face of such an unexpected interruption to his father's funeral and the histrionics of his mother and sisters, who were understandably shocked

"Inspector, I'm glad you called," he said as soon as Daniel was admitted to the study, where the viscount had been attending to his correspondence. The beautifully appointed room overlooked the back garden and was an oasis of privacy and comfort. "Would you like some coffee? Or tea?"

"No, thank you, my lord," Daniel said, although, in truth, he wouldn't have minded a cup of coffee to wash away the taste of the eel pie, but to accept didn't seem appropriate given the man's elevated social position.

"This was my father's study," the viscount said wistfully. "The only time I was ever called in here when I was a child was to be reprimanded or punished for some silly prank." He smiled. "I thought my father would live for years yet, but you never know when someone will be taken, do you?"

"No, you don't," Daniel replied, understanding only too well how Neville Ashford was feeling.

"Everyone seems to think I'm thrilled to be a viscount at last, but I'd much rather have my father back."

"I'm sorry for your loss," Daniel said, and meant it.

"Have you discovered anything more about our man?" Neville Ashford asked.

Daniel fixed the man with a direct gaze, needing to see his reaction to the news. "The man was a woman."

"What?" the viscount cried. "Impossible."

"She was wearing men's clothes and a fake goatee, but she was most definitely female."

"Extraordinary," the man said. "Who was she?"

"We've yet to identify her."

"So, how can I help? I didn't know her," the viscount said after Daniel showed him a photograph of the woman's face.

"Are you quite certain? Anything you tell me will be kept in the strictest confidence," Daniel added, in case the man was concerned about a possible scandal.

"I am. I've never seen her in my life."

"How many keys are there to the vault?" Daniel asked, changing tack.

"There were originally two keys, but one went missing. I have the other. I gave it to Mr. Fielding two days before the funeral, and he returned it to me yesterday."

"How long has the other key been missing?"

"I really don't know. A good while, I think."

"Where was is kept?"

"Here, in this room." The viscount opened the desk drawer and withdrew a small, lacquered box. "The keys were kept in this box."

"Was the desk usually locked? Or the box?" Daniel asked.

"The box doesn't have a key, and I'm not sure about the desk. As I said, I rarely came in here while my father was alive."

"Who was the first person to be entombed in the vault?" Daniel asked.

"My grandfather. That was nigh on twenty years ago."

"Was the second key still in its place then?"

"I wouldn't know. I was only seven at the time."

"Of course," Daniel said, feeling foolish in the extreme. "Who had access to this room?"

"My father kept the study locked, but the housekeeper had a key so the room could be cleaned and aired out."

"Is the housekeeper still employed by your family?"

"My mother hired a new housekeeper three years ago. The key was already missing by then," Neville added. "I know that because my Aunt Verity died right around that time, and my father mentioned that there was only one key to the vault when he arranged her funeral. He meant to have another key made, but I suppose he never got around to it."

"And the servants? Might one of them have taken the key?"

Neville shrugged. "I haven't spent much time in this house, Inspector. I went off to Eton when I was thirteen, then on to Cambridge. I've kept my own residence in Mayfair since returning to London. I don't suppose I'll be needing it now. I will have to move in here with my mother and sisters."

"Has your father's will been read yet?" Daniel asked.

"No. That will happen today, at three."

"Do you suppose there will be surprises?"

The viscount's eyebrows lifted in astonishment. "You know, I've never considered the possibility. I simply assumed I would inherit the lot, being the only son. Of course, my sisters and mother are now my responsibility, as they should be, and aside from small personal bequests, I don't expect there to be anything surprising in my father's will. I will certainly let you know if there are any unexpected clauses, such as bequests to bastard children and the like," he added with an amused smile.

"Are such clauses a possibility?" Daniel asked carefully. "Could the deceased have been your father's daughter?"

If the unidentified woman in the mortuary was the late viscount's illegitimate daughter, that would certainly explain why she'd been left hanging in the vault on the day of the viscount's interment, but not who'd killed her or why? Neville Ashford had little to gain by disposing of an illegitimate sister. She'd have no legal claim on the estate, even if she had been conceived within wedlock and before the birth of the current viscount. As the only son, he would inherit both the estate and the title.

"One thing I have learned, Inspector Haze, is never to assume anything, but I really don't think my father had any illegitimate children. He was devoted to my mother, and she to him. They were that rare phenomenon—a genuinely happy marriage."

"May I have the name of you solicitor, your lordship?" Daniel asked.

"Of course." Neville pulled out a clean sheet of note paper and wrote down the name and address.

"Richard Singleton. I've heard of him," Daniel said as he read the name.

"Yes, the firm is quite popular in certain circles."

"May I speak to her ladyship?" Daniel asked as he pocketed the folded sheet.

Neville Ashford threw him a questioning look. "Only if you promise not to ask my mother if my father had any illegitimate children."

"You have my word, sir."

"Very well, then. But I will ask you not to interview my sisters. They're traumatized enough after what occurred yesterday. They're still very young, and I promise you, they know little of the business of adults. They are not yet out of the schoolroom."

"Of course. I understand," Daniel replied. He would have insisted had he thought the two girls might know something, but at twelve and fourteen, Daniel highly doubted they were privy to anything important enough to influence the investigation.

Neville Ashford consulted his watch. "Mother should be up by now. I'll ask her to join us in the drawing room."

Daniel had hoped to speak to the widow privately. With her son present, she might not be as forthcoming, but he was grateful to be allowed access to the woman. The viscount could have easily refused. Daniel was shown to the drawing room, while Neville Ashford went to speak to his mother. The two appeared a few minutes later and settled across from Daniel, the viscount obviously intending to remain for the duration.

Lady Ashford was in her late forties and had the same dark hair and hooded eyes as her son. Her black gown and black lace cap did little to disguise the fact that she was still an attractive woman, and younger than Daniel had first assumed when he'd seen her yesterday at the cemetery.

"I wonder if I might ask you a few questions, my lady," Daniel said, keeping his tone deferential.

"You may," Lady Ashford replied tersely.

"Do you recall when the second key to the vault went missing?"

Lady Ashford made a show of thinking. "First I heard of it was when Verity died. That was three years ago, but I can only assume it had been missing for some time before that. The last person to die before Verity was the late viscount's younger brother, but he wished to be buried in Scotland, so the subject of the key never came up."

"My lady, may I show you the photographs of the deceased?" Daniel asked.

"That's rather macabre, isn't it?" Lady Ashford asked, but Daniel could see that she was curious to see the deceased close up.

"Yes, but I need to ascertain if you knew her."

Lady Ashford didn't appear surprised when Daniel referred to the victim as a woman, so her son must have told her of the latest development when he'd gone up to speak to her.

"All right," she conceded. "I will do as you ask, Inspector."

Daniel showed her the two photographs and she looked at them carefully, studying the victim's features. "I'm sure I've never met her," she said, handing the photographs back.

"Do you think she might have been connected to your family in some way?" Daniel asked, phrasing the question as delicately as he could.

"No," Lady Ashford replied sharply. "She's a stranger to us. Isn't she, Neville?"

"I have already told the inspector, Mama, that I have no idea who she was."

"Thank you, my lady," Daniel said, and replaced the photographs in his breast pocket.

"What a very difficult job you have, Inspector," Lady Ashford said, shaking her head. "And so very unpleasant."

"Someone's got to do it," Daniel replied, wondering what she expected him to say.

"Yes, I expect they do. Well, I do hope you find whoever killed this poor young woman and reiterate to the press that she had nothing to do with us." She didn't wait for Daniel to reply and turned to her son. "Neville, do speak to Cressida. She's most upset by what happened yesterday."

"Yes, Mama."

Thus dismissed, Daniel left, this time by the servants' entrance, and headed to the offices of Singleton and Marsh, Esquires.

Chapter 11

Richard Singleton had to be nearing seventy. He had a ring of gray curly fuzz encircling his egg-shaped head and rheumy blue eyes nestled in a puddle of wrinkles, but his gaze was sharp and his smile genuine.

"How can I help you, Inspector Haze?" Mr. Singleton asked when Daniel was escorted into his office by a clerk who looked like he'd just sucked on a particularly sour lemon.

"I need to know the terms of the late Viscount Ashford's will," Daniel said.

The old lawyer sat back in his chair and grinned. "I'm sure you know that's confidential information, and as far as I can tell, you don't have a warrant."

"I don't," Daniel admitted.

"So, let's try this another way," Mr. Singleton suggested. "You tell me what you suspect, and I will tell you if your hunch is valid or not."

"All right," Daniel agreed, grateful not to have been dismissed out of hand. "A young woman dressed as a man was found hanging in the Ashford vault yesterday morning. Contrary to appearances, she didn't take her own life; she was murdered. Poisoned. Neither the new viscount nor the late viscount's widow seem to know who she was or what her connection to the family might have been. Is it at all possible, Mr. Singleton, that the woman was the viscount's natural daughter, or even his mistress?"

The lawyer smiled wryly. "I draw up many wills, Inspector, and believe me when I tell you, I've seen it all. Even in your line of work, you'd still be surprised what people get up to, but Viscount Ashford was a family man. He loved his wife and as far as I know was never unfaithful to her in any way that would impact future generations. There was no mistress and no love child, and if there were, he didn't leave them a farthing. The will is exactly what you'd expect it to be. He left everything to his son, except for a few small bequests to loyal retainers and the staff at his gentlemen's club."

"Do you have any ideas who the woman might have been?" Daniel asked, sorely disappointed to learn that the viscount had been the model husband and father.

"I'm sorry, but I don't. I have provided legal counsel to the Ashford family for over forty years, and not a whiff of scandal in all that time."

"What about the son?" Daniel asked, not quite ready to drop the Ashford line of inquiry. "Might the woman have been Neville's lover?"

"If she was, I know nothing about her and can't help you," Richard Singleton replied.

"Thank you for your time," Daniel said, and stood.

"Good luck with your inquiries, Inspector Haze. I hope they lead you far from my client."

I bet you do, Daniel thought as he left the law office.

Stepping outside, Daniel consulted his watch. There was no point in returning to Scotland Yard. The victim's photo would run in tomorrow's edition of the *Illustrated London News* and the *Daily Telegraph* so there was bound to be a response, but he didn't expect anything had come into the Yard in the past few hours. Feeling at a loose end, Daniel decided to call on Jason. He might have thought of something since last night, especially if he'd discussed the case with his wife. Katherine Redmond had a keen mind and was always eager to involve herself in their investigations, if only in a peripheral way. Besides, Daniel was hungry despite the pie he'd had less than two hours ago and hoped Jason might join him for a spot of lunch.

Decision made, Daniel set off for the hospital.

Chapter 12

Jason looked tired and upset when he came out to meet Daniel in the foyer. The patient he'd operated on had developed a fever, so Jason had remained on hand in case his condition worsened. The two men stepped outside to talk, settling on a bench beneath a leafy maple. It was a beautiful autumn day, and it was pleasant to just sit for a while, since they'd both been on their feet since early morning.

"What are the man's chances?" Daniel asked, studying Jason's worried expression.

"It's too soon to tell," Jason replied. "I'll know more within twenty-four hours. The fever could be the body's natural reaction to the amputation, or it could be a sign of an infection, which will either clear up or turn septic. The instruments had been sterilized before the surgery, and I had washed my hands in carbolic to reduce the possibility of contaminating the area."

"Have you ever lost a patient?" Daniel asked. "Not during wartime, but in a hospital setting."

"Of course. Quite a few. But it never gets easier. You always think you might have saved them if only you'd operated sooner or done something differently. I found myself endlessly second-guessing myself. After losing my first patient, a boy of fourteen, I even considered walking away from medicine altogether."

"And now?" Daniel asked.

"And now I know that you can't save everyone. Most patients recover, some do not, but they would all likely die without surgical intervention, so I comfort myself with the knowledge that I save the majority of those who put their faith in me," Jason replied with a tired smile. "But enough about me. Have you learned anything about our victim?"

"Not a thing. If the woman was any relation to the Ashford family, they're not admitting to knowing her. And according to the family lawyer, there are no unexpected bequests in the late viscount's will, which doesn't mean she couldn't have been his illegitimate daughter, or his mistress. Perhaps she'd approached the family after the viscount had died, demanding a settlement or she'd reveal the truth. Rather than part with the money or risk scandal, Neville Ashford killed her, or more likely had someone else do the deed. Although I don't see the point of displaying her body in the family tomb if avoiding scandal was the goal," Daniel mused. "Perhaps it was a warning to anyone else who might come forward in the hope of reaping financial rewards from their association with the late Viscount Ashford."

Daniel sighed heavily, his frustration getting the better of him. "Before calling on the viscount, I visited at least ten tailoring establishments as well as several shoemakers, but no one was able to shed any light. Same goes for the cufflinks. They are the sort of trinket anyone who's gainfully employed might be able to afford. Perhaps they were even a gift," Daniel speculated. Somehow, relating the information to Jason made his efforts seem more worthwhile. Not every avenue of inquiry led to a result, he reminded himself, his mood improving somewhat. It was early days yet.

"Anyhow, the photographs of the deceased are set to run in tomorrow's edition of the *Illustrated London News* and the *Daily Telegraph* so we might have a lead before the day's out. Someone is bound to recognize her," Daniel said. "Until then, I find myself at a loose end."

Jason looked thoughtful at he turned to face Daniel. "I think I might know who she was. Or more accurately, who he was."

Daniel's mouth fell open at this unexpected statement. Jason had let him prattle on for the better part of ten minutes when all along he might have been in possession of crucial information about the case.

"How could you possibly know? You've been at the hospital all morning," Daniel sputtered, wishing Jason would have just come out with it.

"I overheard something in the operating theater, one of the surgical students asking about the whereabouts of his cousin. I thought nothing of it at the time, and then the patient was brought in, and all my attention was focused on the procedure for the next few hours. It was only once I was finished, and the students had begun to leave, that the memory slid into place. I clearly recalled seeing the two men at previous surgeries and realized that the cousin he'd spoken of bore a striking resemblance to our victim. I intended to speak to the man, but he'd already gone by the time I had cleaned up."

"Are you going to keep me in suspense?" Daniel exclaimed. "Who was he…eh, she?"

"The man in attendance this morning was Edward Gray. And I think the person on the slab in the mortuary might be Alexander Gray."

"What makes you think so? Did this Mr. Gray say his cousin was missing?"

"Not in so many words, but he seemed concerned because Alexander was meant to be there this morning and never showed."

"Do you know where I can find this Edward Gray?"

Jason's expression turned smug. "As it happens, I do." He pulled a folded sheet of paper out of his breast pocket and handed it to Daniel. "This is his address. The hospital maintains a record of all the attending medical students and their details. Alexander Gray resides at the same address."

"I'm going to head over there right now," Daniel said, fervently wishing Jason could come along. The fact that Edward Gray knew, and presumably respected Jason would be an invaluable asset in an interview, but he couldn't ask Jason to leave his patient at this crucial stage. Jason had a greater responsibility to the man upstairs than he did to Daniel, who had come to rely on Jason's input in any investigation that wasn't a straightforward case of wrongdoing.

"Can you wait an hour?" Jason asked, surprising Daniel out of his reverie. "I would like to change the dressing on the amputation patient myself. I know the nurses will do a competent job, but I need to examine the incision for signs of infection. Once I issue instructions for follow-up care, I'll be able to join you."

"I will get something to eat and return for you in an hour," Daniel said, bolstered by the prospect of Jason's assistance and the promising potential of this new lead. At least he'd have something to report to Superintendent Ransome this evening instead of admitting that he'd come up empty after a full day of investigating the murder.

"There's an excellent chophouse just around the corner. All the doctors go there."

"Then that's where I'll go," Daniel said in parting.

Chapter 13

They found Edward Gray at his lodgings in Blackfriars. Two young men were leaving just as Daniel and Jason arrived, so it seemed there were several other lodgers besides the Grays staying at the boarding house. The landlady, Mrs. Fleet, who was as wide as she was tall and had a penchant for lace-trimmed ruffles that cascaded from her ample bosom like the waters of a frothing waterfall, invited them to wait in the parlor while she informed Mr. Gray he had visitors. Judging by the smugness of her smile, she clearly considered them to be gentlemen of quality who might elevate the reputation of her establishment merely by stepping through the front door.

The parlor was small but clean and cozy, with a carpet worn by numerous feet and outdated furniture that had been well used during its long lifetime. There were framed needlepoint samplers on the wall and an arrangement of porcelain figurines on the mantelpiece, their painted eyes looking slyly at the visitors from beneath beribboned bonnets and shiny black tricorns Their outfits were about a century of out of date and the figurines had probably been keeping vigil on the mantel for about that long.

Jason clasped his hands behind his back and turned toward the door, a part of him desperately hoping that he was wrong and Edward Gray would not be able to identify the victim. It would be a setback for Daniel, but Alexander Gray, from what little information Jason had been able to glean since that morning, was a gifted surgeon, one of the top students in his class at the Royal College of Surgeons, and a generally well-liked young man. Surely the woman he'd autopsied couldn't be one and the same, but the queasiness in his gut and the tension in his shoulders told him otherwise. There was a strong possibility that his hunch was correct.

Edward Gray, who arrived shortly. was a fair-haired young man with pale blue eyes and a slender build. He strongly resembled the deceased and seemed more shocked to find Dr.

Redmond waiting for him in Mrs. Fleet's parlor than an inspector from Scotland Yard. He stopped short, staring at Jason with an apprehensive expression.

"Dr. Redmond," he exclaimed. He looked like he was about to say something else but then thought better of it and opted to wait for an explanation.

"Shall we sit down?" Jason invited, smiling kindly at the young man.

Edward Gray sank into a chair and faced the two men, his face growing paler by the second. "Is something wrong? Is it Alex?" he asked, his voice quavering.

"Do you have reason to believe something's happened to your cousin, Mr. Gray?" Daniel asked.

"I haven't seen him since Monday. I knocked on his door this morning, and then again when I returned from the hospital, but there's no answer. And Mrs. Fleet said she saw him go out on Monday night."

Daniel extracted a photograph of the deceased in her disguise and passed it to Edward Gray. "Is this Alexander Gray?"

The young man's hand flew to his mouth as he stared at the photograph. Being a medical student, he understood only too well what he was looking at, even though the photograph had been taken after the deceased had been cut down and laid out on the floor of the vault. "What happened to him? Where was this taken?" Edward whimpered.

"This was taken at Highgate Cemetery. The body was discovered when the vault was opened to receive the late Viscount Ashford's remains."

"No!" Edward cried, his eyes brimming with tears. "No! Why would anyone hurt Alex? He was the kindest of men."

Jason felt overwhelming sympathy for Edward Gray, especially since he was about to inflict further suffering on the poor man. "Mr. Gray, I performed the postmortem on your cousin," he said, giving Edward to understand that he knew the truth.

The young man went white to the roots of his hair. It obviously hadn't occurred to him that an autopsy had been ordered and that his cousin's secret was now out in the open. He nodded miserably and fixed his gaze on his folded hands.

"Mr. Gray, I think an explanation is in order," Daniel said. He was raring to ask his questions, so Edward Gray's grief would have to wait until he was on his own.

Edward sighed heavily and raised his eyes to meet Daniel's inquiring gaze. "Alex was not my cousin. She was my sister. Alexandra," he said softly.

"Why was your sister dressed as a man?" Daniel asked. He'd moderated his tone, clearly willing to exercise patience now that he was getting somewhere with the investigation.

"I think I can answer that," Jason replied, noting the fear in Edward's eyes. He must have just realized that he could be held accountable for his sister's deception. "Alexandra Gray wished to study medicine and, as a woman, found all doors closed to her, so she found a way around the obstacles in her path. Is that correct, Mr. Gray?" Jason asked gently.

Edward nodded. "Ally and I were orphaned at a young age," he said, having composed himself enough to utter more than a few words. "We were taken in by our father's widowed sister. She lived in Truro, so we had to leave London."

A faraway expression crossed Edward's face, as if he were clearly seeing that time of loss and sudden change. "Aunt Eva had no children of her own, and she doted on us. I think she pretended we were hers, and we were happy to allow her to do so, since we were so desperate to feel that we belonged to someone and wouldn't find ourselves alone in the world. Ally was just six at the time, and I was eight," he added. "We just wanted to be loved."

"That's understandable," Daniel said, his Adam's apple bobbing as he swallowed back his reaction to Edward's words, which had no doubt brought Charlotte to mind. "Please, go on."

"Aunt Eva was well off, so once I was old enough, she hired the best tutors for me. I had expressed a desire to study medicine, and she was thrilled. She thought it was a fitting occupation for a young gentleman." Edward smiled wistfully at the memory.

"After a time, Ally asked to join in on the lessons, and Aunt Eva agreed. She didn't believe an education to be detrimental to a woman's prospects. To be honest, I was never as dedicated a pupil as Ally was. She was always berating me for my ambivalence and telling me how fortunate I was to have been born a man. Mr. Cuthbert, our tutor, treated Ally as if she were any other student, but he did tell her outright that if she wished to go into medicine, her only hope was to take up nursing, as no medical school would admit her on account of her being a woman. Ally argued with him and told him about Elizabeth Blackwell, who'd been the first woman to graduate from medical school in America nearly twenty years before."

Edward looked at Jason to see if he recognized the name. He did. He'd been awed by the woman's persistence and courage but didn't think admitting women to medical school was about to become standard practice. He tried to recall if any other women had followed in the lady's trailblazing path but couldn't think of any. He had heard of Elizabeth Garrett Anderson, who'd applied to several British medical schools and had been rejected by them all. But she had been granted a license to practice medicine from the Society of Apothecaries, the first woman in England to do so.

"So, what happened?" Daniel asked, clearly not very interested in Alexandra Gray's inspiration.

"When Aunt Eva passed, Ally talked me into moving to London to pursue my studies. I couldn't afford Oxford or Cambridge and didn't qualify for a scholarship. Edinburgh, being the next best university on the list, was too far away, so I agreed. Little did I know that Ally planned to apply to medical school right alongside me. She told me about James Barry, who'd been born a woman but had passed herself off as a man to enter medical school and had lived as a man until her death decades later. Lord only knows where Ally had unearthed that bit of information, but she was inspired by the woman and thought it could be done. I told her she was mad, but Ally was adamant. She had it all planned. She thought that if we let the house in Truro, we'd have enough money to live modestly in London and always have a bolt hole should we need to leave London."

"How did she prepare for her transformation?" Jason asked, curious about the logistics of such an undertaking.

Edward sighed again, still exasperated with the sister who now lay dead in the mortuary at Scotland Yard. "Ally's friend, Tansy, is a seamstress in Truro, so Ally had her make an entire gentleman's wardrobe for her. I tried to change her mind and point out all the things she'd be giving up, but talking Ally out of anything was like trying to stop a locomotive with one's bare hands," Edward confessed. "Once she had her clothes, Ally ordered shoes, using a cutout of her feet. She told the cobbler the shoes were a present for her brother, so he wouldn't ask any questions or demand that the brother come in person to try them on. She even found a shop that sold theatrical makeup and various props. That was where she purchased the goatee. She bought three, in fact, just in case, and the necessary adhesive. She treated the whole thing like an adventure and tried to prepare for every eventuality."

"What happened when you arrived in London?" Daniel asked.

"I was terribly nervous, but when no one seemed to notice anything odd, not even Mrs. Fleet, who's got a nose like a bloodhound, I began to relax. I actually liked having Ally by my side. We studied together and attended all the lectures and surgeries. We had planned to work together once we qualified."

"Why did you pretend to be cousins rather than brothers?" Jason asked.

"In case we ran into anyone who knew us from Truro. People knew I didn't have a brother, only a sister, so it seemed safer that way."

"And was the money you earned from letting the house enough to support you both?" Daniel asked, his thoughts likely turning toward darker possibilities.

"Aunt Eva left us some money, enough to last until we were able to start earning a living," Edward said, his eyes misting again.

He was now truly alone in the world, a feeling Jason knew only too well, having felt much the same when he'd returned home at the end of the Civil War to learn that his parents were gone, and his fiancée had married his best friend in his absence. If it hadn't been for Micah, Jason might have wallowed in self-pity until he spiraled into self-destructive behavior and met with a bad end. He hoped Edward Gray would continue with his studies and qualify as a surgeon. If his role in his sister's deception came into question, Jason would vouch for him personally to keep him from getting expelled.

"Mr. Gray, did anyone know your sister's secret?" Daniel asked, ignoring the man's misery.

"No. We made a pact to tell no one. That was the only way to retain control of the situation."

"Did anyone wish your sister harm?"

"No," Edward cried. "She was the sweetest, most caring person. No one had any reason to dislike her."

"Did she often go out by herself at night?" Jason asked, recalling what Edward had said about Mrs. Fleet's observation.

"We usually went out together. I don't know where she went on Monday, or whom she'd met with, if that's what you're about to ask." His anxious gaze fixed on Jason, and he squared his shoulders, as if bracing for a blow. "How did she die, Dr. Redmond?"

"I believe she was poisoned with aconite, then hanged once she was dead."

"Did she suffer?" Edward whimpered.

"There's no evidence to suggest that your sister suffered before she died. I believe she died almost instantly."

"Well, thank God for that, at least." The young man's pale hands began to tremble, as though a new thought had occurred to him. "Was she…?" He couldn't finish the question.

"No, Mr. Gray. Your sister had not been interfered with," Daniel hurried to reassure him

Edward nodded. "There's little to be grateful for when someone you love dies, but I'm thankful it was quick."

"Do you know the Ashfords?" Daniel asked.

"No. Our paths never crossed."

"Are you sure?" Daniel persisted. "Perhaps you met in passing."

"Yes, I'm sure. We never met."

"So why would your sister's body be left on display in their family vault?"

"I have no idea," Edward said. He looked dejected and utterly beaten. "A heartless prank?" he suggested bitterly.

Daniel let that line of questioning go for the time being and turned to more immediate avenues of inquiry. "Did your sister have any particular friends here in London?" he asked, his notebook at the ready.

"All our friends were mutual."

"Who are your closest friends?" Jason asked. "People you socialized with outside of lecture halls."

"Ezra Hall, Timothy Latham, and Max Devane." Edward smiled sadly. "Ally had a bit of an infatuation with Max. She called him Max Divine."

"Did your sister hope to marry in time?" Daniel asked.

"Marriage and family were not a priority for Ally. She wanted to be a surgeon, and she was willing to sacrifice personal happiness for her dream."

"Did your sister ever visit Highgate Cemetery?" Jason asked.

"She did, yes. She said she liked to look at the inscriptions and imagine the people's lives. She often wondered if she might have been able to save any of them had she operated on them, or if they had been destined to die."

"Did she go alone?" Daniel asked.

"No, we often went together. I thought it a morbid habit to walk among the dead, but I didn't like Ally going alone."

"Did any of your friends ever join you?"

"No. Max thought it was macabre, and Timothy always rushed home to his wife. He's newly married."

"What about Ezra Hall?" Daniel asked.

"Ezra is not a fanciful man. He sees medicine as a means to an end," Edward replied.

"And what end is that?"

"A comfortable life, Inspector. It's vastly preferable to laying railroad tracks, as Ezra's father had done for nigh on thirty years. The work broke his back, as well as his spirit."

"And what do you see medicine as?" Jason asked, surprised by the direction the conversation had taken. Much like Alexandra Gray, he'd always wondered if he might have saved someone's life had he operated on them in time and often found himself studying the stones in a graveyard, feeling immense relief when he saw that someone had lived a full life and had not been taken in their prime, or worse yet, in childhood. Now that he was a father, he found those deaths most heartbreaking of all.

"I believe that medicine is a combination of the scientific and the spiritual, Dr. Redmond. A person who believes they will get better often does, whereas a person who has no will to live can often die of a non-life-threatening ailment." Edward cast an embarrassed look at Jason. "You must think that's asinine."

"I don't, actually," Jason replied. "I agree with you. The patient's mental state has much to do with recovery, in my opinion."

Edward looked relieved.

"Mr. Gray, do you think any of your friends suspected that Alex Gray wasn't exactly what he appeared to be? Might your sister have said or done something to give herself away?" Daniel asked.

"Ally was very careful. She always wore a cravat to hide the lack of an Adam's apple and the goatee to stem questions about a lack of a beard." Edward became emotional again. "I know you've never heard her speak, but she had a deep voice for a woman, so that worked in her favor. She didn't immediately stand out among other young men."

"What about taking care of her more intimate needs?" Daniel asked, making the young man wince with embarrassment.

"Surely she couldn't avail herself of the ladies' cloakroom when nature called."

"Ally was fanatically strict about her intake of liquids."

Jason nodded, cognizant of the wisdom of Alexandra's decision. Many public areas, such as the hospital and the Royal College of Surgeons, had cloakrooms where a row of chamber pots was separated from the rest of the room with nothing more than a screen. Men often chatted to each other as they relieved themselves, utterly unselfconscious in front of other men. There was no way Alexandra Gray could have availed herself of the facilities without betraying her secret. It couldn't have been easy for her, especially when she had her menses, but she had obviously found a way to manage her personal needs without betraying her true self.

"So, you are certain that no one knew Alexander Gray was really a woman?" Daniel asked.

"I'm certain," Edward replied.

"We'll need the addresses for your friends."

Edward Gray recited the addresses, and Daniel jotted down the information in his notebook.

"Thank you, Mr. Gray. We might need to speak to you again. Incidentally, where were you on Monday evening?"

"Here. Mrs. Fleet can vouch for me. I wasn't feeling well when I came home around three and went directly to my room. She brought me supper on a tray at seven, and then I went to bed around nine. I get migraines sometimes," Edward explained. "When I woke the following morning, I knocked on Ally's door, but there was no answer, so I assumed she'd already left."

"Thank you, Mr. Gray."

"Can I bury Ally?" Edward asked, looking from Daniel to Jason.

"Yes. The body will be released to you tomorrow, but I'm afraid I will not be able to keep the victim's true identity out of the papers," Daniel said. "The story will run tomorrow."

"I understand," Edward replied miserably. "I can just imagine how the journalists will portray her. By the time they're done with Ally, everyone will believe she deserved to be murdered."

Jason couldn't argue with that. This would be a sensational story that would capture the attention of the capital, for a few days at least, until something else newsworthy occurred, and then the press would be onto that. He did hope that someone would compliment Alexandra Gray on her ingenuity and her determination to follow her dream at great personal cost, but he knew better. She would be vilified and made to seem unnatural, a cautionary tale for any woman who thought she could compete in a man's world and get away with subterfuge. Everyone would think Alexandra Gray got her just deserts in the end.

"Mrs. Fleet, might we have a word?" Daniel asked once Edward Gray had left the parlor and Mrs. Fleet materialized in the doorway, ready to see them out. Jason wouldn't be surprised if she'd been listening in on their conversation, but her expression gave nothing away.

"Of course," she replied, and settled in the chair Edward Gray had just vacated.

On closer inspection, Mrs. Fleet was older than Jason had first thought. Possibly in her early fifties. She was a motherly woman whose brown gaze was as warm as it was inquisitive.

"Is Edward in some sort of trouble?" she asked.

Daniel explained about the murder of Alex Gray but left out the most important detail for the time being. Mrs. Fleet let out a strangled cry as her hand flew to her ruffled bosom. "Oh, that dear boy. He was so good. Why would anyone do that?"

"That's what we're trying to discover," Daniel said. "Mrs. Fleet, did you see Alex and Edward Gray on Monday evening?"

Mrs. Fleet sighed as she focused her mind on the evening in question. "Well, Edward came home around three. He looked ill, and I told him so. He said he had a megrim and needed to lie down. He went directly to his room and remained there for the rest of the evening. When I brought him supper at seven, he was in his dressing gown."

"And Alex?" Jason asked.

"Alex came in around four and asked for tea. I brought it up to his room. He had his books spread out on the desk and looked to be studying. He took supper with the other lodgers at seven and returned to his room. He then went out at nine."

"Do you know where he went?" Daniel asked.

"No. I was in my room when he left."

"So how do you know he left the house?" Jason asked.

"My bedroom faces the street, so I saw him through the window. I often sit by the window in the evening. I like looking at the night sky," she explained shyly. "Something of an amateur astronomer."

"Which way did Alex Gray go?" Daniel asked.

"A hansom came by just as he left the house, and he got in. I didn't see which way it went once it turned the corner."

"Did Alex often go out by himself?" Jason asked.

"From time to time. And he was stealthy about it. Didn't want Edward to know."

"How do you know that?"

"He'd creep past Edward's room and then let himself out quietly."

"What time would he normally get back?" Daniel asked.

"In the small hours. I'd always wake when he came in. I'm a light sleeper," she added.

"And did Alex say anything the next morning about where he'd been?"

"No. He'd come down to breakfast as usual, looking no worse for wear."

"How did Alex dress when he went on these outings?" Jason asked.

Mrs. Fleet shrugged her meaty shoulders. "Just his usual. Not in evening clothes, if that's what you mean."

"Mrs. Fleet, did you ever notice anything odd about Alex, or find anything you couldn't explain in his room?" Daniel asked.

"Like what?" Mrs. Fleet asked, clearly horrified by the implication that she had missed something of great importance.

"Like items that might belong to a woman."

"I do not allow ladies on the premises, Inspector Haze. This is a respectable boarding house, and if rules are not observed, then the perpetrator will find himself looking for new accommodation. Neither Alex nor Edward ever brought a woman back with them. Ever."

"Mrs. Fleet, Alex Gray *was* a woman," Jason said. "Alexandra."

"I beg your pardon?" Mrs. Fleet asked, assuming she'd misheard.

"Alexander Gray was a woman," Jason repeated.

"Goodness me," Mrs. Fleet exclaimed, her hand going to her bosom again. "How is such a thing possible?"

Her mouth opened in an O of astonishment as if certain aspects of Alex's needs were just beginning to make sense to her. "Now that you mention it," she said, "I never did see a shaving razor in his room. And I did find…" Her voice trailed off, probably because she didn't care to admit to snooping.

"What did you find, Mrs. Fleet?" Jason asked.

"Cotton cloths, the sort women use…" She went silent again, her cheeks flushing scarlet.

"The sort women use during their time of the month?" Jason asked.

Mrs. Fleet nodded. "She must have washed them out herself and dried them in her room."

"Did you do her laundry?" Daniel asked.

"Yes, it's part of the arrangement I have with the lodgers. I do the laundry for all the young men. But I've never seen anything unusual," she added.

"Did Alex Gray ever have any visitors?" Jason asked.

"Some of the Grays' fellow students came to call. I let them use the parlor and offered them tea and bread when they got hungry. I never charged them for the extra food. I like having young people about. They liven the place up with their passion and idealism," Mrs. Fleet smiled fondly. "They'd talk for hours about things I didn't understand. Not that I was listening," she hastened to assure them. "But they always left by ten."

"But did Alex Gray ever have his own visitors?" Daniel asked.

"No, never." Mrs. Fleet looked thoughtful. "I did notice one odd thing, though."

"And what was that?" Jason asked.

"Not many cabs come down this street. If ever I need one, I must walk to the cab stop near St. Paul's. But a cab always appeared as soon as Alex left the house."

"So, you think it was prearranged?"

"Must have been, or she'd have to walk to the stop on her own at that time of night."

"Thank you, Mrs. Fleet," Daniel said. "You've been most helpful."

"Oh, anytime, Inspector. Dr. Redmond," she said. "Anything I can do to help. Man or woman, no one deserves an end like that."

Chapter 14

Once out in the street, Jason and Daniel headed toward St. Paul's Cathedral, which was just a few streets over, its distinctive cupola visible above the rooftops. As Mrs. Fleet had pointed out, hansom cabs didn't seem to come along as frequently in this area as they did in the more prosperous parts of London, where people didn't think twice about paying for a ride. The less fortunate often chose to walk and save their coin for food and coal.

Daniel didn't mind the walk. He always did his best thinking while walking, and it was a lovely afternoon, the sun shining gently out of a cloudless sky and bathing the city in a golden haze that would give way to the purple shadows of twilight in a few short hours.

"What are your thoughts?" Daniel asked Jason, who was unusually quiet, his face shadowed by the brim of his topper.

"Well, we now know that Alexandra Gray successfully maintained her persona as Alex Gray for a long while, and we know her reasons for doing it. We also know that she kept secrets from her brother and went out alone at night, possibly to meet someone. A lover?" Jason asked, clearly not expecting an answer, since he went on. "If she were having a sexual relationship, was it with a man or a woman, and did that person know the truth of her situation? It's difficult to say if the killer knew she was a woman, since they didn't display her in a way that would make her sex obvious."

"Whoever left her in that vault knew she'd be found as soon as the vault was unlocked in the morning, just as they could be sure a postmortem would be ordered. Perhaps they relished our shock at finding out the truth."

"Yes, that's possible, I suppose. But what was their motive for killing Alexandra Gray? This wasn't a spur-of-the-moment killing. It was premeditated. The killer had come prepared, not only with poison but with a rope to hang the victim. Why? And why go through the trouble of hanging her once she was already dead? They could have just as easily laid her out on the empty shelf. I don't think the shock value would have been diminished, do you?"

"Whoever killed her wanted to make a statement, or send a message, but to whom? It would stand to reason that they were targeting the Ashford family, but if the Ashfords truly didn't know Alexandra Gray, what was the killer hoping to accomplish?"

"And how did they administer the poison?" Jason asked, speaking almost to himself. "There were no defensive wounds on her hands or arms. They didn't try to hold her down, so she must have either taken it willingly or under threat. Or she was tricked."

"Whichever way the poison was given, it points to the fact that she knew her killer and possibly trusted them."

"Or perhaps the killer gave her a choice," Jason suggested. "A final act of compassion, so to speak."

"How do you mean?"

"Let us suppose that for whatever reason, the killer wanted Alexandra Gray's body to be found hanging in that vault. That was the intention all along. But the killer didn't really care how she died, so she was offered a choice. Death by hanging or death by poison. If I were offered the same choice, I'd take the poison every time."

"So, you're suggesting that the killer wished to make it easier for her, which would suggest that there was a relationship of some sort between victim and perpetrator?" Daniel asked.

"Yes, I am. That's the only way I can rationalize hanging the victim once she was already dead."

Daniel nodded. "That certainly makes sense, but we won't know if your theory is correct until we learn more about Alexandra Gray's life and the people in it. I do agree with you, however. This was no random killing, and perhaps the killer did feel a modicum of pity for the victim."

"We're a lot further ahead in the investigation than we were this morning. Now we know the identity of the victim and can establish a timeline of her activities in the days prior to her death," Jason said.

"Mrs. Fleet appears to have been the last person to see Alexandra Gray alive, at approximately nine o'clock. She died a few hours later. That narrows down the window considerably. Still, if Edward Gray has no idea where his sister went that evening, then we must find someone who does."

"If Alexandra Gray had an arrangement with a particular cabbie, he'd know where she went on those nocturnal outings," Jason suggested.

"That's an excellent point," Daniel agreed. "I'll see if I can track the man down, but first, let's talk to her friends. Perhaps one of them knows something her brother doesn't," Daniel said.

"I think we should start with Max Devane. If Alexandra Gray proclaimed an infatuation with him, then it's possible her feelings were reciprocated."

"Which would mean that Mr. Devane would have to know her secret."

"Unless he's homosexual and thought he was romancing a man," Jason pointed out.

"Yes, I suppose that's a possibility, but you said you saw no signs of eh…" Daniel allowed the sentence to trail off, unsure what the correct terminology would be in this case.

"I saw no signs of recent penetration," Jason replied, leaving out the more descriptive adjectives pertaining to such an arrangement between homosexual partners, "but it's not impossible that it had happened in the past."

"Why would any woman permit such a thing?" Daniel exclaimed.

Jason laughed, clearly amused by Daniel's question.

"What's so funny?" Daniel demanded.

"Daniel, human sexuality has been around for as long as humans themselves, and although society, the church, and fear of repercussions have largely controlled people's perceptions of sex throughout the ages, there are always those who are eager to experiment and push the limits of societal norms."

"You're saying she might have liked it?" Daniel asked, incredulous and disgusted in equal measure.

He was always shocked by Jason's matter-of-fact attitude toward behavior he'd always believed to be a sin, but Jason was a doctor and had seen things Daniel couldn't begin to imagine. Not only was he comfortable with nudity and all the intimate functions of the human body, but he was completely unfazed by the most shocking aspects of human nature. Jason was vastly worldlier than Daniel, a realization that made Daniel feel embarrassed by his naivete but also grateful to have been spared certain aspects of the human condition. Even in his job, which exposed him to some of the most loathsome traits of man, he had managed to retain something of his innocence, which he was sure to lose if he continued to muck about in the quagmire that was humanity and its predilection for violence.

"I'm only saying that we need to keep an open mind until we know more of what Alexandra Gray got up to," Jason said, correctly interpreting Daniel's reaction.

The conversation ended abruptly as they approached the hansom stand. There were three cabs waiting for fares, so they approached the first one.

"Where to, guv?" the cabbie asked Daniel, smiling to show a missing front tooth.

Daniel gave the man Max Devane's address in Aldgate. He was more than a little curious to meet Max *Divine*.

Chapter 15

Jason looked around as the hansom turned into Fenchurch Street. Even at this time of day the street was congested with carriages, wagons, and pushcarts. The road was lined with architecturally unappealing buildings, each one with a shop on the ground floor. Colorful awnings shadowed the shopfronts, and there seemed to be constant activity as people went from shop to shop or wove their way through traffic to get to the other side of the street, some pushing their laden carts before them. The general atmosphere was one of chaos, but it reminded Jason of certain parts of New York, and he felt a pang of nostalgia for his hometown. Two men clad in black stood arguing in the street in what Jason thought was Yiddish. He'd heard it spoken on the Lower East Side in New York and could identify if not understand it.

"Lots of Jews here, from Eastern Europe mostly," Daniel said. "If it's not the Irish, it's the Jews."

"You have to feel sorry for people who are forced to leave their homeland to survive," Jason said.

"Oh, I do," Daniel replied with feeling. "Life is difficult enough without being treated like vermin by those who feel you're infringing on what's rightfully theirs. You might have the dregs of society living in some of the worst slums, but even they look down their noses at the immigrants and feel a sense of superiority because they feel they belong. Little do they realize that the immigrants are a plucky lot and will prosper through sheer determination and hard work," Daniel said as the cab turned into Billister Lane. "And if they don't, they'll leave."

"Where would they go?" Jason asked.

"To America," Daniel replied. "Leaving by the boatload, from what I hear. They think they'll have a chance at a better life there."

"Perhaps they will," Jason said, although he wasn't so sure. The lot of the immigrant wasn't easy in any country, especially if they didn't speak the language or possess valuable skills.

The hansom stopped before a red brick building with multiple doorways, all painted black. The Devanes obviously weren't well off, but Billister Lane was far nicer than some areas of London Jason had seen. Being a side street, it wasn't as noisy or dirty as the main thoroughfare, and the houses looked relatively well maintained, if not prosperous.

A woman of middle years opened the door to their knock. She wore a pinafore over her black gown, and her dark hair was threaded with gray beneath a plain linen cap. Her hands were reddened from housework, and there were traces of flour at the cuffs of her gown, but it was clear from her demeanor that she wasn't a servant.

"Mrs. Devane?" Daniel asked.

"Yes."

Daniel held up his warrant card. "I'm Inspector Haze of Scotland Yard, and this is Dr. Redmond, my colleague. We'd like to speak to Max."

The woman went white, her hand flying to her ample breast. "Vat do you vant with my Maxim?" She had an Eastern European accent but seemed fluent enough in English to understand Daniel.

"We only want to ask him a few questions. A friend of his has died in suspicious circumstances."

"Vell, it's nothing to do vis my son."

"I'll be the judge of that, Mrs. Devane. Now, if you could let us in," Daniel said sternly.

The woman's shoulders sagged with resignation, and she finally stepped aside, allowing them to enter the narrow entryway that smelled of boiled cabbage and something else Jason couldn't readily identify.

"You can vait in here," she said after showing them to a small parlor, and went to fetch Max.

The room was clean, not a speck of dust to be seen on any surface, but everything showed signs of wear, except for the green velvet curtains that looked almost new. The furniture had either been bought decades ago or acquired second-hand, and the carpet was still thick, but the colors were faded, and one of the corners looked as if it had been chewed by a dog.

Daniel looked around the room, while Jason turned to examine the only photograph on display. It was yellowed and cracked, probably from being transported without a frame, but it couldn't have been taken that long ago. In it were seven people, an old man dressed in a black coat and hat, and a gray-haired woman, presumably his wife, seated at the center, along with a middle-aged man, also dressed in black, and a somewhat younger incarnation of Mrs. Devane, and three children—a teenage boy, and two little girls, their hair worn in braids. They all stared solemnly into the camera, their faces tense and almost fearful. That was probably the first time they'd been photographed. Jason wondered if the patriarch of the family and his wife were still alive or if this was the only reminder the children had of the grandparents they'd lost.

A dark-haired young man entered the room. "Good afternoon," he said. "I'm sorry if my mother was rude to you. She is nervous of strangers."

"That's quite all right," Daniel said. "It's understandable."

"Please, sit down," Max invited, and did so himself once they were seated. "How can I help you, gentlemen?" He seemed surprised to see Jason but didn't inquire after his presence, preferring to wait for an explanation. There was a watchfulness in him that Jason found telling.

He hadn't known Maxim Devane by name, but he had seen him in the operating theater on several occasions. He was a good-looking young man with intelligent brown eyes and razor-sharp cheekbones. His dark brows spread over his eyes like the wings of a raven in flight, and the short beard he wore made him look somewhat older than he probably was. Jason put him at approximately twenty-seven, a few years older than most of the other students. Unlike his mother, Max Devane spoke perfect English, not a hint of an accent betraying his immigrant status. He must have come to England at a fairly young age if he'd been able to lose his accent so completely. Either that, or he was a good mimic and worked hard to keep people from pegging him as a foreigner.

"Mr. Devane, an individual known to you as Alexander Gray was found dead in Highgate Cemetery on Tuesday morning," Daniel said.

Max paled. "You mean the body in the vault? That was Alex?"

"It was," Daniel said. "We've only just identified him."

"But what happened? Who'd want to hurt Alex?"

"That's what we're trying to find out. How long have you known Alex Gray?" Daniel asked.

"About two years now. We met at Guy's Hospital."

"Did you two ever spend time alone together?" Jason asked.

"No, not really. We mostly went out as a group, with other students."

"And where did you go?" Daniel asked.

"For a drink or a quick meal. That's all any of us can afford. And sometimes we gathered at the Grays' lodging house. Mrs. Fleet—that's the landlady—allowed us to use the parlor."

"Did you like Alex Gray?"

Max Devane seemed surprised by the question. "Yes, very much. He was a good friend."

"Was that all he was?" Daniel demanded.

Max stared at Daniel, clearly not comprehending the question. "What else could he have been?" he finally replied, his worried gaze sliding to Jason in search of an explanation.

"What Inspector Haze is asking is whether the two of you might have had a romantic relationship," Jason clarified.

Max's mouth fell open, and his brows lifted in astonishment. "A romantic relationship?" he echoed. "Was Alex homosexual?"

Max's shock seemed genuine, so Daniel moved on, no doubt intending to circle back to the question of sexuality later.

"Is Devane an alias?" Daniel asked.

Max's expression hardened, as if he had been expecting that very question. "Yes. Our real name is Devansky. My family is from Russia. We came to England nearly ten years ago so that I could study medicine."

"Could you not have studied medicine in Russia?"

"Jews are not admitted to the universities, not even if we have Russian-sounding names. The authorities know exactly who we are and keep tabs on us."

"How old were you when you left Russia?" Jason asked.

"Seventeen. It took me some time to learn enough English to be proficient enough to apply to medical school."

"Your English is flawless," Jason said.

"Thank you," Max replied, clearly pleased with the compliment.

"What do your sisters do?"

"My sisters are both married. The older sister's husband works in my father's textile shop, and the younger sister's husband is a baker."

"When was the last time you saw Alex Gray, Mr. Devane?" Daniel asked, moving the interview along. Dealing in textiles might explain the new curtains, but the family business could have no relevance to the death of Alex Gray.

"Monday. We attended a lecture together. Edward Gray was there as well."

"Did Alex tell you what his plans were for the rest of the day?"

"No. I assumed he was going to go home and study," Max said.

"Was Alex particularly friendly with anyone?" Jason asked.

"Are you asking me if he had a lover?" Max asked, turning toward Jason. "I didn't know he preferred men, not until you told me just now."

"We don't know that he did," Daniel replied, compounding Max's confusion. "But did he ever single anyone out? Was he closer to anyone in your group?"

"He seemed to feel the most comfortable with Edward, but I suppose that's only natural, given that they'd known each other their whole lives. I don't think he cared for Timothy Latham, but he kept his feelings to himself."

"Why do you think he disliked Timothy Latham?" Jason asked, trying to place the man and failing.

"Timothy can be a bit brash and overbearing in his opinions," Max replied. "He's also newly married."

"What bearing does his marital status have on his relationship with Alex?" Daniel asked.

"Timothy often spoke of his wife, Belinda, in rather unflattering terms. I think Alex thought his behavior ungentlemanly."

"What was it he said about his wife?" Jason asked.

"It wasn't anything overtly cruel or derogatory, just that she was timid and fearful and needed things explained to her in the simplest of terms, but then he'd backtrack and say that her lack of intelligence was the result of her being a woman and it ensured that she knew her place."

Jason nodded. This wasn't anything he hadn't heard from men of his acquaintance many times over. A wife should be an ornament, a credit to her husband, a womb to be filled as many times as the man saw fit. A few men hoped their spouse would be a true companion, a life partner, but those men tended to have a more romantic nature and a deeper emotional need to be loved and understood.

He knew there were those who spoke cruelly of Katherine behind his back, saying she wasn't beautiful or elegant enough to be Lady Redmond. But then they remembered that Jason was American, and a surgeon to boot, which to some was one step above a common butcher, and decided that he didn't know any better than to marry a country vicar's daughter instead of searching farther afield for a woman of his own station. Jason found their snide comments of little interest or consequence. Katherine was fiercely intelligent, loving, and loyal, the only qualities he wanted in a wife. And if she wasn't considered conventionally beautiful, with her dark coloring and bookish spectacles, she had a beauty all her own, and to Jason, she was the star he would follow for the rest of his days and the only woman he wanted as the mother of his children.

"Did Alex and Timothy ever argue?" Jason asked, wondering if Alexandra had felt the need to defend Timothy Latham's wife.

"No, but it was obvious to me that Alex disapproved of Timothy's comments and found them disloyal."

"Had Alex ever met Belinda Latham?" Daniel asked.

"Not that I know of. Timothy never introduced her to anyone in the group."

"Were you not invited to the wedding?" Jason asked, recalling the weddings of his own medical school friends.

"They were married in some small village in Suffolk. That's where both Belinda and Timothy are from. They've known each other since they were children. I can't say I blame Belinda for feeling overwhelmed by her new life. I remember only too well what it was like when we first arrived in London. My mother thought we'd be murdered in our beds and had my father move the dresser against the door every night to keep out would-be assassins," Max said with a sad smile.

"Did you ever notice anything odd about Alex, Mr. Devane?" Daniel asked, his flinty gaze fixed on the young man.

"How do you mean, Inspector?"

"Perhaps something didn't seem quite right," Daniel prompted.

"I don't know what you mean," Max insisted. "Not right in what way?"

"Alex Gray was a woman."

Max Devane blanched, his eyes widening in disbelief. "A woman?" he choked out. "No. That's not possible."

"She was Edward Gray's younger sister," Daniel elaborated.

"I… I didn't know."

"Are you sure?"

"I'm sure. I would never describe Alex as masculine, but I never imagined he was anything but a man."

"Do your friends and lecturers know you're a Russian Jew?" Daniel asked.

"I'm sure they do, but I don't advertise the fact," Max replied warily.

"Why is that?"

"Because people can be prejudiced against those who are different from them," Max said, a note of defensiveness creeping into his tone.

"Would you feel threatened if someone were to reveal your secret?"

"It's not a secret, Inspector, and no, I wouldn't kill to keep my true identity from coming out, if that's what you're suggesting. I've never hidden the fact but simply didn't feel the need to publicize it. When someone asked me where I was from, I told them."

"But did you also tell them you are Jewish?" Daniel pressed, curious to see if Max Devane would rise to the bait and lose his temper.

"No, I didn't. Is that a crime?" Max challenged, but there was no anger in his eyes, only wariness.

"No, it isn't, but do you think your lecturers and fellow students would treat you differently if they knew?"

"Without a doubt, but to be honest, that doesn't matter. Once I qualify, I plan to practice medicine right here, in my neighborhood, and in other poor areas. I never went into medicine for the money. I want to help people who will otherwise perish or suffer needlessly. And believe me, Inspector, when you are poor and in agony, you don't much care if the man who's willing to help you is Jewish or not."

Daniel nodded, satisfied with Max's answer. He turned to Jason, silently inquiring if he had any more questions for Max.

"You didn't ask how Alex died, Mr. Devane," Jason pointed out.

"No, I didn't, because I had read about it in the paper. It said the victim was found hanged inside the Viscount Ashford's vault."

"Alexandra Gray was poisoned. Aconite, most likely."

"Did she suffer, or was the dose high enough to kill her instantly?" Max asked.

"She would have died almost instantly."

"Thank God," Max said. "Man or woman, Alex was a good friend, and I will miss her very much."

"Is there anything you can tell us that would help us to understand what happened to her?" Jason asked.

"Sadly, no. Alex was a brilliant student and would have made an intelligent and compassionate surgeon. Her death is a loss to the medical profession."

"You are not shocked that a woman would wish to be a doctor?" Daniel asked.

Max shrugged. "Why shouldn't a woman be a doctor if she has the intelligence and the determination to do the work?"

"That's a very progressive point of view," Daniel remarked, somewhat acidly.

"The world is changing, Inspector, and one day all the prejudices and limitations will be swept aside and any person, man or woman, will be free to follow their dreams."

"A radical, are you?" Daniel grumbled.

"No, just a dreamer," Max replied.

Daniel nodded. "I'm not sure I agree with your prophecy, but we all need to dream from time to time. Thank you, Mr. Devane. We may need to speak to you again."

"I'll be happy to help in any way I can."

"I would appreciate it if you didn't tell your friends about our conversation, or about Alex Gray's true identity," Daniel said.

Max's grin was sarcastic. "You want to take them by surprise, like you did me?"

"I do. I need to see their reaction to the news for myself."

Max sighed. "You have my word. In fact, I won't be seeing them for a few days."

"You are not attending tomorrow's surgery?" Jason asked.

"No. I have a previous commitment."

"What commitment is that?" Daniel asked, no doubt wondering if Max Devane would take the time to cover his tracks if he'd been careless enough to leave any.

"My sister gave birth to a son last week, and tomorrow is the circumcision. I must be there to honor my nephew and his parents."

"I see," Daniel said, although it was obvious to Jason that Daniel wasn't at all sure what that entailed beyond the obvious and how Max's presence would honor anyone. Daniel didn't bother to ask and signaled to Jason that he was ready to go by pushing to his feet.

Daniel and Jason said goodbye to Mrs. Devane, who was hovering just outside the door, looking anxious, and left.

"What did you make of him?" Daniel asked once they were outside.

"Sensitive, earnest, ambitious," Jason said.

"Think he's capable of murder?"

"Everyone is capable of murder when their own life or future is at stake. But what would be his motive?"

"Perhaps he's not as open about his background as he says he is. Does the College of Surgeons allow Jews in?"

"I honestly don't know," Jason replied. "I don't see why they wouldn't."

"You're as much of a dreamer as Max Devane. Dear God, can you imagine anyone being anything they want to be?" Daniel sputtered. "A woman detective. Or, better yet, a Member of Parliament or a High Court judge. I hope I'm safely dead by the time such a thing comes to pass. I bet you'd like to see that."

"I would," Jason teased. "Wouldn't you want Charlotte to have opportunities that weren't open to women before?"

"I would want Charlotte to find a good man and have a family, as a woman should," Daniel replied. "Are you hoping Lily will follow in your footsteps?"

"Only if she doesn't have to pretend to be a man to do so," Jason replied.

"You are a radical, Jason Redmond," Daniel said affectionately.

"I'll take that as a compliment," Jason replied. "Better a radical than a stodgy proponent of age-old injustices."

"Is that what I am?" Daniel asked, clearly wounded by Jason's description.

Jason grinned. "You're more of a free thinker than you realize, Daniel."

"But I just don't know it yet?" Daniel asked, grinning back.

"You know it. You're just not ready to embrace it," Jason replied, chuckling when Daniel rolled his eyes.

"Well, I think that's all we can do for today," Daniel said once they found a hansom. "I will continue with the interviews tomorrow." He pulled out his watch and consulted the time. "I think there might still be time to stop Alexandra's photograph from appearing in the morning edition of the *News*. No sense running it now that we know who the victim was. And I would like to preserve something of her privacy," Daniel added. "Contrary to what you think, I do admire her courage and determination."

"She certainly had courage in spades," Jason agreed. "Not many women would go all in like that."

Daniel nodded. "Try explaining that to Ransome."

"Ransome understands ambition, be it in a man or a woman," Jason said. "As it happens, I have a cesarean section scheduled for eight tomorrow. I have a feeling you might find the two men you seek in the operating theater."

"Excellent," Daniel said. "I'll see you at the hospital, then. Goodnight, Jason."

"Goodnight, Daniel."

Chapter 16

John Ransome leaned back in his chair and studied Daniel across the vast expanse of his desk, his gaze thoughtful.

"The lady had courage, I'll give her that," he said at last. "But admitting that doesn't bring us any closer to identifying her killer. Someone obviously had it in for her to go through the trouble of poisoning her, then stringing her up inside the vault. There were some very strong emotions at play here."

"I agree, sir. I will be questioning her friends tomorrow," Daniel said, wishing Ransome would just compliment him on a job well done and allow him to leave. He was tired and hungry and hoped to get home in time to see Charlotte before Miss Grainger put her to bed.

"It's not her friends you need to question but her enemies," Ransome replied.

"I won't know who her enemies were until I question the friends," Daniel pointed out.

"What have you done, Miss Alexandra?" Ransome mused as he looked ceilingward. "Whose feathers have you ruffled?"

"I think we're dealing with a bit more than ruffled feathers here, if you don't mind my saying, sir," Daniel interjected.

"Might she have been one of them lesbians?" Ransome asked, leveling his gaze at Daniel.

"I really couldn't say."

"She would have had to be," Ransome went on. "She was unnatural in the other aspects of her life."

"How do you mean, sir?"

"Why would a woman want to give up her God-ordained role in favor of pursuing the goals suitable only to a man?"

"She was a brilliant student, by all accounts."

"I'm not saying that a woman can't be blessed with above-average intelligence, rare though it happens, but why would she want to sacrifice all the things that would bring her personal fulfilment?"

"Perhaps practicing surgery was all the personal fulfilment she craved," Daniel pointed out.

Ransome smiled in that condescending way Daniel found so infuriating. "I like my job, Haze. I relish the sense of accomplishment and personal satisfaction it brings me, but I still get to go home to my wife and children and leave the ugliness and injustice behind for a time. What would this Alexandra Gray go home to at the end of the day? Her trusty scalpel? No, this woman was unnatural, and she had to have had unnatural urges. Find her lover, and you'll find her killer."

"If she had a lover, I'll find him. Or her," Daniel added for Ransome's sake. "Now, if you have no further questions..."

"Go on, Haze. And well done today," Ransome added. "Give my best to his lordship. He came up trumps again."

"I will pass on your compliments," Daniel said as he pushed to his feet. "Goodnight, sir."

"Goodnight, Haze." John Ransome suddenly smiled in a way that seemed entirely genuine. "If you hurry, you'll get home in time to read a bedtime story to your little one."

Daniel nodded and fled, unnerved by Ransome's comment. How did he know that Daniel rushed home every day to spend time with Charlotte, when Daniel had never mentioned it to anyone? And what else did he know about him? It wasn't a secret at Scotland Yard that Daniel's wife had died this past June, but did he know Sarah's death had been a suicide? The idea of John Ransome knowing made Daniel's stomach twist with anger, but he forced the thought from his mind.

Ransome had been a constable, then a detective before his promotion to superintendent two years ago. He was a clever man, and an observant one. And if he thought Alexandra Gray might have been murdered by her lover, maybe he had a point, Daniel decided as he stepped out into the rain that had begun to fall in drenching sheets. He found a cab and gave the cabbie his address. He couldn't wait to get home.

Chapter 17

Thursday, September 17

Thursday morning found Daniel at St. George's Hospital, waiting for Jason to finish the surgery so he could interview the remaining two men. He paced the corridor before the operating theater, his mind teeming with questions. What must it have been like for Alexandra Gray to find herself surrounded by men all the time, with no women to talk to or offer support? Had she relished the subterfuge, or had she felt intimidated, doing her best to push down her fears and focus on the end result? And how long would she have been able to get away with the pretense? Surely sooner or later she'd slip up or find herself in circumstances beyond her control.

Was that what had happened on Monday night? Had she let down her guard because she was lonely and had allowed someone in, believing them to be an ally? Would she have risked taking a lover when finding herself with child would threaten the life she'd created for herself? Or had her lover been a woman, as John Ransome had suggested? With a woman, there'd be no risk of pregnancy and she could still pass herself off as a virgin if she meant to wait until a union with a man to sample the delights of the marriage bed. Perhaps the relationship was platonic, a way for Alexandra Gray to spend time with another woman without fear of exposure.

At this stage, it was impossible to tell. Even her brother, who seemed to be the only person she trusted, didn't know where Alexandra had gone. Or maybe he did and had decided to keep it to himself for fear of causing more harm to his sister's reputation. She was dead, so the only thing he could do was protect her memory and keep her name from being dragged through the muck of public opinion. But Daniel's gut feeling told him Edward Gray had been telling the truth. He'd been shocked and heartbroken. Surely he'd want to see justice done.

Finally, the doors swung open, and the students began to file out. There were about thirty men, some walking alone, others coming out in small groups, discussing what they'd just witnessed. There was no sign of Edward Gray.

"Ezra Hall and Timothy Latham," Daniel called out before the men had a chance to walk away.

Two young men broke away from the group and moved toward him, their expressions wary. He wondered if they knew who he was and why he was there. Had Edward Gray summoned his friends to his side in his grief, or had he isolated himself, needing time to come to terms with his loss?

Daniel held up his warrant card. "I'm Inspector Haze of Scotland Yard. I would like to speak to you for a few minutes."

"Of course," the dark-haired man said. "What's this all about, Inspector?"

"I'm afraid I have a previous engagement," the second man said.

"This won't take long," Daniel assured him, glad to see Jason emerge from the operating theater, sans apron and cap, hastily buttoning his coat. "Dr. Redmond will join us," Daniel said.

The two men looked perplexed but followed Jason to an empty office at the end of the corridor. There was a desk, two guest chairs, and several bookcases filled with medical tomes. Daniel supposed it was someone's consulting room, but as long as it was empty, it would serve his purpose. He turned to the two men.

"We'll speak to you one at a time. Which one are you?" Daniel asked, addressing the dark-haired man.

"Ezra Hall."

"Please, Mr. Hall," Daniel said, gesturing toward one of the chairs. "If you'll kindly wait outside, Mr. Latham."

"Of course," Timothy Latham replied, and walked over to the window in the corridor, resting his hip against the windowsill. He took out his notes to study while he waited.

Daniel shut the door and sat behind the desk, while Jason took the second guest chair and moved it to the side of the desk, turning it so he could face Ezra Hall. Hall was of average height, solidly built without appearing stout, and neatly dressed in a suit of gray tweed. He was clean shaven, and his dark eyes were warm, his expression one of friendly patience. Resting his hands on his thighs, he leaned back in his chair, looking for all the world like he was about to enjoy a musical performance or listen to a lecture.

"How well did you know Alex Gray, Mr. Hall?" Daniel asked, watching the man for a reaction.

"Did?" Ezra Hall echoed, his expression turning to one of dismay.

"Alex Gray was found dead on Tuesday morning, his body hanging in a vault in Highgate Cemetery."

"That was Alex?" Ezra cried. He seemed devastated by the news but quickly collected himself. "Does Edward know? He's Alex's cousin."

"We spoke to Mr. Gray yesterday afternoon," Jason interjected.

"That explains why he didn't show this morning," Ezra muttered. He looked at Daniel, his gaze filled with pain. "Alex was a good friend."

"Did you two ever spend time alone together?" Daniel asked.

"No. Alex and Edward went everywhere together. They were inseparable."

"Did either of them ever mention Neville or the Viscount Ashford?"

"Not that I can recall. Alex and Edward grew up in Truro, so they didn't know many people in London. Most of their friends were chaps they met over the course of their studies."

"Did Alex have any enemies?" Jason asked.

"If he did, he never mentioned them to me. I suppose there were those who might have been less than keen on him."

"Why would that be?" Daniel asked.

"Alex was clever and confident. He didn't suffer fools gladly, and one comes across many fools in this area of study."

"Why is that?" Daniel inquired. Noticing the look on Jason's face, he took Ezra Hall's statement to be true, since Jason clearly agreed with him.

"Not everyone's cut out to be a doctor, Inspector. That goes double for anyone wishing to become a surgeon. Merely understanding anatomy is not enough. A surgeon must be intuitive and compassionate." His gaze strayed to Jason, whom he obviously admired. "A patient is not a piece of meat but an intricate, marvelous creation to be respected and revered. A great surgeon must be an artist, his scalpel as delicate as a brush."

Daniel noticed Jason nodding in agreement. "And you're saying that Alex Gray had what it took to be a great surgeon?" Daniel asked.

"He was a natural," Ezra said.

"And Edward?"

"Edward understands the mechanics of surgery, or will by the time he qualifies, but it's not in his soul. For Edward, it's a means to an end."

"And for you?" Jason asked, watching the young man intently, his head cocked to the side.

"And for me, it's a lifelong ambition," Ezra replied, his gaze turning steely. "My mother died in childbirth when I was eight. The child was breech, the umbilical cord wrapped around its neck. A competent surgeon, or perhaps even an incompetent one, might have saved her had a cesarean section been performed in time, but my father couldn't afford the services of a surgeon, so he stood by helplessly as his wife and unborn child passed from this world. I would love to be the man who performs the first open heart surgery or removes a brain tumor without killing the patient, but if I can save some boy's mother or some man's wife, I will be just as glad, knowing I had made a difference."

Daniel felt a lump in his throat as he recalled the night Charlotte was born. Sarah might have died had Jason not been there, so he understood Ezra Hall's loss only too well. A child never got over losing their mother, regardless of how she died.

Clearing his throat, Daniel proceeded with the interview. "Did you ever notice anything odd about Alex Gray?"

"Odd in what way?"

"Like anything that stood out."

"Sorry, I don't know what you mean, Inspector," Ezra replied.

"Mr. Hall, Alex Gray was a woman," Jason said, both he and Daniel watching Ezra Hall as he absorbed the news.

Ezra let out a low whistle and nodded to himself, as if something finally made sense. "Well, that explains it, then."

"Explains what?" Daniel asked.

"Alex was the most himself when he was at a lecture or attending a surgery." Ezra paused. "Is it all right if I refer to Alex as a he? I just need a bit of time to accept that he wasn't what I believed him to be."

"By all means, Mr. Hall," Daniel replied. "You knew Alex as a man, so describe her in terms that are most comfortable for you."

Ezra nodded. "Thank you. I know it's odd, but it's not easy to make the switch, especially when speaking of the past."

"Please, go on," Jason invited.

"Alex was completely focused on what he was seeing or hearing, but when we were in a group, he often seemed to hang back, especially in noisy, crowded places. When we went to a public house or a tavern, Alex tended to sit with his back to the wall, preferably in the corner. I just thought he was intimidated by crowds, but now I understand that as a woman, being in a roomful of inebriated men was probably very frightening."

"Did you ever notice anything else?" Daniel asked.

"Well, he always kept quiet when the conversation turned to women," Ezra said. "I simply thought he'd never been with a woman and was too embarrassed to admit it. I even offered to help him with his problem."

"What exactly did you offer to do?" Jason asked.

"I offered to take him to a brothel, but he politely refused, so I never brought up the subject again."

"Mr. Hall, did Alex Gray have any enemies?" Daniel asked.

"Not enemies, precisely, but rivals. Have you heard of Hiram Bosworth?" he asked Jason.

"Of course. He's a highly respected surgeon. I believe he operated on a member of Her Majesty's cabinet recently," Jason said.

"Yes. And he also consulted on a case for the royal family when the Surgeon to the Queen was taken ill and wasn't able to attend to his duties."

"What does Hiram Bosworth have to do with Alex Gray?" Daniel asked.

"Hiram Bosworth is offering a place in his practice to one of the students recommended by John Hilton, the president of the Royal College of Surgeons," Ezra said. "Mr. Hilton has put forth several possible candidates."

"Yes, I have heard that," Jason said. "Was Alex Gray in the running?"

"Mr. Hilton spoke to Alex only last week. He was a serious contender." Ezra's smile was bittersweet. "Alex was so happy. He...eh, she had worked so hard for this."

"And who was in direct competition with Alex?"

"Aubrey Dixon. He's the son of a butcher, so he knows his way around a carcass," Ezra added spitefully. "Very ambitious, and very determined to get the position."

"I've met Mr. Dixon on several occasions," Jason said. "He sought me out to ask some questions."

"And kiss arse?" Ezra asked, a cynical smile tugging at the corner of his generous mouth.

Jason chuckled. "You might say that. Can't say I enjoyed the experience."

"Anyone else you can think of who might have had a rivalry with Alex Gray?" Daniel asked.

Ezra Hall shook his head. "For what it's worth, I think Alex would have been an asset to Mr. Bosworth's practice."

"You don't like Aubrey Dixon much, do you?" Daniel asked, wondering if a new name would be put forth now that Alex Gray was dead. Was Ezra hoping he'd have a chance, and was that chance worth killing for?

"No, I don't, which is not to say he's not a good surgeon," Ezra admitted grudgingly. "The recommendation was well deserved."

"Do you think another candidate will be named now that Alex Gray is no longer in the running?"

Ezra shrugged. "I don't know. You would have to ask Mr. Hilton."

"Mr. Hall, who do you reside with?" Daniel asked.

Ezra Hall seemed surprised by the question but answered promptly. "I used to live with my father, but he passed three years ago now, so I live alone."

"And who helps with your domestic needs? Or do you do it all yourself?" Daniel glanced at Ezra Hall's elegant hands, which were the hands of a surgeon, not of someone who did his own laundry.

"A neighbor's wife, Mrs. Christie, comes in three mornings a week. The arrangement suits us both."

"She has her own key?"

"Yes," Ezra replied, clearly perplexed by the direction the questioning had taken. "Why does that matter?"

"It doesn't," Daniel replied. "Just looking to get a clearer picture of your daily life."

"I'm out for most of the day, and I eat wherever I happen to be at the time," Ezra explained. "When at home, I study and read for pleasure, and occasionally have a friend over to supper. That's my life, in a nutshell."

"And do you ever entertain women at your home, or do you prefer brothels?" Daniel asked pointedly.

"What I said about taking Alex to a brothel was just a joke. I don't suppose it seems funny now that she's gone," he added bitterly. "I don't frequent brothels, Inspector, nor am I courting anyone. Until I finish my studies, I prefer to remain unencumbered."

"Where were you on Monday night?"

"I was at home."

"Can anyone vouch for you?"

Ezra Hall's gaze slid toward the window, his expression speculative, as if he were weighing his options. "I wasn't alone," he said at last.

"Who were you with, Mr. Hall?"

"I was with Rhona."

"And who is Rhona?"

"Mrs. Christie," Ezra said, his cheeks and neck turning a mottled red, his gaze sliding to Jason as if he were expecting to be rebuked.

"So, not just a charwoman, then?" Daniel quipped.

"No."

"Did you not say she's married?"

"Her husband is an invalid. He's been bedbound for several years. We all need a bit of comfort, Inspector."

"All right for some, I suppose," Daniel said.

The fact that Ezra Hall was having an affair with a married woman said much about his character, but many a man found comfort with a woman who wasn't his wife, especially a man who was unencumbered, as Ezra Hall had put it. "And will Mrs. Christie confirm your alibi?"

"She will," Ezra replied. "We were together all night. She went home at six."

"Can I have the address for Mrs. Christie?" Daniel asked.

"Of course."

Daniel jotted down the details. "Thank you, Mr. Hall. You're free to go."

"Another one who didn't ask how Alexandra died," Daniel pointed out once Ezra Hall was out of earshot.

"Probably read it in the paper and put two and two together now that he knows the body found in the vault was of his friend," Jason replied.

"Oh, I do resent the press sometimes," Daniel fumed. "They really do interfere with an investigation. I've asked the editors not to run Alexandra's photograph today, but I've no doubt my request fell on deaf ears. It's too good a story to pass on."

"Would you pull the story if you were in their shoes?" Jason asked.

Daniel scoffed. "No. Good thing the surgical students were already in the operating theater when the morning editions hit the streets. The surgery bought us a few hours, but time's just run out."

Daniel turned toward the door as Timothy Latham entered the room. They'd have to wait until he left to discuss the case in private.

Chapter 18

Timothy Latham was an average-looking person, the sort you'd pass over in a crowd. Sandy brown hair, pale blue eyes, a neat beard, and a physique more suited to a farmer than a future surgeon. When he sat down, the chair seemed to groan beneath his bulk, and Daniel couldn't help but look at the man's hands. They were large, with stubby fingers that were nothing like the delicate fingers of Alex Gray or the elegant hands of Max Devane. Daniel wondered how Timothy Latham fit into the group and if he had disliked Alex Gray as much as she was said to have detested him.

"It was Alex in that vault, wasn't it?" Timothy Latham said as he looked from Daniel to Jason, whose presence at the interview he was obviously still trying to work out.

"How do you know?" Daniel asked, but it really didn't matter. The cat was out of the bag, and the woman was out of her trousers.

"Someone just handed me this," Timothy said, and held up a copy of the *News.* Alex Gray's photograph in his masculine attire was printed beneath the headline. "Says the corpse was hiding a devastating secret. I've no doubt sales will be awe-inspiring tomorrow," Timothy added bitterly.

Jason and Daniel exchanged looks, equally surprised that Alex's secret hadn't been splashed across the front page. They had one more day before Alex Gray's gender became a matter of public knowledge and they lost their element of surprise.

"Mr. Latham, how well did you know Alex Gray?"

"Not well enough to be privy to his secret, if that's what you're asking," Timothy Latham replied crossly.

"But were you two close friends?" Jason asked.

The man shrugged. "We were part of the same group. We had our studies in common. Would we have become friends if we had met under different circumstances? I really don't think so."

"Why do you say that?" Daniel asked.

"I'm a simple man, Inspector. And I want simple things. Alex was a bit more highbrow, if you know what I mean."

"In that he liked refined things?"

"Alex wanted to be top of his field. His ultimate ambition was to perform open heart surgery. He was always talking about that," Timothy Latham scoffed. "Never been done, and likely never will be. At least not with the patient living long enough to make it worthwhile. The only person who thought Alex could succeed was Ezra Hall, but then he's a bit of an idealist himself. Thinks he can save every patient if he sets his mind to it. Will never happen, if you ask me."

"Never say never, Mr. Latham," Jason said. "The surgeries we perform routinely today would have been unfathomable a hundred years ago."

"Perhaps, but Alex wasn't going to live a hundred years, was he? He wanted to do it within the next ten years. Well, I don't suppose he'll get to do it now, poor sod. What a waste of a young life."

"Mr. Latham, did you and Alex Gray ever spend time alone?" Daniel asked.

Timothy Latham shook his head. "I did go for a drink with the lads from time to time, but I always went home to my wife after one jar."

"Did you dislike Alex Gray?" Jason asked, obviously sensing the same scorn Daniel had picked up on as soon as Timothy Latham walked in.

"At times," Timothy replied.

"Why?" Jason asked.

"Not for the reason you think."

"And what reason is that?"

"You think I was jealous of Alex because he was more skilled, or because he was better looking than me. He was both; I admit that. But the reason I disliked Alex was because he was a shit."

Jason's eyebrows lifted in astonishment, but Daniel only gripped his pen harder. Now this was what he'd been hoping for—honesty. Alex might have been brilliant, ambitious, kind, and loving, but those were generally not the qualities that got a person killed. Jealousy, greed, fear of exposure, and just plain old hatred were what mattered in a murder investigation, and Timothy Latham looked ready to spew.

"Why do you say that, Mr. Latham?" Daniel asked, hoping not to spook the man into clamming up.

"Alex was smarter than most, I'll grant him that, but he was also the sort of person who always rubbed a chap's nose in his shortcomings. He liked to taunt and belittle. Oh, he wasn't obvious about it; he was too clever for that. But there were the snide comments, the sneering looks. He thought I never noticed, but I did."

"What did he taunt you with?"

"Alex thought there was no worse fate than mediocrity. He aspired to greatness and thought everyone should do the same."

"What do you aspire to, Mr. Latham?" Jason asked.

"I aspire to being a competent surgeon, Dr. Redmond. I don't think there's anything wrong with that. I also aspire to having a family. Alex didn't want a family. He said it would interfere with his work."

"So, you think he looked down on you because you chose to marry?"

"I think so. He didn't like it when I spoke about my wife. It irritated him, and he once said that I have no respect for women."

"Do you?" Jason asked.

"Women have their place," Timothy replied bullishly. "And as long as my wife knows hers, we'll coexist in peace and harmony."

"Why did you continue to be friends with Alex Gray if you didn't enjoy his company?" Daniel asked.

"I like and respect Edward Gray, and I'm quite close with Max Devane. I could hardly ask them to exclude Alex just because we didn't get on. Besides, Alex inspired me to do better, to try harder. I'm grateful to him for that."

"Was Alex particularly close to anyone in the group?" Jason asked.

"He was close to Edward. They had a bond, but I suppose that was to be expected. I thought he felt a bit shy around Max Devane."

"Shy?" Daniel asked.

"Yes. There was an awkwardness there, but I'm not sure that anyone else noticed it."

"Why do you think that was?"

"I really couldn't say. Max is a quiet, self-effacing person who's kind and respectful to everyone."

"Did Alex ever make snide comments to Max?" Jason asked.

"No. Never."

"What about Ezra Hall? Did he ever taunt Ezra?"

"From time to time, but their interaction was more friendly banter than barbed exchanges. I think Alex respected Ezra, both as a friend and as a surgeon."

"Do you think their relationship went beyond mutual respect?" Daniel asked.

Timothy Latham fixed Daniel with an inquisitive stare. "What are you getting at, Inspector Haze? Are you suggesting that there might have been more to Alex's relationships with his friends than mere friendship? I think I would have known if Alex was a molly."

"Mr. Latham, Alex Gray wasn't a molly; he was a woman."

"Wha'?" The man's mouth hung open. "Are you having me on?" he asked, squinting at Daniel.

"I'm not. That's the devastating secret the *Illustrated London News* is titillating its readers with. Dr. Redmond performed the postmortem, so there's no doubt."

"Oh, I see. So that's your role in this," he said, nodding at Jason. "I was wondering why you were present for the interview."

"Does it surprise you that a woman was able to pass for a man for so long?" Daniel asked.

"It does, but given Alex's desire to be a surgeon, I can't say I'm surprised. She could hardly waltz into the Royal College of Surgeons and expect to be admitted. She did what she had to. To be honest, I have newfound admiration for her. I only wish I'd had a chance to tell her so."

"Would you have told her so, or would you have felt angry and betrayed?"

"If you're suggesting that I killed her because I discovered her secret, then you're wrong. Yeah, I would have felt duped, I admit that, and I probably would want nothing more to do with her, but what Alex Gray chose to do with her life is none of my business."

"Did it make you angry that she was recommended to Hiram Bosworth, and you weren't?" Daniel asked.

"Not in the least. Besides, if the esteemed Mr. Bosworth ever found out the truth, he'd have tossed her out on her ear."

"Mr. Latham, can you think of anyone who disliked Alex Gray? Besides you, that is."

"Aubrey Dixon, but I'm sure you already know that. I suppose Mr. Guthrie had it in for him. Her," Timothy corrected himself.

"Who's Mr. Guthrie?"

"Harold Guthrie is one of the surgeons at Guy's Hospital. We attended several of his surgeries this past year."

"Why did he not like Alex?"

Timothy Latham smiled at the memory. "Because Alex questioned his judgement and implied, quite openly, that he always chose the most drastic alternative when sometimes a less invasive approach would work just as well."

Jason chuckled at that.

"You find that funny?" Daniel asked.

"I've known surgeons like that, and they don't like to be accused of butchery, especially by a student."

"Mr. Guthrie threw Alex out of the operating theater. Twice. Told him…her not to come back again."

"Anyone else?" Daniel asked.

"No one comes to mind," Timothy replied. "May I go now? I'd like to pay a condolence call on Edward. He must be devastated to lose his cousin so suddenly."

"Alexandra was his sister," Daniel said.

"All the more reason."

"Do you know where I might find Mr. Dixon?" Daniel asked as Timothy Latham made to leave.

"He often goes to the Coffee Brewery after theater. Says watching a surgery gives him an appetite. If he's not there, the Royal College of Surgeons will have his address on file."

"Thank you for your candor, Mr. Latham," Daniel said. "Can I have your home address?"

Timothy Latham looked abashed. "Why do you need my address? I told you everything I know."

"Just for our records. I can obtain it from the RCS, as you just pointed out."

Timothy Latham recited his address and sprang to his feet, eager to leave now that the interview was finished.

"Are you free to accompany me?" Daniel asked Jason once Latham was gone.

"Yes. I will return later in the day to check on mother and baby and my amputation patient, but I have a few hours to spare. And with any luck, we'll catch Aubrey Dixon at the coffeehouse."

"What are your thoughts on Hall and Latham?" Daniel asked as they walked down the now-deserted corridor.

"I didn't get the sense that either of them was lying," Jason replied. "Timothy Latham clearly felt threatened by Alex Gray, but I don't see him going through the trouble of committing murder, especially one as elaborate as the one we're dealing with. I doubt he'd see the point."

"You don't think he's capable of killing a rival?"

"I'm sure he is, but there will always be those who'll make him feel small, out of step, or even obtuse. That's the nature of the profession. Killing every person who forces you to question your ability is not the answer, and I'm sure Timothy Latham realizes this. I'm not ruling him out entirely, but I don't believe he's our man."

"He seemed awfully reluctant to give his address," Daniel pointed out.

"Perhaps he doesn't want us to question his wife. If she is as timid as he has implied to his friends, she might be frightened by a visit from a police inspector."

"Timid or not, I still need to confirm Latham's alibi."

"You would be remiss in your duties if you didn't," Jason agreed.

"What did you think of Hall?" Daniel asked.

"Ezra Hall clearly liked and respected Alexandra Gray, and I think his reaction to the news that she was a woman was genuine."

"Unless he's a consummate actor," Daniel argued.

"If he knew Alexandra was a woman, it's quite possible they were having an affair, which would be a good reason to lie. He lives alone, and we know he's not averse to enjoying a casual relationship. Perhaps the arrangement suited them both. If they were romantically involved, it would explain where Alexandra was going on the nights she sneaked out of the lodging house. I doubt Edward would approve of the liaison, so she kept it secret from him."

"Yes, that does fit the facts, but why would Ezra kill her?"

"Perhaps one of them wished to end the affair and things became acrimonious, or there was professional rivalry, but, again, I don't see the need for all the theatrics. Surely there are easier ways to murder someone. And how did the killer gain access to the vault?"

"That's what I'd like to know," Daniel said as they stepped out into the street. "How are the Ashfords connected to this murder?"

"We won't know the answer to that question until we establish the motive," Jason replied.

"And we're no closer to doing that than we were two days ago," Daniel replied sourly.

"But we'll get there in the end," Jason said confidently.

It was easy to be self-assured when one didn't have to answer to John bloody Ransome, Daniel decided as they headed toward the Coffee Brewery.

Chapter 19

The Coffee Brewery was a quaint little coffeehouse with a half dozen round tables flanked by spindly chairs, dreamy landscapes on the walls, and stained-glass windows that had to be a remnant of the building's previous incarnation. Perhaps it had been a chapel in its heyday. Nearly all the tables were occupied, since it was nearly noon, and the patrons were ready for something to eat. The sweet aroma of freshly baked treats permeated the small space, and the clinking of china and cutlery filled the room with a low din.

Aubrey Dixon sat alone at a corner table illuminated by sunlight streaming through the antique window, a silverplate coffeepot before him. Steam rose from his half-full cup, and a plate painted with delicate violets held the remnants of his cake. Dixon's wheat-blond hair gleamed, and his deep blue gaze betrayed his confusion when Daniel and Jason approached his table.

"Dr. Redmond," Aubrey said, his gaze straying to Daniel, who had yet to identify himself.

"Mr. Dixon, this is Inspector Haze of Scotland Yard," Jason said. "Mind if we join you for a minute?"

"Eh…no," Dixon said, eying them with obvious suspicion and clearly wishing they'd leave.

Jason and Daniel sat down and were immediately approached by the waiter.

"A pot of coffee and a plate of scones with clotted cream and strawberry jam," Daniel said without missing a beat. He wasn't going to miss an opportunity to fortify himself, since it was time for luncheon.

"And you, sir?" the waiter asked Jason. Jason considered a moment, then ordered coffee and a ham sandwich.

"How can I help you, gentlemen?" Aubrey Dixon asked once the waiter had gone. "Surely you didn't come here just for the pleasure of my company."

"No, we didn't," Daniel said, annoyed by the young man's sarcasm. "Alex Gray was found dead on Tuesday morning."

"So I heard," Aubrey Dixon replied. "Poor chap," he added without much feeling.

"He was your rival for the position with Hiram Bosworth," Daniel said, watching Aubrey Dixon closely.

The man laughed bitterly. "You think I killed him in order to get the position?"

"Did you?"

A slow smile spread across Aubrey Dixon's face. "No need, Inspector. I'm going to get the position anyway. Mr. Bosworth intimated as much when we met on Monday afternoon."

"And if he hadn't?" Jason asked.

"Alex was a worthy opponent, and if he got the position, I would congratulate him and set my sights on something else. Life is full of opportunities if you're clever enough to recognize them. Hiram Bosworth is not the only respectable surgeon in town. Might you be in the market for a partner, Dr. Redmond?" Dixon asked, smiling winsomely at Jason.

"Not at this time, Mr. Dixon, but I'll be sure to keep you in mind."

Daniel waited with his next question while the waiter unloaded his tray and filled the little table with china, pots of coffee, and plates. Once satisfied that everything was in order, he left them to enjoy their meal.

"Were you and Alex Gray friends?" Daniel asked.

"No, we weren't, but we were on good terms," Aubrey Dixon replied, then looked to Jason. "How did he die, Dr. Redmond?"

"Alex was poisoned, then strung up to make his death look like a hanging," Jason replied.

"Would he have suffered?"

"I don't believe so."

Aubrey Dixon nodded as if relieved to hear that. Daniel thought it wasn't a very convincing act.

"Would you have preferred him to suffer?" Daniel asked.

Aubrey looked genuinely surprised by the question. "Why would I have preferred him to suffer?"

"Perhaps you thought he got what was coming to him."

"I felt no animosity toward Alex," Aubrey sputtered. "Just because we weren't friends doesn't mean I wanted to see him hurt or dead."

"And what if I told you that your archrival was a woman?"

"I would say you're trying to trick me, Inspector Haze," Aubrey said. He lifted his cup delicately to his lips, but his gaze never left Daniel's face.

"Well, he was. Dr. Redmond can confirm that. He performed the postmortem."

Aubrey Dixon turned to Jason, awaiting confirmation. Jason nodded.

"Well, then I suppose whatever happened to her was probably well deserved," Aubrey said.

"That's rather harsh," Jason said sharply, and Dixon instantly relented, obviously worried about losing Jason's good opinion.

"I'm sorry. I really didn't mean that. I only meant to say that she obviously found herself in a situation she couldn't handle. A woman should never be out alone at night without the protection of a male relative or her husband."

"What makes you think she was out alone?" Daniel asked.

"Wasn't she?" Dixon countered.

"Given that she was murdered, I think it's safe to assume she was with someone. Probably someone she trusted."

"Well, if that's the case, then she wasn't with me, because she didn't trust me one bit. She thought I had no honor."

"And why was that?" Jason asked.

"Because I will do whatever it takes to rise to the position I seek. Whether it be with Hiram Bosworth or with the Surgeon to the Queen," Aubrey Dixon said loftily. "I intend to be top of my field, and I won't apologize for that, not to anyone."

"Nor should you," Jason remarked. "As long as you treat your colleagues with consideration and respect."

"Consideration and respect have to be earned, Dr. Redmond," Aubrey Dixon said. "Just because someone thinks they can wield a scalpel doesn't mean they should. I've met many a man who'd be better suited to butchering an animal carcass, and I've told them as much."

"Hopefully, you don't think that of me," Jason said, a small smile playing around his lips. He was mocking the pompous youth, but Aubrey Dixon took the question seriously.

"Of course not, sir. I attend all your surgeries. I have great admiration for your skill and sensitivity to the patients."

Jason inclined his head but didn't thank the young man.

"Are you married, Mr. Dixon?" Daniel asked.

"No, but there's a young lady I've been courting," Aubrey replied. "Why do you ask?" Understanding dawned, and he looked utterly appalled. "You think I was involved with that woman?"

"Were you?"

"I didn't know she was a woman, did I? And if I had, I would have reported her to the RCS. She had no business being there. She made a mockery of us all."

"Those are fighting words, Mr. Dixon," Jason said.

"I have no doubt you'll hear worse in the coming days," Aubrey said. "I'm only saying what any other medical student and professor will say once they find out the truth."

"But you just said Alex Gray was a worthy opponent. Has your opinion of her ability now changed?"

"Of course it has changed," Aubrey hissed. "She was a woman, for God's sake. She should have become a nurse if she was so desperate to enter the medical profession."

"But she was clever enough to be a surgeon," Daniel pointed out, partially to rile the man to see how deep his anger ran. "She might have been chosen for the position you coveted."

"Yes, she was clever. And she would have made an excellent surgeon. But then she would have met some man, fallen in love, and given it all up to stay at home and have babies, because that's what women are meant to do, aren't they?"

"Alexandra Gray didn't want to have a family. She wanted to be a surgeon," Jason said quietly.

"She might not have wanted to have a family now, but that's a lonely life she chose for herself," Aubrey said. "The isolation would have got to her in the end. I don't suppose we'll ever know now."

"Who do you think killed her, Mr. Dixon?" Daniel asked, watching the man intently.

"I have no idea."

"Where were you on Monday night?"

"I was at home, celebrating my sister's engagement. The party started at seven and didn't break up until just before midnight, at which point I went to bed. There are at least ten people who can vouch for my whereabouts, and that's not counting the servants," Aubrey Dixon said smugly. "Now, if you will excuse me. I have a lecture in a half hour," he added, and fled after leaving several coins on the table.

"Good. Now we can eat in peace," Daniel said. "What an arrogant prig."

"I wonder if Hiram Bosworth has actually offered him the position or if Dixon felt safe to make that assumption now that his rival is dead," Jason said as he added cream to his second cup of coffee.

"I think we should ask him," Daniel replied. "These scones are wonderful, by the way. I'm almost tempted to order two more."

"Treat yourself. You deserve it."

Daniel ordered more scones and turned back to Jason. "Aubrey Dixon would have the most to gain from Alexandra Gray's death, but unless we can disprove his alibi, he's out of the running."

"Not necessarily," Jason replied. "The time of death is an estimate. It's entirely possible that Dixon might have quietly left the house after everyone went to bed and killed her then."

"Might he have killed her before seven and then moved the body to the vault after everyone had left?"

Jason shook his head. "I don't think so. Taking into account the temperature inside the vault, I believe the victim died sometime between ten and two in the morning. Anything outside that is possible, but Dixon would have had to have killed her at least four hours prior to my earliest estimate."

Daniel exhaled loudly. "What on God's earth did Alexandra Gray do that evening? Where did she go? Did she meet someone intentionally, or had she been lured to the place of execution? Or had she been killed elsewhere and left in the vault for dramatic effect? We know from Mrs. Fleet that she went out alone at night without the knowledge of her brother. What was she trying to hide if not a love affair?"

"I tend to agree that a love affair seems like the most obvious answer, but trusting someone with her secret would be a risky venture in her situation. If her lover betrayed her, her entire future would be at stake."

"In which case, it would make more sense if she killed her lover than the other way around."

"How do you wish to proceed?" Jason asked.

"I will start by verifying the alibis."

"And if they check out?"

"Then I will attempt to locate the cabbie who collected Alexandra Gray from her lodging house. They clearly had an arrangement of some sort."

"How will you go about finding him?" Jason asked.

"There are several cab yards on the outskirts of London, and I will visit them all. I will show the cabbies a photograph of the victim and hope someone recognizes her in her guise of Alex Gray."

"What is the probability of locating one cabbie in a city this size? It's like searching for a needle in a haystack."

Daniel shrugged. "I won't know until I try, but it's imperative that I find him."

"And I will call on Hiram Bosworth and Mr. Guthrie later today, after I check on my patients," Jason promised. "I am at the hospital for most of the day tomorrow. May I call on you tomorrow evening?"

"Of course. I should be home after six."

"We'll speak then."

Chapter 20

Having said goodbye to Jason, Daniel went to see the Dixons. A pretty maidservant invited him to wait in the parlor while she summoned her mistress. The room was spacious and elegantly decorated, the furnishings showing no signs of wear. Dixon Senior had certainly done well for himself to afford a nice house and several servants. Daniel had seen two different maids pass by the open door while he waited.

Mrs. Dixon entered the room in a cloud of cloying perfume. She appeared to be in her mid-thirties and wore a fashionable gown of apple-green satin worked with exquisite embroidery at the neckline, hem, and sleeves. Unlike her son, who was fair, she was dark-haired and exotic, possibly even foreign-born. An emerald necklace and matching earrings sparkled against her olive skin and had probably cost more than Daniel had earned in the past decade. Mrs. Dixon was more suitably attired for the opera or a lavish supper party than a St. John's Wood drawing room in the middle of the afternoon.

"How can I help you, Inspector?" she asked once they were seated and Daniel had declined an offer of refreshments.

"I am investigating the murder of one of Aubrey's fellow students, a man by the name of Alexander Gray. Have you ever heard Aubrey mention him?"

"Yes, I have," Mrs. Dixon replied, her brows knitting. "But that hardly means Aubrey had something to do with Alexander's death."

"I didn't say he did, but it is my duty to speak to Alex's friends, and rivals, to see if I might learn something that might lead me to his killer."

"And have you spoken to Aubrey?" Mrs. Dixon asked. She appeared more curious than worried about her son's possible involvement.

"I have. He told me he was at an engagement celebration for your daughter on Monday evening," Daniel replied.

Mrs. Dixon smiled and nodded. "That's right. Isabella is Aubrey's half-sister," she clarified. "Aubrey is my stepson, but I love him as if he were my own," she added, which was probably stretching the truth just a little given Aubrey Dixon's bristly demeanor, but then again, perhaps he was more amiable when at home.

"How old was Aubrey when you married his father?" Daniel asked, curious about Aubrey's home life. There was something theatrical about Mrs. Dixon, as if she were on stage, playing a part, and Daniel wondered how she truly felt about her stepson and his father. If she was thirty-five, then Aubrey was only twelve or thirteen years younger than her, probably closer to her in age than her husband.

"Aubrey was four. And I was all of sixteen. He was the most darling little boy," Mrs. Dixon gushed. "Positively cherubic."

"Where are you from, Mrs. Dixon?" Daniel asked, certain that Mrs. Dixon had not been born in England despite her flawless pronunciation. He had a feeling she wouldn't mind talking about herself, and he was right.

"I'm originally from Naples," she said, brightening. "I came to England as a child. My mother was an opera singer," she explained.

"How did you meet your husband?" The question had nothing to do with the investigation, but Daniel was curious how the daughter of an Italian opera singer wound up married to a butcher.

Mrs. Dixon folded her hands in her lap as if about to deliver a monologue and began speaking, her voice pleasantly melodious. "My mother was in high demand when she was a young woman, but as she grew older, she got fewer parts. She liked to smoke cheroots, you see. Her voice became hoarse, and she'd developed a cough that could disrupt a performance. She was also hopeless with money, so I took over the running of the household by the time I was thirteen. Every week, I would go to our neighborhood butcher and ask him for scraps, which I would make into a stew that would last us for days."

She sighed dramatically. "The butcher was kind to me. And so was his son, Charles," she added with a melancholy smile. "After my mother died, Charles asked me to marry him. His first wife had died, leaving him to raise Aubrey alone, and I needed someone I could rely on. I thought we'd make a good team."

"And did you?" Daniel asked.

"We did, yes. Charles was more ambitious than his father and opened a second shop as soon as he was able. Then a third. He has done very well for himself, and although he was disappointed that Aubrey didn't want to join him in the business, he is immensely proud, nonetheless."

"What time did your guests arrive, Mrs. Dixon?"

"Everyone was invited for seven, and the last couple left just before midnight," Mrs. Dixon added before Daniel had a chance to ask.

"And Aubrey?"

"Aubrey went up to bed. He had an early lecture the following day."

"Are you certain he remained in his room all night?" Daniel asked.

Mrs. Dixon seemed taken aback by the question. "Inspector, Aubrey in not an infant, and we don't check on him during the night, nor would it be appropriate for me to go into his bedroom." She gave Daniel a knowing smile that suggested she wasn't immune to her stepson's charms. "I saw him go up, and I saw him come down the following morning. He joined me at breakfast, in fact, and we discussed the party, but I cannot swear on my life that he had remained in his room all night."

"Does Aubrey ever go out in the evening?" Daniel asked. Most young men found much to amuse them in London. There was something for every taste, and Daniel was sure that Aubrey Dixon found something to his liking, even if he was devoted to his studies.

"Of course. He goes out with his friends, and he enjoys the theater and the occasional supper party or a musical evening. And he recently began to court a young lady his father and I highly approve of."

"Does he stay out late?"

"He is a twenty-two-year-old man, Inspector. Of course he stays out late."

"Did he ever mention meeting Alexander Gray outside of lectures?" Daniel asked.

"Not that I can recall, but that doesn't mean they didn't meet. I believe they had friends in common." Mrs. Dixon cocked her head to the side, fixing Daniel with a penetrating stare. "Assuming Aubrey was capable of such a thing, why would he want to kill this young man, Inspector? What would he have to gain?"

"I have yet to figure that out, Mrs. Dixon."

The woman gave Daniel a sad smile. "Aubrey wants to be a surgeon. Personally, I think it's not that different from being a butcher and he'd be better off working with his father, but he's determined. He's very excited about this position with Hiram Bosworth. He talks about the man incessantly. If I know Aubrey, and I do," she added, "he's cautious and analytical. He's not the sort of person who does things on the spur of the moment. It simply isn't in his nature. Aubrey would never jeopardize his future over a minor rivalry."

"Sounds to me like he would be devastated if he lost out to Alexander Gray," Daniel said.

Mrs. Dixon shook her head. "He'd be upset, certainly, but then he'd simply find another opportunity. Aubrey will get what he wants in the end, but it won't be through murder. He's not that stupid."

"Thank you for your candor, Mrs. Dixon. Now, I'd like to speak to the servants," Daniel said, clearly taking Mrs. Dixon by surprise. She'd assumed he was about to leave.

"By all means, Inspector, but they will tell you much the same thing," she replied, feigning indifference.

"Nevertheless," Daniel insisted.

"Of course. I will send them in one by one."

"How many are there?"

"There's an upstairs maid, a parlormaid, a cook, a scullion, and a hall boy. There's also our coachman, but he was not in the house on Monday night."

"He still might have seen something. I'd like to speak to him as well."

"As you wish," Mrs. Dixon said.

Daniel wasn't at all sure that Mrs. Dixon was above coaching her servants on their responses, but he could hardly ask her to remain. They wouldn't speak truthfully in front of their mistress, not if their positions were at stake. Daniel hoped he'd be able to tell from their demeanor if they were telling the truth. He leaned back in his chair and closed his eyes for a moment, bracing himself for the round of interviews, but sat up straighter and raised his pencil in readiness as the first servant entered the room, the young woman who'd opened the door to him when he had arrived. Taking her name, Daniel began.

When he left the Dixon house more than an hour later, he had nothing in his notebook to contradict Mrs. Dixon's statement. The servants had been extremely busy on Monday night, but yes, they had seen Master Aubrey throughout the evening, and no, they hadn't seen him leave the house after the guests had departed and the family had retired for the night. The last of the staff had gone to bed well after two, having been clearing the dining room and putting the kitchen to rights, tasks that required them to traverse the ground floor repeatedly in the hours after the party. No member of the family had come down the stairs, nor had anyone opened either the front or the back door. Everyone had seen Aubrey Dixon go up. No one had seen him come down. Did that mean he was innocent? Perhaps. Could the servants be lying to avoid getting the sack? Also possible. Daniel didn't get the impression that any of them had been trying to deceive him, but that wasn't to say he was correct.

The same could be said for Mrs. Dixon. Perhaps the woman did love Aubrey, Daniel mused as he weighed her responses to his questions. She'd defended him as if he were her own son and seemed to know him better than most natural mothers knew their children.

As Daniel took his leave, he wondered how well his own mother had known him at that age and how much of her love had been based on the child he'd been rather than the restless, often angry young man he had become after his father had died so suddenly at the age of forty-two. She hadn't understood his desire to join the police, nor had she thought he should marry Sarah. Helen Haze had thought Sarah was weak and selfish and would not make Daniel happy in the end. Well, his mother had turned out to be right about that, at least, if not about his decision to join the police service. Daniel couldn't see himself teaching as his father had done or becoming a shopkeeper or a clerk. Policing was in his blood, just as Sarah had been until a few months ago.

Chapter 21

Once outside the Dixon residence, Daniel checked Timothy Latham's address. It would make sense to stop by now, since it wasn't too far, and he hoped to catch Belinda Latham alone. He doubted she would be too forthcoming under the watchful eye of her husband, and Daniel wanted to get an unimpeded impression of the woman and Timothy Latham's marriage. There had been something in Latham's demeanor toward the end of the interview that had made Daniel want to dig a little deeper, even if only to put his mind at rest. Reluctant to waste time, Daniel found a hansom and was at the Latham door within a quarter of an hour.

The Lathams lived in one of the recently constructed houses in Camden Road. The location would have been more desirable five years ago, before the mainline railway had been slated to cut through Kentish Town and overshadow the newly laid-out square to accommodate Camden Road station, which had opened just that year. The railroad tracks were clearly visible from certain vantage points, and the sound of the approaching train utterly dispelled the aura of genteel tranquility that the builders had originally hoped for when choosing to build in this part of London.

Daniel knocked on the door and was surprised when a woman in her thirties opened the door. She had to be at least ten years older than Timothy Latham, so perhaps she was a servant. He produced his warrant card and smiled in a friendly manner to put her at ease.

"I'm Inspector Haze of Scotland Yard, and I would like to speak to Mrs. Latham."

"I'm Mrs. Latham," the woman replied.

"Belinda Latham?"

"Yes. Please, come in, Inspector."

Mrs. Latham led him to a comfortable parlor and invited him to sit. "Would you care for some tea?"

"Thank you, no. I'm not staying long," Daniel said. "I just need to ask you a few questions, and then I'll be on my way. I have a few more people I need to call on today."

Mrs. Latham sat across from him and folded her hands in her lap, waiting for him to explain the reason for his visit. Daniel took a moment to study her. She had light brown hair, parted in the middle and wound into a neat bun at her nape. Her dark brown gaze was calm and introspective, and her round face had a fresh, country look about it, not the often-unhealthy pallor of those who'd lived their whole lives in London and breathed in coal smoke and the oppressive stench from the river since birth. Her gown was of dark blue calico, a modest lace collar its only decoration. She wore no jewelry except for a thin wedding band that glinted in the sun from the window.

Mrs. Latham's eyebrows furrowed in confusion when Daniel failed to speak, and he roused himself from his reverie and smiled at her again, hoping he hadn't put her on her guard with his watchful stare.

"A friend of your husband was found dead on Tuesday morning. Murdered."

"You mean Alex Gray?" Belinda Latham asked, seeming unperturbed.

"Yes. Have you ever met him?"

"No, but Timothy has mentioned him on several occasions."

"Did he like Alex Gray?"

Belinda shrugged delicately. "Timothy is not the sort of person who easily warms to people. He's very private by nature and keeps himself to himself."

"I was told you are newly married," Daniel said.

Mrs. Latham wasn't unattractive, but it was difficult to see Timothy and Belinda as a married couple. There was something motherly in her, and he didn't at all get the impression that she was timid or scatterbrained. She looked calm and composed, and Daniel could see in her gaze that she was weighing her options, which instantly made her more interesting.

"We are not married, Inspector," Belinda said after a long pause. "But I told you the truth. I am Mrs. Latham."

"I'm afraid I don't understand," Daniel said.

"I'm Mrs. Bertram Latham. I am Timothy's brother's widow."

She clearly expected Daniel to comment, but he decided to remain silent, hoping she'd feel the need to explain. Most people were uncomfortable with silence and tended to fill it with chatter. In this case, the chatter could be telling.

Daniel's hunch hadn't been wrong. Belinda let out a heavy sigh, and when she finished, her shoulders were considerably lower than they had been, as if a great weight rested on them now that she'd told him the truth, or part of it.

"Bertram and I were married nearly ten years ago," she began. "We weren't blessed with children and were eventually desperate enough to consult a doctor. Bertram always blamed me. He said it was the woman's fault when there were no children. He assumed I was barren."

Daniel could see the pain in her eyes. These were clearly unpleasant and hurtful memories. "The doctor found nothing wrong with me, but he concluded that our childlessness was caused by an accident Bertram had suffered as a boy. He'd been kicked by a horse, you see." At this, Belinda's cheeks turned a mottled red that made it clear just where her husband had been kicked. "He was only nine at the time and he'd recovered quickly, but the impact had done enough damage to render him sterile."

"I'm sorry to hear that, Mrs. Latham," Daniel said, although he had no idea what any of this had to do with the present situation. He refrained from asking and waited for Mrs. Latham to speak again.

"Upon finding out the reason, Bertram drowned himself. The vicar, who was a kind man and felt sympathy for us when he found out what had happened, explained Bertram's death away as a terrible accident and allowed us to bury him in the graveyard, but many suspected the truth. Bertram was a suicide, and I would have to live with that for the rest of my life. Besides that, I was now too old to bear children, so my future looked bleak."

"How did you wind up living with Timothy?" Daniel finally asked.

"Timothy is the only family I have left, and he felt responsible for me. He couldn't afford to maintain two residences, so he suggested that I move to London and look after him as a wife would. We don't share a bed," she added, her cheeks growing even redder. "We live as brother and sister, but it's easier for people to think we're married. That way, we need not explain. That's part of the reason Timothy never invites any of his friends home and likes to give them the impression that I'm a country bumpkin. I don't mind, really," she added, her violent blush beginning to fade. "I'm happy to have a home with a man who cares about me. I would be all alone and destitute otherwise."

"Mrs. Latham, where was Timothy on Monday night?" Daniel asked.

"He was here. We had supper together at seven, and then Timothy studied while I tidied up and darned my stockings. I must make what I have last as long as I can," she added wistfully. "Timothy can't afford to buy me new things. Once he qualifies as a surgeon, perhaps then."

"What time did you retire?"

"I went to bed around nine-thirty. Timothy was still at his books, but I heard him come to bed around midnight. I couldn't sleep," she explained. "I often lie awake for hours, thinking of how my life turned out. I'm not bitter," she said, her eyes misting with tears. "I just can't help but wonder if it was something I did that has led me to this. I'm grateful to Timothy, I really am, but I had hoped for so much more when I married Bertram."

"I'm sorry, Mrs. Latham," Daniel said, and meant it. He might not have felt sympathy before, but given that he often lay awake long into the night, wondering much the same thing, he felt a sad kinship with the woman. "What if Timothy decides he wishes to marry?"

What would become of Belinda then? Would she be relegated to the role of housekeeper for the newly married couple or be expected to go away and let them enjoy their matrimonial bliss? What would she live on? He supposed she could always find a position as a domestic servant if she had no other choice.

"I don't think he will. That's why he was happy to allow me to pose as his wife. Timothy doesn't like women, Inspector," Belinda confided, lowering her voice. "He says he has no use for them. Not all men are cut out for marriage."

"No, I don't suppose they are. Does he have any close friends? Anyone he spends time with privately?" Daniel asked.

"No. He enjoys the camaraderie of the other students, but he never stays longer than it takes to have one drink. Like I said, he's a private person, a bit of a loner. That seems to be enough for him."

"And is it enough for you?" The question had just popped out, and Daniel felt awful for asking it. It was none of his business, and there was nothing he could do to help Belinda even if he really wanted to.

"I have a roof over my head, food on my plate, and a man who cares enough not to leave me out in the world on my own. For now, that's enough. If the good Lord sees fit to put a good man in my path, I won't say no," Belinda Latham said, allowing herself a small smile.

Daniel didn't bother to ask how she might meet a good man if any man she encountered believed her to be married to her brother-in-law. That had nothing to do with him, and if she believed such a thing was possible, then he hoped she was right.

"Thank you, Mrs. Latham. I appreciate you taking the time to speak to me."

"Timothy would never hurt a fly," Belinda said in parting. "He's a bit gruff, but he's a good man at heart."

Daniel bid her a good day and left, heading toward Clerkenwell on foot.

He hadn't warmed to Timothy Latham when they met and would have liked to paint him as a suspect, but his gut instinct told him to leave Latham alone, at least for the time being. If Belinda Latham had been telling the truth, then Timothy had an alibi for Monday night and couldn't have killed Alexandra Gray, nor did he seem to have a motive. He hadn't known she was a woman, nor had Timothy seemed to like her much as a man. Their dealings had been cordial in a group setting, which was not to say that a deep hatred for Alex Gray hadn't seethed in Timothy Latham's breast. He seemed like the sort of man who would easily feel slighted and allow his anger to fester—but enough to kill and stage the murder scene? Daniel didn't think so.

As he quickened his stride, he couldn't help but wonder if Timothy Latham was homosexual. Was that the reason he had installed his brother's widow in his home, using her as a cover? To hide behind a fictitious wife made for a convenient arrangement if he had no interest in women and no plans to marry. Belinda wouldn't dare question him if he went out alone and didn't tell her whom he was seeing, nor would she ever confront him, fearful of the consequences to her own future.

Or maybe Timothy was just one of those men who felt no need for female companionship. Not every man craved a woman's touch or wished to have children. Timothy Latham was still young and might change his mind, but that had nothing to do with the case, as far as Daniel could see. For the moment, Latham had no discernable motive and had an alibi. Daniel was happy to leave it at that.

Chapter 22

Daniel's next port of call was Rhona Christie, who lived two doors down from Ezra Hall in Clerkenwell, but his attention wasn't entirely focused on questioning Ezra Hall's charwoman as he approached the Christie residence. It was often true that murders were committed by those closest to the victim, the friends and lovers more apt to feel jealousy or resentment and have the most to gain from the person's death, but there were plenty of times when the crime was perpetrated by someone outside the deceased's circle.

Daniel was convinced, given the method of the murder, that Alexandra had known her killer and had sparked a murderous rage in their heart, but it was entirely possible that the person responsible wasn't known to any of Alexandra's friends. She'd obviously kept secrets from her brother, and none of her friends appeared to know that she had been a woman, their reactions sincere enough to attest to the fact that they were telling the truth. There was a part of Alexandra's life no one seemed to know anything about, and no amount of checking alibis was going to point Daniel toward the truth.

He was missing something, and he found his thoughts returning to Aubrey Dixon. Even though Dixon could have technically left home after the party and met Alexandra at Highgate, or wherever they'd arranged to meet, Daniel had to agree with Aubrey's stepmother that Aubrey murdering Alexandra Gray seemed unlikely. He was an ambitious young man and would be foolish to risk his own life to eliminate a rival for a position he might get on his own merit. If Jason was able to confirm that Hiram Bosworth had indeed chosen Aubrey Dixon for the position in his practice, then Aubrey's motive would evaporate into thin air. There had to be someone else, someone who had nursed a hatred against the young surgeon, their desire to destroy her so powerful that they had not only taken her life but had needed to humiliate her in death with the staged hanging. The killer had wanted Alexandra's secret revealed. They had wanted the world to know that Alexandra Gray had been a fraud, a woman who had stepped out of line and had paid for her daring with her very life.

The killer had known Alexandra's secret; Daniel was in no two minds about that. So, who was it? A secret lover? A rival surgeon who had been threatened by Alexandra's impressive prospects? But why? Alexandra Gray had yet to complete her studies and qualify as a surgeon. She might have been competent and intuitive, but there were plenty of other surgeons in London. Why would she make whoever killed her feel so threatened? Unless this was simply a hate-filled crime against a woman. Might the killer have wanted to punish her for daring to reach for something she had no right to? A religious zealot, perhaps? Had there been any similar crimes committed against women who dared to question the status quo?

Nothing sprang to mind. It might help to consult John Ransome on the matter. He'd been in London since the start of his career with the police service a decade ago. Perhaps he would remember. But unless this person killed systematically, the information would be of no help because to tie one murder to another was no easy thing.

Daniel let out a grunt of frustration. His mind was going in circles, his reasoning bringing him back to where he'd begun. Someone had hated Alexandra Gray enough to plan her murder and carry it out in a unique and dramatic way. But what was the motive? Love? Jealousy? Betrayal? A desire to watch someone die without having any reason to select that particular person?

Daniel stopped walking, astounded by the magnitude of that latest supposition. What if the killer had not known Alexandra at all and had selected her at random, the victim just happening to cross paths with someone bent on murder? What if the killer was some attention-seeking lunatic who simply wanted his deeds to get into the papers and toy with the police for the sheer pleasure of watching them fail? Might it be someone who wanted to see John Ransome humiliated, for it would be Ransome who'd take the fall if the case failed to get solved? It was Ransome who'd receive the bad press and possibly a rebuke from the commissioner. But then, not every case got solved. Everyone knew that, the commissioner included.

Cold sweat broke out on Daniel's face, his anxiety rising with every unanswered question that seemed determined to undermine his faith in his detecting skills. There was only one thing to do, and that was to doggedly pursue every lead, question everyone who'd known the victim, and hope that someone, intentionally or unwittingly, might drop a hint that would be the loose thread that would begin to unravel this mystery.

Daniel stopped in front of the house and drew several deep breaths to combat his agitation. He had to verify Ezra Hall's alibi. Dogged police work was what solved crimes, he reminded himself as he walked up the steps and knocked on the door. Dogged police work.

Chapter 23

Daniel was relieved to find Rhona Christie at home. She wasn't at all what Daniel had expected—a dowdy, emotionally wrung-out wretch who'd grab a bit of affection anywhere she could get it. She was a handsome woman of about thirty, with thick chestnut hair that curled becomingly around her heart-shaped face, and pale green eyes fringed with thick lashes. She had a trim figure, and although her gown was neither new nor fashionable, it was neatly pressed and accented with what appeared to be a new lace collar. If not for the haunted expression in her eyes, Daniel might have mistaken her for a woman content with her lot.

"How can I help you, Inspector?" Mrs. Christie asked once Daniel introduced himself and they were seated in the tiny parlor that smelled of wood polish and loneliness.

"I'm investigating the murder of Alexander Gray. He was a friend of Ezra Hall. Did you ever meet him?"

"No, but Mr. Hall mentioned him in conversation," Mrs. Christie replied. "He told me about all his friends."

"You two have an unusually close relationship," Daniel said, smiling in an understanding manner to take the sting out of his words.

"We're friends. Have been these many years," Mrs. Christie replied, appearing unperturbed by Daniel's insinuation.

"Mr. Hall alleges that you and he spent the night together on Monday. Is that true, Mrs. Christie?"

The woman fixed him with an unflinching stare. "Yes, it is. I spend several nights a week with Ezra."

"What about your husband?" Daniel asked.

"What about him?"

"Does he not mind?"

"My husband no longer minds anything, Inspector Haze. There was an accident at the docks three years past. A crate filled with bottles of Jamaican rum broke loose as it was being unloaded, crushing the men who were standing below."

"I remember reading about it in the paper," Daniel replied. "Two men died."

"Yes. And a third survived, and very unfortunate it was too because my husband is now a cabbage," Mrs. Christie said bitterly. "He'd have hated living like this and would have preferred to have died that day."

"I'm very sorry, Mrs. Christie. It must be exceedingly difficult for you both."

She inclined her head in acknowledgment. "So, yes, Inspector, I was with Ezra on Monday night, and I can promise you that he never left his bed. I made him breakfast in the morning and went on home."

Daniel looked around the room. He hadn't noticed the photographs before, but now he stared at them, intensely sorry for the smiling young couple in the silver frame. The photograph had presumably been taken to commemorate their wedding day, since Rhona Christie was at least a decade younger than she was today. The second photograph was of a young girl, perhaps five years of age. She looked very much like Mrs. Christie and was smiling shyly, her hand clutching a cloth dolly.

"Is that your daughter?" Daniel asked.

"Was my daughter," Mrs. Christie replied. She had sounded bitter when speaking of her husband's accident, but now her voice caught, and her eyes filled with tears. "She died recently."

"I'm terribly sorry," Daniel said, intensely sympathetic toward the poor woman. "Was she ill?"

"No. She was in fine health. And then, that day, she said she was feeling tired and asked to go to bed. I tucked her in and told her to rest, and that I'd have sausages for her supper when she woke. Except she never did. When I came to wake her, she was gone." The tears flowed freely now, the expression in those green eyes going from haunted to bewildered. "She'd just turned eight," Mrs. Christie whimpered.

"Did you summon a doctor? What was the cause of death?" Daniel asked, even though he was probably causing the poor woman more pain with his pointless questions.

Mrs. Christie took a moment to collect herself, then looked at him, her gaze telling him that he clearly had no understanding of her situation.

"There seemed little point to spend money on a doctor, Inspector. Nothing he said would bring my Veronica back, would it? I used the money I had put by to pay for her funeral and to buy white lilies to put on her grave. She would have liked that. Lilies were her favorite." Mrs. Christie's gaze shifted toward the window, where a bright, sunny day was so at odds with her grief. "So you see, Inspector Haze, it doesn't really matter what I do. There's no one left to care."

"Doesn't Ezra Hall care?" Daniel asked, although it really wasn't any of his business. Their relationship was their own, whatever they considered it to be.

"He does, but not enough to offer me a future. He'll meet a fine young woman someday, and she'll be the famous surgeon's wife and the mother of his children. And I'll be the drab who'd once washed his drawers."

"Perhaps you'll marry again one day," Daniel said. He had no idea why he'd felt the need to comfort the woman, but something about her grief resonated with him. If not for Charlotte, no one would care what he got up to either. Charlotte was the anchor that kept him moored to his life.

"I doubt that very much," Rhona Christie said on a heartfelt sigh. "Todd's not right in the head and can't get around on his own, but his heart is strong. As long as I keep feeding him and changing the soiled linens, he'll go on like this for ages. I tell you, Inspector, if it weren't a crime against the Almighty, I'd hold a pillow over his face and be done with it, just to spare him the suffering and humiliation of having his wife wipe his arse and spoon-feed him porridge. He hated porridge," she said wistfully. "Said it was for old folk as had no teeth."

Daniel nodded. Perhaps the Almighty would take pity on her and call Todd Christie to him sooner rather than later, giving the poor woman an opportunity to still make something of her life. She was too young and attractive to feel such hopelessness at the prospect of the future.

"Thank you, Mrs. Christie," Daniel said. "I hope life has some pleasant surprises in store for you."

Rhona Christie laughed at that. "I don't believe in fairy stories, Inspector, but I'm more than ready to be proven wrong."

Just like Belinda Latham, Daniel reflected, saddened by these women who had nothing to look forward to in their lives except the possibility of a miracle that would rescue them from the impossibility of their situation.

Leaving the Christie house, Daniel found a hansom and instructed the cabbie to take him to Scotland Yard. Superintendent Ransome would be expecting an update on the case and wouldn't appreciate being kept waiting.

Chapter 24

John Ransome leaned back in his chair and sized up Daniel in a way that implied he'd be happy to sack him on the spot if he had someone more qualified to take over the case. Daniel had heard from Sergeant Meadows upon arrival at the Yard that Commissioner Hawkins had stopped by not an hour ago, likely to remind Ransome in person that it was in his best interests to solve the case quickly and clear the Ashfords of any wrongdoing.

There had to be some connection to the Ashfords, and the new viscount was young, handsome, and not above suspicion where an attractive young woman was involved. Perhaps he liked to play twisted games with his victims, or maybe it had been a love affair gone wrong. Daniel didn't think the man was stupid enough to leave a woman he'd killed in the vault on the morning of his father's interment, but maybe that had been the whole point. No one would believe him to be responsible, not when the answer would be so blatantly obvious as to be discounted on the spot in favor of some elaborate conspiracy. In any case, Ransome was always skating on thin ice when it came to the more upstanding members of society, those who could have a quiet word with the right person and have him put out to pasture, replaced with someone who would do what they were told and turn a blind eye when the situation called for it.

As much as Daniel resented John Ransome's abrasive manner, he felt confident that Ransome would back him up when the evidence pointed to a member of the peerage, or a well-respected civil servant, as had been the case only a few months ago. But Ransome was a political animal, and if he could find an alternative solution to putting his head on the block, he would, preferably swapping his own head with Daniel's.

"So, you have nothing," Ransome stated once he'd heard Daniel's report.

"I wouldn't say that, exactly," Daniel countered out of sheer obstinacy. Ransome was right. He had nothing of substance to go on.

"All right," Ransome replied, beginning to fold down the fingers of his left hand with the index finger of his right as he itemized Daniel's failures. "No clear motive. No obvious suspects. No known witnesses to the crime. No idea if there's a connection between the Ashfords and the victim. And no viable leads to pursue." He grinned in that condescending way he had, more a baring of the teeth than a smile. "I seem to have run out of fingers," he said nastily.

"Lord Redmond is going to speak to Hiram Bosworth and Harold Guthrie this evening," Daniel said.

"And what do you expect they'll say?" Ransome demanded.

"Hiram Bosworth will either confirm or deny Aubrey Dixon's assumption that he's won the position in Mr. Bosworth's practice. Harold Guthrie has been publicly embarrassed by Alexandra Gray on several occasions. If he has no alibi for Monday night, he's a suspect."

"The way I see it, your only possible suspect is Aubrey Dixon. He had a motive, and he had an opportunity. His stepmother could only alibi him until midnight. She clearly told you she couldn't confirm that he'd remained in his bedroom after she saw him go up. What he did after midnight is anyone's guess."

"No one saw Aubrey Dixon leave the premises after he'd gone up to his bedroom," Daniel reminded Ransome.

"Doesn't mean he didn't. He could have climbed out the window for all you know."

"All right. Let us suppose that Aubrey Dixon did indeed leave the house after he was seen to retire. Mrs. Fleet saw Alexandra Gray leaving the lodging house around nine o'clock. Aubrey Dixon was at his sister's engagement celebration until midnight. That's three hours of Alexandra's time that are unaccounted for, hours during which she might have been murdered."

"Well, then I suggest *you* account for them, Haze. Find the cabbie who collected her from her lodgings and find out where he took her. What on God's green earth was this woman doing at the cemetery at night? Did she go directly to Highgate, or had she gone somewhere else entirely and was either lured or brought to the cemetery, before or after death? My money is on Dixon. You said yourself that the man is ambitious and clearheaded and stated that if one opportunity didn't work out, he'd simply find another. Or create another, most like." Ransome paused for breath before continuing.

"This was no crime of passion, an unforeseen result of someone losing their temper and doing something they'd likely regret for the rest of their days, if only because they'd be soiling their drawers at the prospect of facing the hangman. This was premeditated. Planned. Aubrey Dixon sounds like just the sort of chap who'd plan the murder of his archrival to the last detail, making sure no one could connect him to the crime."

Daniel opened his mouth to respond, but Ransome forestalled him.

"A party where a dozen people saw him? Check." Ransome was folding fingers again.

"No one who can definitively say that he'd left the house after midnight? Check." Another finger folded.

"Nothing to connect him to the scene of the crime? Check. Hiram Bosworth, who'd confirm that he'd already told Dixon he had the position? Check. Of course he'd have the position if he were the last man standing."

The last finger came down. "Dixon thought it all through and made sure no one could refute his alibi. It all fits, Haze."

"So does a square peg into a round hole if you use a sledgehammer to drive it in, sir," Daniel retorted.

"If you don't come up with anything to disprove my theory by this time tomorrow, we're charging Dixon. Now, if you don't mind, I have a previous engagement, so off with you."

Thus dismissed, Daniel left the Yard, rudely ignoring Sergeant Meadows' wishes for a good evening, and practically trotted home to St. John's Wood. By the time he arrived, he felt slightly less murderous than he had an hour ago.

Chapter 25

Jason found Hiram Bosworth at the Athenaeum Club in Pall Mall after being directed there by the man's very helpful valet. The Athenaeum Club was geared toward men with an interest in arts and sciences and was often patronized by those in the medical profession. Jason had, in fact, been invited to join once he'd relocated to London but had yet to respond to the invitation, since he wasn't sure he wished to belong to a club. To him, it seemed like an outdated practice favored by stodgy older men, but he supposed a membership might foster certain professional relationships that could be not only beneficial but intellectually stimulating.

Hiram Bosworth was said to be close to sixty but didn't look a day over forty-five. He was tall, slim, and fit. Rumor had it that he still fenced with a private instructor several days a week and belonged to a gymnasium that he attended as often as he could, given his hectic schedule. His dark hair was gently threaded with gray, and his dark blue gaze probably missed very little. Bosworth was intelligent and well respected without being pompous or self-absorbed, the sort of colleague Jason was eager to cultivate.

"Lord Redmond," Hiram Bosworth exclaimed when Jason was shown to the library where Bosworth had been reading. "It's a surprise to see you here. I've grown accustomed to meeting you in a hospital setting."

"I'm actually here on a mission," Jason replied, settling into a club chair across from Bosworth.

"In that case, allow me to buy you a drink. What's your tipple of choice?"

"A brandy, please," Jason said to the waiter who had materialized by his side.

"Make that two, Simpson," Bosworth told the man. "Now. How can I help?"

"I'm assisting Scotland Yard with the investigation into Alex Gray's death," Jason explained. "There was a suggestion that Aubrey Dixon had a motive to dispose of his rival. Would you say that's an accurate assessment of the relationship between Dixon and Gray?"

"Yes and no," Hiram Bosworth said. "I did make it known that Gray and Dixon were my top candidates for the position in my practice, but I intimated to Aubrey Dixon that he would ultimately be my choice."

"May I ask why?"

The older man nodded. "I like…liked Alex Gray immensely. He was a gifted young man who would have made an excellent surgeon, but there was something about him that put me on my guard."

Jason watched the man. Had Hiram Bosworth suspected that Alex Gray wasn't what he had seemed? Had he perhaps known for certain?

"What was it that alarmed you?" Jason asked, once Simpson had brought their drinks and taken himself off on silent feet.

"Aubrey Dixon comes off as a pompous, overconfident dandy, but underneath his bluster, he's a man of great intelligence and dogged persistence. He is also able to detach himself from the patient emotionally and focus entirely on the medical aspect of the situation. I think an apprenticeship with me would make him happy, and he would work hard to justify my trust in him. If he proves as competent as I believe he will be, I will feel safe to leave my practice to him once I'm ready to retire."

"And Alex Gray?"

"Alex Gray was the most ambitious young man I'd ever met. He wouldn't be happy to remain in my employ for long, only long enough to learn what he could. His ultimate goal would be not to live up to my expectations but to surpass me as a surgeon. I would be nothing more than a step on his ladder to success."

"And what of Edward Gray? Is he as ambitious as his cousin?" Jason asked, wondering if they might have underestimated Edward Gray's desire to succeed.

"Not as ambitious or as gifted as Alex," Hiram Bosworth replied. "Edward will make a decent surgeon, but he'll never be brilliant."

"So, he was never a possibility?"

"Not for a second."

"Was there anyone else you had considered?" Jason asked.

"Yes. Ezra Hall. He's dedicated and eager to learn."

"Does the death of Alex Gray alter his prospects?"

"Not with me. I like Ezra, but there's an arrogance in him I find off-putting." Hiram Bosworth chuckled. "I wager you're thinking that Aubrey Dixon is as arrogant as they come, but the truth is, Ezra would readily sacrifice the patient to find a new method or prove he can succeed where someone else has failed. I don't believe in using my patients for research. My only job as a surgeon is to help them and improve the quality of their life, or what's left of it."

"In other words, you didn't trust either Alex Gray or Ezra Hall to uphold your values as a surgeon," Jason summarized.

"Precisely. I need a man I can trust, someone I would feel safe leaving my patients with."

"Mr. Bosworth, would it shock you if I told you that Alex Gray was a woman?"

Jason watched the man carefully for any hint of subterfuge but saw none, only genuine surprise as Jason's words penetrated the thick façade of self-assurance and finally settled in, the suggestion morphing into rock-solid awareness. "Yes, it would," Bosworth said slowly, as if still struggling with the revelation. "I always thought him somewhat effeminate, but it never occurred to me he was actually female. I suppose I assumed he was a molly. Well," he exclaimed. "She certainly fooled me."

"You and everyone else," Jason said.

"Is that why she was killed, do you think?" Bosworth asked. "Someone discovered her secret?"

Jason answered the question with one of his own. "Do you think any of the students would kill her if they found out?"

"It's a possibility, I suppose, but I think it would be easier and safer for their own prospects to simply out the woman rather than kill her."

"It might have been a crime of passion," Jason suggested.

"It might, but surgeons are a practical, analytical bunch," Bosworth said with an amused smile, no doubt implying that Jason also fit that description. "Why poison someone, then go through the trouble of hanging them in a place they'd be discovered the following day? Much easier to toss the body in the Thames and be done with it. By the time the corpse would be fished out, there'd be no evidence left to incriminate them. No, there was something more at play here than mere rivalry, Lord Redmond. I'd say what we are dealing with are intense personal feelings harnessed into coolheaded calculation."

"You think it was a love affair gone wrong?"

"Or gone right," Hiram Bosworth replied with a sly grin.

"How do you mean?" Jason asked.

"Say one of the other students, who happens to be of a homosexual persuasion, had developed tender feelings toward our young Mr. Gray. What if his feelings were reciprocated, the budding relationship so intense that Miss Gray found the courage to confide in her admirer, foolishly believing her sex wouldn't matter, since she was prepared to live as a man and to accommodate him physically without ever expecting any sexual gratification for herself? Shocked and humiliated, the man might feel a murderous rage toward the woman who'd played him for a fool and was a more competent surgeon to boot. That might drive an insecure young buck to murder."

"Yes, I suppose it could," Jason agreed. "Especially if the young buck in question feared exposure."

"Well, they'd both have something to hide," Bosworth pointed out, "but wounded pride can incite a man to do terrible things."

"I will certainly convey your theory to Inspector Haze," Jason said as he finished his drink and set the empty glass on the conveniently placed table at his elbow. "Thank you for seeing me, Mr. Bosworth."

"It was my pleasure, my lord, and I would gladly give Mr. Dixon the boot if you would consider joining me as a partner," the older man said, his eyes twinkling with amusement.

"I thank you for the offer, but if I were to go into private practice, I think I'd prefer to establish my own."

"Fair enough," Bosworth said. "You have a fine reputation as both a surgeon and as a man. There are those who find you most intriguing, the ladies of the ton in particular. I hope that wife of yours knows how to keep your interest from waning," he added without bothering to hide the insinuation that Jason could have done better when choosing a wife than a woman with no pedigree and no fortune.

"My wife is in no danger of losing my affections, Mr. Bosworth." Jason was insulted by the suggestion that he would betray Katherine if a more desirable prospect presented itself and would have liked to walk out of the library, but he had one more interview to conduct and wouldn't allow his personal feelings to get in the way. "Are you acquainted with Harold Guthrie, by any chance?"

"I am. He's a good friend, and if I'm not mistaken, you can find him in the dining room. He prefers to sup early due to a severe case of acid reflux. Can't sleep a wink if he eats anything after five. Would you care for an introduction?"

"I would. Thank you."

Hiram Bosworth raised two fingers, easily getting the attention of Simpson, who was hovering nearby.

"Another drink, sir?"

"Another drink?" Bosworth asked Jason.

"Thank you, no."

"Please ask Mr. Guthrie to join us once he's finished his supper."

"Of course, sir."

Bosworth consulted his gold watch. "He'll be along in precisely seven minutes," he said with a wink. "Like clockwork, our Harold."

Chapter 26

As predicted, Harold Guthrie appeared less than ten minutes later and dropped into a chair, as if exhausted beyond words. Unlike his friend, Guthrie was short and quite rotund, his silver hair and beard giving him a grandfatherly appearance, even though he was probably no more than fifty-five. It was difficult to imagine him as a criminal mastermind, but Jason had to ask his questions regardless. Just because someone looked innocent didn't mean they were.

"I'll leave you gentlemen to it," Hiram Bosworth said diplomatically once he'd made the introductions, and took himself off to another room.

Jason explained the reason for his visit and asked for Mr. Guthrie's impressions of Alexander Gray, then watched as the man paused to consider his response.

"Annoying," he said at last, surprising Jason with his vehemence. "Annoying as heck."

"How so?"

"Arrogant, disrespectful to his betters, and full of confidence he had no right to possess at such a young age."

"I believe he questioned your methods," Jason said gently, wondering if the spark he'd lit was about to set off an explosion.

"He did. On more than one occasion," Guthrie admitted, shaking his head in disbelief. "And do you know what the most irritating part was? Gray was right. I have become set in my ways, relying on experience rather than challenging myself to learn new methods and techniques. A dinosaur, some students call me behind my back."

"And how does that make you feel?" Jason asked, surprised Mr. Guthrie wasn't more annoyed. He almost seemed amused.

"Sad. Old. Past my prime. But would I kill a student because they had questioned me? Heavens, no. Alex Gray forced me to take a good, long look at myself, and what I decided was that I'm not ready to go gentle into that good night, Lord Redmond. I intend not only to hone my skills as a surgeon but to invite the students to theorize on what they would do in a particular instance rather than tell them what I would do. My job is to teach, to inform, not to suppress ambition or knowledge. Was Alex Gray annoying? A resounding yes. Correct in his criticism of me? Also yes. I can admit when I'm wrong," Harold Guthrie said, and Jason believed him because he saw no evidence of animosity. The man seemed most annoyed with himself.

"Thank you, Mr. Guthrie. I appreciate you taking the time to speak to me."

"I do hope you'll join the club, your lordship. I would enjoy talking with your further."

"Perhaps I will," Jason said, and meant it. He enjoyed conversing with like-minded men, especially if they weren't as stodgy as he had originally believed them to be. Perhaps he was becoming set in his own ways as well, and that was not something he was prepared to tolerate.

Chapter 27

Friday, September 18

Friday dawned cool and gray, but the rain held off. The sun seemed to be trying valiantly to break through the clouds, piercing the gloom like arrows shot directly from heaven. Daniel wished he could join Miss Grainger and Charlotte on their outing to the park. Grace had saved some breadcrumbs for Charlotte so she could feed the ducks, and Charlotte was excited to get going, even though it was still early and there wouldn't be too many people about. Charlotte always looked for other children to share her breadcrumbs with so that they could feed the ducks together.

"Shall we wait until later?" Miss Grainger asked anxiously, her blue gaze fixed on Daniel as he joined them in the nursery before heading out for the day.

Daniel couldn't help smiling at her. She seemed as eager as Charlotte. "Why wait for anything?" he replied, feeling reckless. "If you're happy to take her, then please go now. I just want her to be happy." *And you*, he thought suddenly, envisioning Miss Grainger and Charlotte at the park, laughing and playing.

Miss Grainger grinned. "I agree. Why wait? People are always putting things off, and so often they never come to pass for one reason or another."

"I wish I could join you," Daniel said wistfully.

"Can't you come with us for a short while?"

"I would like nothing more, but I'm afraid I can't take any time off until this investigation is at an end."

"And is it likely to come to an end soon?" Miss Grainger asked, still looking up at him.

There was genuine interest in her gaze, and Daniel wished he could talk to her about his work, but it wouldn't be appropriate, so he shook his head instead.

"It's difficult to say. Sometimes a break in the case comes at just the right time, and at other times, the waters grow murkier, and eventually one must give up and move on to another investigation. Not every crime gets solved."

Miss Grainger's smile was full of pride. "You will solve this case, Inspector Haze. I know you will. I have great faith in you."

"Thank you, Miss Grainger. I hope I don't disappoint you."

"Never," she answered pertly, and turned away from him, looking down at Charlotte, who was pulling impatiently on her hand.

"Go now?" Charlotte demanded, her dark eyes pleading.

"Your papa says it's all right, so let's get our coats and hats," Miss Grainger said. "Wave goodbye," she added as Daniel turned to leave the nursery.

"Bye," Charlotte sang, but her attention wasn't on him. She had more important things to do.

After leaving the house, Daniel walked to the nearest hansom stop, where he found three cabbies sharing a companionable smoke as they waited for fares. They were all of middle years, one with a crooked nose and a missing front tooth, noticeable only because he smiled brightly at Daniel, unlike the other two, who looked at him in a surly manner. Always one to appreciate a friendly gesture, Daniel approached the grinning man.

"'Allo, guv," the man said. "Where can I take ye this fine morn?"

"What's your name?" Daniel asked.

The other two men sniggered, glad Daniel hadn't approached them since they clearly expected some unpleasantness to unfold, but the man removed his hat and held it against his chest in a gesture of humility.

"Name's Josiah Brown. Pleasure to make yer acquaintance, guv."

"Daniel Haze," Daniel replied with a smile of his own, and held out his hand to the man. He didn't think telling the cabbie he was with the police would work in his favor. People tended to clam up, especially if their conscience wasn't crystal clear.

The man shook Daniel's hand gingerly, probably wondering what on earth Daniel was up to.

"I need a bit of help, Mr. Brown. I wonder if you might be the man to supply it?"

Mr. Brown's gaze narrowed as he considered Daniel's question, but then he nodded. "What sort of 'elp ye be needing, Mr. 'Aze?"

"My wife…" Just saying that made Daniel feel as if all the air was momentarily squeezed from his lungs, but he took a deep breath and continued. "My wife left her reticule in a hansom cab the other day. How would I go about tracking down the cabbie who'd driven her?"

Mr. Brown nodded, clearly appreciating Daniel's predicament. "Well, there are a fair few cab yards outside the city. I reckon ye can visit them all and ask after yer wife's reticule, but— and I 'ate to say it, guv—I 'ardly think ye'll get it back, 'specially not if there were anything of value inside."

"I understand, but I must try, Mr. Brown. I don't care about the money she carried, but there was a photograph…" Daniel allowed the sentence to trail off, letting the cabbie come to his own conclusions. "It wouldn't be worth much to anyone who found it," he said at last. "But it means a great deal to us."

"I reckon yer chances are not awful good, and I tell ye that honest-like, but if ye want, I'll take ye to every yard so ye can at least tell yer lady ye tried."

"I would appreciate that, Mr. Brown."

Daniel had never given much thought to the lives of hackney drivers, but now he was interested, and the more he knew, the better equipped he'd be to talk to the men he encountered.

"Do you own this cab?" he asked as Mr. Brown turned to climb onto his perch behind the carriage.

The man laughed. "If only."

"So, how does it work?"

"I work for Mr. Smithson. 'E owns ten cabs. 'E maintains 'em, stables the 'orses and pays for their upkeep and such. I turn my earnings over to 'im at the end of the day, and 'e pays me a weekly wage based on the takings."

"How many hours a day do you work?" Daniel asked.

"Twelve at the very least," Mr. Brown replied.

"That's a long day."

"It is," Mr. Brown agreed. "But it pays the bills and keeps me out of me missus' 'air," he said with a phlegmy laugh. "Now, are ye ready, guv? Ye won't find yer photo by standing 'ere."

The cabbie waited until Daniel was settled inside before moving away from the curb. Daniel noted the sour expression on the other two cabbies' faces with a certain degree of satisfaction. They'd missed out on a hefty fare, given how many hours Mr. Brown would be driving Daniel around from yard to yard. And they were quick enough to surmise that there would be a nice little something in it for him at the end of it all. Daniel sat back and allowed the motion of the cab to lull him into a more relaxed state. He was under no illusions. His quest would take hours and probably prove fruitless, but he had to try.

Chapter 28

Four hours later, Daniel knew more about operating a hansom cab in London than he'd ever thought possible, but he hadn't found the man who'd driven Alex Gray to her assignations. There were few cabbies around; only the ones whose horses had gone lame or whose cabs needed immediate cleaning or repair were hanging about the cab yards during the daylight hours. Everyone else was out earning their keep.

Daniel didn't need to pretend to look for his wife's missing reticule, since Josiah Brown remained with the cab, waiting patiently for Daniel to complete his inquiries. Daniel asked after the man who'd picked up a fare at Mrs. Fleet's lodging house and then showed the men a photograph of Alexander Gray. They all denied ever having seen him, alive or dead, nor could any of them recall being asked to go to Highgate Cemetery after dark. With every shake of the head and every squinty-eyed look at the photo, Daniel felt less hopeful of finding the driver he was searching for, probably all the more so because the driver wouldn't care to be found once he knew the man was dead and the cabbie might be implicated in the murder.

And then there was the morning edition of the papers, which screamed in bold block print that the victim had, in fact, been a woman, and asked all the questions Daniel had asked himself when he had first found the victim. Who was she? Why had she been dressed as a man? What had she been doing at Highgate Cemetery after closing hours? And who'd go to such lengths to end her life? There were paragraphs of speculation about the life she might have led, each suggestion more lurid than the last. At least the press hadn't yet learned the truth of her identity or the reason she'd dressed as a man. Once they did, the Royal College of Surgeons would be named, as would Alexandra's friends and tutors. No one would be safe from the press, not when this was the most scandalous story to hit the pavement in weeks.

"Any luck, guv?" Josiah Brown asked Daniel as they were about to leave the last yard they'd visited in Bermondsey.

"No," Daniel replied. He was tired and frustrated, and wished he had something more to show for more than four hours of crisscrossing the city and talking to people who had no real desire to help him.

"Tell ye what, guv. Why don't ye leave that photograph with me and give me the address of the lodging 'ouse. I'll put the word out and let it be known where to find ye."

Daniel stared at the man, wondering how he knew.

Josiah Brown grinned, revealing his missing tooth. "I ain't as thick as ye might imagine." He held up a copy of the *Illustrated London News* that he must have picked up somewhere along the way because he hadn't had it that morning when they'd set off. Perhaps one of the cabbies had passed it to him, having finished with it. "I can read. Ye're looking for the cabbie as drove this cove to Highgate on Monday night. Could 'a just told me, Inspector Haze of Scotland Yard," he said, his smile growing more amused. "Says yer name right 'ere." He pointed a stubby finger at the second paragraph.

"You're correct, Mr. Brown. I should have been straight with you."

"Don't matter," the cabbie replied. "Ye got yer job to do, and I'm sure ye know best how to go 'bout it. But since ye hit a dead end, so to speak, let me 'elp."

Daniel considered the proposition and agreed. He paid the hefty fare and gave the man an extra five shillings on top.

"Thank ye kindly, guv," Josiah Brown said, and pocketed the money. "Much obliged. Where to now? It's on the house-like."

"Scotland Yard."

Chapter 29

"Any response to the newspaper articles?" Daniel asked the desk sergeant once he returned to the Yard.

Sergeant Meadows nodded gravely. "More than you might imagine, Inspector. People who claim to have come across the victim have been coming and going all morning long."

"Any possible leads?"

"Constable Napier has been sifting through the lot," Sergeant Meadows said. "Best ask him."

Daniel found Constable Napier in one of the interview rooms, speaking to an elderly woman who seemed to be in the midst of a lengthy narrative. Judging by the young constable's expression, she wasn't telling him anything of interest.

"Excuse me, madam," Constable Napier said when he saw Daniel.

"I'll wait, sonny," the woman promised. "I wasn't finished yet."

"Thank you for coming in, but I believe I have everything I need, Mrs. Baggot," Constable Napier said as he held the door in a suggestive manner.

"Well, that's the last time I'll take time out of my day to help the police," Mrs. Baggot said angrily, and walked out the door, head held high.

"I think you've earned a break, Constable," Daniel said as he looked at the young man's exasperated expression.

"I'll be all right to continue, as soon as I make a cup of tea."

Daniel followed the constable to the back room, where the kettle was already on the hob, Sergeant Meadows having anticipated their need. Daniel was starving, but food would have to wait until he was fully briefed.

Constable Napier made two strong cups of tea, added sugar, complained bitterly about the lack of milk and the right selfish sods who'd used it all up, and handed a cup to Daniel.

Daniel took a grateful sip and sank into a chair. Constable Napier sat across from him and blew on his brew, grumbling under his breath that it was too hot to drink without the milk.

"Anything?" Daniel asked.

"I must have spoken to at least twenty people this morning who think they know something of Alex Gray," the constable complained.

"And were any of them on the level?"

"Only one," Constable Napier replied, finally taking a sip of his tea. "A Mr. Elgin. Owns a broker's shop."

Daniel sat up straighter. "What did Mr. Elgin have to say? Did you take down his address?"

"'Course, I did," Constable Napier replied, his feathers ruffled by Daniel's insinuation that he'd made an error. "He said that Alexander Gray came into his shop about six months ago, just after Easter or thereabouts. He bought two scalpels and…" He pulled out his notebook to check the rest of the items. "Ah, here we go. And a metacarpal saw, bone cutting forceps, and a trocar. He also bought two pewter bowls."

"Surely such items are not readily available in a broker's shop," Daniel said.

"It seems Mr. Elgin bought the lot from a retired surgeon of his acquaintance. The articles were in fairly good condition, according to Mr. Elgin," Constable Napier added. "Only a hint of rust on the scalpels and the metacarpal saw."

Daniel set his mug on the table and leaned back in his chair, considering this new information. Mr. Elgin's account aligned with Alexandra Gray's chosen profession and wasn't in itself concerning. She had been a surgical student, so it made sense than she would invest in instruments—second hand if she couldn't afford to buy them new—but Jason would never use a rusted instrument on a patient. Daniel considered this angle. Perhaps the students were only allowed to practice on cadavers, so the condition of their instruments wouldn't much matter. He'd have to ask Jason when he came by that evening.

"Did Mr. Elgin recall anything else? Had Alexander Gray come in alone?"

Constable Napier glanced at his notebook again. "He came in with another medical student. Mr. Elgin had never seen the other man before, nor had he asked for his name, since Alexander Gray paid for the lot."

"Was Mr. Elgin able to describe the second man?"

"He said the man was dark-haired and had dark eyes, but that was all he remembered."

"So why would he remember Alexander Gray?" Daniel asked under his breath.

"I can answer that," Constable Napier said happily. "Mr. Elgin said that Alexander Gray seemed to be urging the second man to buy the second scalpel. He was excited, while the other man seemed to hang back, noticeably reluctant."

"Did Mr. Elgin know why?"

"He thought perhaps the second man couldn't afford the purchase but was too embarrassed to say so, even though Mr. Elgin suggested a very reasonable price, given that he wasn't likely to find another buyer anytime soon."

"But Alexander Gray paid for them both," Daniel pointed out.

"He did. He bought both scalpels, which was what had embarrassed the second man."

"Generosity is not a crime," Daniel said. "It's safe to assume the second man wasn't Edward Gray, since I've no doubt they shared their finances, and Edward is fair-haired."

Daniel smiled despite himself. The second man had to be Max Devane. According to her brother, Alexandra had nursed romantic feelings for Max, and Max's financial circumstances were clearly strained, since the whole family seemed to rely on one shop to support them all. Perhaps Alexandra had wished to do something nice for her friend but had embarrassed him instead. Hardly a reason for murder, but it would need to be verified just the same.

"Was there anyone else who had pertinent information about the case?" Daniel asked.

Constable Napier shook his head. "Unfortunately, no. Everyone else was making up wild tales about the victim, none of them even remotely relevant to the case."

"What sort of wild tales?" Daniel asked. There could be a kernel of truth in even the craziest lie.

"That Alexandra Gray was unnatural in her desires, an actress, a dupe."

"A dupe?" Daniel asked, unsure he understood what the constable meant.

"There was one fellow, a photographer—don't worry, I got his contact details," the constable rushed to add, "—who thought maybe she was paid to dress like a man and approach a particular woman or man with the intention of a photographer taking a photograph at just the right moment. The photograph would then be used to claim infidelity for the purpose of obtaining a divorce."

"Surely it takes more than an image of two people standing next to each other to prove infidelity in a court of law," Daniel said.

Constable Napier blushed like a girl. "He'd do more than stand. Perhaps he'd offer the man a…" He appeared to choke on his tea and turned an alarming shade of purple.

"A what, Constable?" Daniel asked once the constable seemed to recover somewhat.

"A vulgar act," Constable Napier choked out. That was all he seemed prepared to say.

"All right. What about the women? Surely a respectable woman wouldn't agree to a stranger offering…" Daniel wasn't quite sure what a stranger could offer a susceptible woman that wouldn't frighten the life out of her and send her running and screaming toward the nearest bobby.

"He'd maybe push her up against the wall and kiss her against her will, to make it look like a romantic encounter," Constable Napier explained.

"I see," Daniel said, not seeing at all. Surely it would be obvious that the woman was unwilling, but perhaps it didn't really matter, if the husband were determined to rid himself of his unwanted wife.

"The dupes are paid handsomely, from what the photographer said," Constable Napier explained. "Enough to pay for surgical instruments, I reckon."

"Let me have the addresses, Constable Napier."

The constable tore the page out of his notebook and handed it to Daniel, his expression suddenly reminding Daniel of Charlotte when she expected praise.

"Well done," Daniel said.

The young man's face lit up. "Thank you, Inspector."

Daniel left his unfinished tea for the constable to deal with and headed back out. He had just enough time to speak to Edward Gray, if he found him at home.

Chapter 30

"Edward's been unwell, Inspector. I cannot allow you to see him," Mrs. Fleet announced, her ruffles bouncing with the strength of her conviction.

"I'm afraid I must insist, Mrs. Fleet," Daniel replied. "I require no more than five minutes."

"He's very fragile," Mrs. Fleet tried again, but Daniel stood his ground.

"I need Mr. Gray's help in solving his sister's murder," Daniel said. "I will wait for him in the parlor."

Daniel pushed past Mrs. Fleet and entered the parlor, taking a seat in one of the wingchairs. Mrs. Fleet huffed like a set of bellows but took herself upstairs to fetch Edward Gray.

She hadn't been exaggerating the state of him, Daniel decided when the young man walked into the parlor and dropped onto the settee like a particularly heavy stone. He was pale, dark circles shadowing the skin beneath his hollow eyes. His skin looked clammy, and he appeared to have lost weight since Daniel had last seen him.

"How can I help, Inspector?" Edward Gray asked morosely.

"You look dreadful." Daniel hadn't meant to say so out loud, but somehow the words just bubbled to the surface.

"I feel responsible for Ally's death," Edward replied. "I should have stopped her from pursuing this mad scheme. I should have done what any other older brother would do—find her a suitable husband and see her safely wed."

"And would she have gone along if you had?"

"Probably not," Edward admitted, a ghost of a smile tugging at his lips. "She was too stubborn to do anything I said.

But I should have tried. I should have refused to come to London with her."

"Would she have come by herself?"

"Most likely. She was as obstinate as a mule."

"Mr. Gray, do you have surgical instruments?" Daniel asked.

"Pardon?" Edward asked, looking confused.

"Do you own your own set of surgical instruments?"

"Eh…no. Why do you ask, Inspector Haze?"

"Your sister bought several second-hand instruments from a Mr. Elgin. His broker's shop is located in Wardour Street. She was accompanied by a dark-haired man. Do you know anything about that?"

Edward Gray looked momentarily confused, but then nodded, as if he'd remembered something vital. "Alexandra hated using communal instruments. She wanted to have her own set, even if it came used. When practicing on cadavers, it doesn't make much difference if the scalpel is bent or rusted."

"Can I see her instruments?" Daniel asked. It was a hunch on his part, but he didn't think Edward would be able to produce them.

"I…eh, don't have them, Inspector."

"Where are they? Are they not in her room?"

"No."

"So, where would she have been keeping these instruments?"

"I don't know. Perhaps the man she was with was keeping them for her," Edward suggested.

"And can you think of who that man might have been?"

"It would have to be Max. He often bought second-hand items."

"But you're not certain?"

"No. She never mentioned going to the shop with Max," Edward admitted.

"Seems like there are many things your sister hadn't mentioned. Like where she went at night when you thought she was in her room."

"Alexandra was a strong-willed woman. She did what she pleased. I hate to admit that, but there it is. I held no sway over her."

"Is there anything you haven't told me, Mr. Gray?" Daniel demanded.

Edward shook his head. "I told you all I know, Inspector."

"Good day, then," Daniel said, and left the lodging house.

Chapter 31

Daniel had just enough time to wolf down his supper and read a bedtime story to Charlotte. He knew he was doing wrong, but as soon as Miss Grainger left the room, he took Charlotte out of her cot and held her in his lap until she fell asleep, only then transferring her back to her bed. She was a little girl, and she needed a cuddle from time to time, something she could no longer get from her mother, who'd decided that mourning for a dead child was more important than tending to the needs of a live one.

He'd tried again and again to cool his anger toward Sarah, but his resentment burned bright, the depth of her betrayal endlessly feeding the flame. He wouldn't hurt Charlotte for the world, but one day, when she was old enough, he'd tell her the truth. It was important that she understood the need to choose a partner who would be just that, a fellow traveler on life's journey, not someone who would simply give up and decide they no longer wished to continue, leaving a grieving husband and a small child behind. Love was important, yes, Daniel thought bitterly as he watched Charlotte sleep, but strength and commitment were just as imperative in a spouse.

Daniel could never imagine Katherine Redmond slugging down a bottle of laudanum and leaving Jason and Lily to go on without her. No, Katherine was strong and faithful. She would do what it took to protect her family and raise her own child, and if she couldn't, she'd make sure that neither Jason nor Lily ever had a moment's doubt about how much she had loved them. Daniel brushed a strand of dark hair out of Charlotte's face, the face that reminded him so much of Sarah. Was he being unjust? Perhaps. But he couldn't find the strength to be fair. All he could do was move on, putting one foot in front of the other until he no longer felt like he was walking barefoot over broken glass. Someday the loss wouldn't hurt so much, nor would he feel such crippling anger. One day, he'd be happy again, with a woman who had a spine forged of steel and who would be a true partner to him.

Pushing aside the thoughts that crowded his mind every time he found himself alone, Daniel tucked Charlotte in bed and made his way downstairs. Jason was always punctual, and Daniel looked forward to spending a quiet hour with him discussing the case. Jason's unwavering friendship was the only thing that felt secure in his world, and Daniel would do anything to nourish it and hope that it lasted a lifetime.

Once Jason arrived, the two men settled in the drawing room. As if by unspoken agreement, Jason always took the chair on the right, Daniel the one on the left. Jason also always brought a bottle of whisky or brandy for them to enjoy. Daniel opened the brandy bottle and poured three fingers' worth of the amber liquid into cut crystal tumblers, a housewarming gift to him and Sarah when they'd first moved into the house in St. John's Wood.

"Were you able to verify the alibis?" Jason asked as he accepted his glass. Daniel belatedly realized that they hadn't seen each other since interviewing Aubrey Dixon at the Coffee Brewery. It was only yesterday but felt like an age.

"Yes, for what it's worth. Rhona Christie confirmed that Ezra Hall was with her. Aubrey Dixon was at his sister's engagement supper until midnight and then went up to bed, and Timothy Latham was also at home for supper, then went to bed around midnight in a room next to his sister-in-law's."

"He lives with his sister-in-law? I thought he was recently married," Jason said. "Were you not able to speak to his wife?"

"Timothy Latham has a rather unorthodox domestic arrangement. Belinda Latham is his brother's widow, not his wife. The brother committed suicide, and Timothy, being the woman's only living relative, took her in and decided to present her to the world as his wife."

"Did she say why?"

"To ward off any uncomfortable questions about them living together," Daniel replied.

"Are they living together as husband and wife?"

"She says not, but it's possible, I suppose. It would be one of several options I can think of."

"The other being?" Jason asked. Clearly he could think of a few himself.

"Timothy Latham might be homosexual and using his sister-in-law as a front," Daniel said, suddenly tempted to start folding fingers like John Ransome. He overcame the urge and continued. "He might be a truly decent human being who feels responsible for his brother's widow but hasn't the means to allow her to live independently. Or he's simply being practical and saving a pretty penny on having to hire a servant to look after his needs, since his sister-in-law has no choice but to keep house for him. As he seems disinclined to marry anytime soon, this is a convenient arrangement."

"It might be more convenient than we realize," Jason suggested. "Perhaps they have a sexual relationship that no one would think to question, living as a married couple for as long as it suits their, or more likely his, purposes."

"So, he has a woman to warm his bed and keep his house without having to marry. The question is, would he kill to keep his secret?" Daniel asked.

"Seems unlikely. Alexandra would need proof to make trouble for Latham, and why would she? Her secret was a lot more explosive than his, so why threaten him with exposure?"

"Maybe he threatened her first," Daniel countered.

"In order to gain what?"

"Might he have been blackmailing her?"

"Then why kill her? A dead man pays no debts," Jason replied. "I can't see a good case for Timothy Latham killing

Alexandra Gray, especially in such a creative manner. He didn't strike me as a man of imagination."

"I would have to agree with you there, but his domestic situation took some imagining, didn't it?" Daniel said.

"It's really not such a stretch for a practical man. His arrangement with Belinda serves a purpose. To kill Alexandra Gray would serve none, as far as we can see."

"I agree. Let's move along, then," Daniel suggested.

"Did you have any luck at the yards?"

"No. The cabbie who took me to the yards promised to put the word out, but I highly doubt anything will come of it. There are hundreds of cabbies in London. Even if word reaches the right one, he might decide not to come forward for fear of losing his livelihood, or worse yet, being arrested for the murder. Ransome is chomping at the bit to get a result and intends to arrest Aubrey Dixon if no new evidence comes to light. How did you make out with Bosworth and Guthrie?" Daniel asked.

"Guthrie said nothing that would make me suspect him, and Bosworth backed up Aubrey Dixon's statement. He is planning to give Dixon the position."

"Did he say why?"

"He did, as it happens. He thought Alex Gray was too ambitious to appreciate it and settle into the practice for long and would move on as soon as a better opportunity presented itself."

"Interesting, that," Daniel replied, taking a generous sip of the brandy.

"Why?"

"It's rare for a woman to be so driven."

"I don't know if I agree," Jason replied. "Plenty of women are ambitious. They just don't always show their hand. They're taught never to appear competitive."

"And as a man, Alex Gray felt no such restraint," Daniel mused.

"Precisely."

"I wonder if it was her ambition that got her killed," Daniel said. "It would certainly give someone a motive."

"Perhaps," Jason replied. "Hiram Bosworth thinks the murder was a crime of passion coated in cold logic."

"It was premeditated," Daniel argued. "That rules out a crime of passion, or at least as it's usually defined."

"Can a crime of passion not be premeditated?"

Daniel chuckled. "The motive was driven by passion, the crime itself by cool common sense."

"And a desire for revenge," Jason supplied.

"Why do you think so?"

"Whoever killed Alexandra Gray made sure her secret would be revealed. They wanted her to be humiliated in death and remembered as a fraud. There was a lot of anger in this killing."

"I agree. I just can't figure out what she had done to infuriate someone to such a degree. But I do have a new lead," Daniel said, eager to share his findings with Jason. "Alexandra Gray and an unnamed dark-haired man bought second-hand surgical instruments from a Mr. Elgin, who has a shop in Wardour Street. What do you make of that? Would she have needed her own surgical instruments for her practical courses?"

"Do you know what she purchased?" Jason asked.

"I do," Daniel replied, and pulled out the sheet of paper Constable Napier had torn from his notebook. "Two scalpels, a metacarpal saw, bone cutting forceps, a trocar, and two pewter bowls. Some of the items were beginning to rust, according to Mr. Elgin."

Jason cocked his head to the side as he considered the list. "A surgeon in training might wish to use their own scalpel when working, but I can't imagine that they would require their own metacarpal saw or bone cutting forceps."

"What is a trocar used for?" Daniel asked. The other items were fairly self-explanatory.

"It's an instrument used for drainage of a body cavity or to puncture a bladder."

Daniel didn't bother to ask why anyone would wish to puncture a bladder and went on. "Would a student be permitted to use a rusted scalpel?"

"Not on a live patient, but then the students work mostly on cadavers until they're considered ready to operate on a patient."

"Jason, are you thinking what I'm thinking?" Daniel asked. He tossed back the remainder of his brandy before reaching for the bottle to refill his glass.

Jason refused a top-up. "You think Alexandra Gray was supplementing her practical education?"

"She might have been. We know that she was fearless, ambitious, and fiercely determined. She also wanted to be the best in her field, and what would give her the edge she needed? Hands-on experience. She might have learned the mechanics of surgery on the cadavers, but operating on live subjects would have given her a wider perspective."

Jason nodded. "I'm sure finding live patients wouldn't be too difficult, especially if the surgeries were performed free of charge and in the poorer areas of the city."

"My thoughts exactly. And if in the course of her extracurricular activities she happened to kill someone, that would give the patient's family a motive for murder."

"Yes, that's certainly plausible. If Alexandra Gray used rusted instruments, she might have introduced infection into the blood, which could lead to tetanus or even sepsis."

"Would she have realized the risk, do you think?" Daniel asked.

"Of course, but perhaps she simply didn't care. If she operated on patients who were likely to die either way, she might have thought herself blameless. She may have also convinced herself that cleaning the instruments would prevent contamination and her efforts would ultimately help the patient. And perhaps they did. She may have saved countless lives, for all we know."

"Except the one that mattered," Daniel mused.

"But why display her in Highgate Cemetery?" Jason asked. "That seems rather symbolic, don't you think?"

"Perhaps to remind other surgeons where they will end up if they use live subjects for their experiments."

"If that is the case, then her accomplice might be in danger of retaliation."

"Or he might be the one who killed her. Perhaps she was becoming too reckless and jeopardizing his future."

"Edward Gray, Timothy Latham, and Aubrey Dixon are fair-haired and have light eyes, so it couldn't have been one of them. Max Devane and Ezra Hall are both dark-haired and have dark eyes."

"Indeed they do," Daniel agreed. "And Max's family sells cloth. Perhaps Alexandra purchased the instruments, but Max provided the bandages and the silk thread needed to stitch up the incisions."

Jason seemed to consider this for a moment. "I don't think Max is our man," he said at last.

"Why do you say that?"

"Because he's an immigrant. He would be too conscious of the risk and frightened of letting his family down after the sacrifices they'd made for him. A foreigner never feels the same sense of belonging as a man who was born and bred in England; take it from me."

"You are hardly discriminated against," Daniel pointed out.

"Not discriminated, exactly, but I'm always treated with a degree of suspicion and reminded in the subtlest of ways that I don't belong here."

"Still?" Daniel asked, recalling with a pang of guilt how he'd treated Jason the first time they'd met.

He hated to admit it, but Jason was right. The English had an inherent mistrust of foreigners, even wealthy, titled ones like Jason Redmond. Being an immigrant as well as a Jew, Max Devane would likely think twice about breaking the law in his adopted country.

Daniel was just about to say so when Grace knocked on the door and entered. "You have a visitor, Inspector Haze."

Daniel glanced at the carriage clock on the mantel. "Really? Who is it?"

"A man named John Mumford."

"I don't know anyone by that name, but show him in," Daniel said, curious as to who this stranger might be.

The man that entered the room was tall and barrel-chested, his thick dark hair falling into his face and his muttonchops as thick and wooly as the sheep they were named after. He wore a sand-colored sack coat and scuffed boots. His bowler hat was in his hands, and he looked furtive, as if unsure if he should be there.

"Good evening, Mr. Mumford. I am Inspector Haze, and this is my colleague, Dr. Redmond. How may I be of service?" Daniel asked.

"It is I that may be of service to ye, Inspector," the man replied. "'Eard ye'd been looking for me on account of the dead cove in Highgate. Josiah Brown put the word out 'mong the lads."

"Are you the cabbie who collected Mr. Gray from his lodgings?" Daniel asked, amazed that the man had shown up on his doorstep.

"I am, indeed, sir," John Mumford replied. He looked uncomfortable, standing there, hat in hand, forelock falling into his eyes, as if he were a serf waiting on his master's pleasure.

"Please, sit down, Mr. Mumford. Would you care for a brandy?" Daniel asked, hoping to put the man at ease.

"Don't mind if I do," Mumford replied as he perched on the edge of the settee.

Daniel splashed a generous amount of brandy into a glass and handed it to John Mumford, who accepted it carefully and cradled it in his large hands before taking a sip and nodding in appreciation. "Fine stuff, this."

"Mr. Mumford, can you tell us how you came to know Mr. Gray?" Jason invited.

"Well, I didn't know 'im, exactly. I picked 'im up once, and 'e asked if I'd be willing to collect 'im when 'e were done. I says sure thing, sir, for a price, I would. 'E said money were no object and 'e'd pay me double the fee if I were to wait for 'im where 'e said."

"And where precisely did he wish you to wait?" Daniel asked.

"By the gates of Highgate Cemetery, at two in the morning," the man replied. "I live on me own, guv, so not like anyone'd miss me, so I agreed. Small price to pay to put a few extra coins in me pocket."

"Did Mr. Gray say what he'd been doing at the cemetery?"

"No, 'e didn't, and I didn't ask. None of me business, if ye know what I mean. I pocketed the extra money and had me a fine supper at the Pig and Whistle the next day."

"Mr. Mumford, did you have an arrangement with Mr. Gray?" Mumford nodded solemnly.

"How did that come about?" Daniel asked.

"Well, that first time when I took Mr. Gray 'ome, 'e said to me 'e needed a trustworthy man to take 'im there and back on certain days. I said, 'I'm yer man, guv. Ye just say the word and I'll be there.' So, 'e said 'e don't know the days in advance like, but 'e'd send a message to me cab yard with a street lad. And 'e did. Sent it round noon on the days 'e wanted me, so I 'ad plenty of warning."

"And you took him to Highgate Cemetery every time?" Jason asked.

"Aye, sir. I did."

"How long did he usually stay there?"

"From ten to two, or thereabouts. A few times I 'ad to wait a while, but 'e warned me 'bout that and asked that I don't leave till 'e came out."

"And how did he look when he returned?" Daniel asked.

"Same as afore, but there was this glee 'bout 'im. I'd say 'e were right pleased with 'imself."

"Were his clothes clean when he came out?" Jason asked.

John Mumford considered this. "I s'pose so. I didn't look too close, mind."

"How did Mr. Gray get into the cemetery?" Daniel asked.

"Gates were unlocked. I saw 'im push 'em open when 'e arrived."

Daniel and Jason exchanged looks. According to the Ludlows, the gates were locked every night and unlocked again the following morning, so someone else was definitely in on what Alexandra Gray had been doing.

"When was the first time you took Mr. Gray to the cemetery?" Daniel asked.

"'Bout six months ago now."

"Mr. Mumford," Daniel asked as he generously topped up Mumford's glass, "how many times would you say Mr. Gray sent for you since that first time?"

The man shrugged his massive shoulders. "I really couldn't say for certain, guv. Mebbe a dozen."

"Did you ever see anyone else while there?"

Daniel was growing desperate. Unless Alexandra Gray was a ghoul who had insomnia and liked to walk through a deserted cemetery at night, there was no reason for her to spend hours in Highgate Cemetery. She certainly wouldn't be performing surgery in the middle of the night, and if she were involved in bodysnatching, Daniel highly doubted she'd be doing the snatching herself. It would take her days to dig up a body, and she would need the means to transport it to wherever she'd be taking it.

Daniel turned back to John Mumford, whose gaze was lovingly fixed on what was left of the brandy. "Mr. Mumford? Did you ever see anyone with him?" Daniel asked again.

"Just the once," Mumford replied. "I couldn't see the man's face proper-like. 'E never came near the gates."

"What were they doing when you saw them?"

"They looked to be having a row."

"What about?"

John Mumford shook his head. "I couldn't hear most of what they was sayin', but I think Mr. Gray wanted to do summat and the other fellow didn't. It looked heated, but it ain't me business. Why should I go sticking my oar in?"

"Is there anything at all you can tell us about the other man?" Jason asked, leaning forward in his eagerness to learn something of what had taken place.

John Mumford drained his glass, and Daniel immediately reached for the bottle. John Mumford would keep talking as long as the brandy kept flowing. He held out his glass, watching intently as Daniel emptied the bottle, then took a sip and sighed with contentment before finally replying.

"I didn't see 'is face, but I 'eard the name Mr. Gray called 'im."

"Well, what was it, man?" Daniel exploded, wondering why the cabbie had kept such an important tidbit to himself.

"Ezra. An unusual name, innit?"

Daniel let out the breath he'd been holding. Ezra Hall. Jason had been right in assuming Alexandra's accomplice hadn't been Max Devane, and now they had proof of Ezra's involvement. A solid lead at long last.

"That name mean anythin' to ye, guv?" John Mumford asked as he set the empty glass on the low table before him.

"Yes, it does, Mr. Mumford. It means a great deal. Can you tell us what happened on Monday night?"

"I took Mr. Gray to Highgate as normal."

"And then?" The man really was thick, Daniel thought, exasperated by having to draw out every piece of information as if from a great depth, since the dolt wouldn't volunteer a single morsel without being prompted.

"I left and came back later as arranged, but he weren't there."

"What did you do?" Daniel pressed.

"I waited."

"How long did you wait?" Jason asked.

"Oh, a long while," Mumford said, nodding as if recalling the hours spent in the shadow of the cemetery.

"What did you do when Mr. Gray did not return?" Daniel asked, wishing he could shake the details out of the man and watch them roll out of his head like colorful marbles.

"Why, I went 'ome, guv. What else would I do? 'Ad to get up for me shift the next day, didn't I?"

"Mr. Mumford, Mr. Gray was murdered while you were waiting for him," Daniel said, doing his utmost to contain his irritation. "Did you see anything or anyone? Did you hear anything?"

"Like what, guv?"

"Like anyone calling for help. Like the signs of a struggle. Like someone running away," Daniel sputtered.

"'Ave ye seen the size of the cemetery, Inspector?" Mumford asked, lifting an eyebrow as if Daniel were daft. "Not very likely I'd 'ear something all that way away, is it? I 'eard an owl 'ooting. 'Eard the chiming of a clock and the nightsoil men going 'bout their business. Didn't 'ear no one call for 'elp, though."

"Did you see anyone at all leaving the cemetery while you waited for Mr. Gray?"

"Neh."

"Did you ever consider going to look for Mr. Gray before leaving?" Jason asked.

"Why would I? I weren't paid to look for 'im, only to wait and take 'im back. Not me business what 'e were up to. I figured 'e got 'eld up or mebbe the other fellow took 'im 'ome if 'e were there. Not like I left yon cove stranded. 'E could'a walked or found 'isself 'nother cab. Why, if I were to worry 'bout every fare, I'd worry meself into the grave." He chuckled at his clever metaphor. "Not me business what people get up to, guv, and not me business to sit up all night waiting on them."

"Mr. Mumford, did you happen to see this morning's edition of the *Illustrated London News*?" Daniel asked. Mumford seemed to have no notion that Alex Gray had been a woman.

"Never learned me letters, guv, so I've no use for newspapers unless it's to wipe me arse, but I 'eard some blokes talking 'bout it. Said Mr. Gray were a broad."

"But you didn't believe them?" Daniel asked, watching the man closely.

"Made no difference to me, guv. I been a cabbie these past twenty years. Seen it all, and then some, if ye know what I mean. As long as I get me fare, I keep mum." He tapped the side of his nose to indicate his discretion. "I were paid 'andsomely for me services, so all I can say is, may Mr. Gray rest in peace."

"Thank you, Mr. Mumford. Where can I find you if I need to ask you more questions?" Daniel asked.

"Cab yard in Bermondsey. I heard ye was there earlier today asking 'round. 'Ad ye come later, ye'd 'ave found me."

Daniel expected John Mumford to take his leave, but he just stood there, waiting. Daniel reached into his pocket and pulled out two shillings, which he handed to the cabbie, who pocketed the money and inclined his head.

"Much obliged, guv. And I do 'ope ye find the cove as done for the poor woman. She didn't deserve what 'appened to 'er, even if she were up to no good."

"How do you know she was up to no good?" Daniel asked as he followed John Mumford to the front door.

The man's eyebrows lifted in time with the corners of his mouth. "Ye know a lot of folk who do lawful business in Highgate at midnight?" he asked, making Daniel feel foolish in the extreme for asking the question. "Thanks for the brandy, guv. Most 'ospitable of ye."

"Glad you enjoyed it," Daniel replied, wishing there were some left to toast their newfound knowledge.

"Well, well, well," Daniel said once he resumed his seat. "So, Alexandra Gray was meeting Ezra Hall at the cemetery. They must have been having an affair."

Jason's skepticism was underscored by the comical lifting of one dark brow. "Are you suggesting they were at it for four hours at a time?"

Daniel shrugged. "Maybe they enjoyed moonlit walks among the graves or read romantic poetry to each other. The point is, Ezra Hall not only knew her secret but was her lover, which gives him a motive for murder."

"The motive being?"

"Sexual jealousy, rejection, betrayal, and in this case, it could even be professional rivalry."

"I'm not convinced," Jason replied. "Ezra lives alone. Why meet in the cemetery when they could have a clean, comfortable bed? And why go through all the trouble of staging Alexandra's death? Why poison her, then hang her when he could have killed her in any number of less obvious ways? He could have strangled her or slit her throat with her own rusted scalpel. Or he could have bashed her head in and left her body atop a grave. Or even buried her. Lord knows it's not hard to find a shovel at a cemetery. No one would be the wiser. Alexandra Gray would have just fallen off the face of the earth, and no one would ever have reason to suspect him. And how did the two of them get a key to the cemetery gates and then gain access to the Ashford vault?" Jason demanded in support of his argument. "There are too many unanswered questions."

"Perhaps Ezra wanted to keep the relationship a secret from Rhona Christie," Daniel suggested.

"Why? Rhona Christie knows Ezra will never marry her. She told you as much herself, and unless she was in the house while Alexandra Gray was there, she'd have no way of knowing the two were engaging in sexual congress."

"Now there you are wrong, my friend," Daniel countered. "Rhona Christie does Ezra Hall's laundry. She'd know if he'd had a woman in his bed."

"But she wouldn't know the woman was Alexandra Gray."

"No, but it wouldn't be too difficult to find out once she became suspicious."

"All right. Let us assume that Ezra wanted to keep his women far away from each other, although given what we know of Alexandra Gray, she wasn't looking for marriage. That still doesn't explain how he managed to get into a locked cemetery or opened the Ashford vault. There were no signs of forced entry, so he must have had a key. And he would have had to lock the cemetery gates after leaving or the London Cemetery Company would learn about the trespass and hire a night watchman at the very least to protect the sanctity of the cemetery."

"I don't know the answers to those questions yet, but I do know that Aubrey Dixon is not the killer. Do you have early morning surgery tomorrow?"

"No. I'm entirely at your disposal. I'll stop by the hospital later in the day to check on my patients."

"Good, because we are going to question Ezra Hall, and we're going to do it in a formal setting. I mean to arrest him for the murder of Alexandra Gray."

"Ransome will be thrilled to have a suspect in custody," Jason said as he stood to leave.

"That he will. And he'll take all the credit, as usual," Daniel grumbled. "Meet me at the Yard at nine. I'll have Hall picked up first thing in the morning, before he leaves the house."

"I'll be there," Jason promised.

Chapter 32

"You're a million miles away tonight," Katherine said as she rested her head on Jason's shoulder, her hair spilling onto his bare chest. Jason wrapped his arm around his wife and pulled her closer, inhaling the lovely smell of her hair and leaning into her soft nearness.

"I'm sorry. I was just thinking about the case."

"Do you not think Daniel's got the right man?" Over dinner, Jason had filled her in on his visit to Daniel's house and the plan to arrest Ezra Hall in the morning.

"All the evidence points to Ezra Hall, even if we have yet to understand his motive for the murder."

"Is that what's troubling you? The lack of a clear motive?"

"No. People kill for all sorts of reasons, and their motives are not always clear. But this case got me thinking about Lily."

"Lily?" Katherine exclaimed, taken by surprise. "What's she got to do with anything?"

"Alexandra Gray was willing to risk it all just for the chance to pursue her goal. She was prepared to live as a man for the rest of her life, give up any sanctioned form of companionship and the possibility of ever having children, just to be a surgeon. No man has to make such sacrifices to follow his dreams."

"Isn't that the way it's always been?" Katherine asked, a tang of bitterness in her voice.

"But we live in such a progressive society. Surely some of the strides we've made should apply to women."

"Do you think Lily might want to pursue an occupation suitable only to a man?" Katherine asked.

"I don't know. She might want nothing more than to marry and have babies, but what if she craves more?"

"Jason, Lily is six months old. She needs milk, a dry nappy, and lots of love. Why don't we address the rest later, like in about twenty years?" Katherine said, smiling up at him.

Jason shook his head stubbornly. "But don't you see, Katie, we have to address this now. How do we raise her? Do we tell her she can do anything she sets her mind to, or do we erect walls around her and make her feel that if she wants to leave, she has to find a sledgehammer and make her own door? And will she be safe on the other side?"

Katherine reached up and cupped his cheek, her gaze loving and kind. "My dear, Lily will let us know how she needs to be raised. We can build all the walls we like, but if Lily wants to, she'll knock them down. It'll be nearly the twentieth century by the time she's my age," Katherine added dreamily. "The twentieth century. Imagine that."

"And you think things will be so different?" Jason asked.

"I don't know, but I do know this. We never know how our lives will turn out. Had someone told me two years ago that a dashing American doctor was going to come into my life and make me Lady Redmond, I would have thought they were quite mad. But here I am. With you. And you probably never imagined you'd be making a life in England after the horrors of the American Civil War, and standing up in church with a vicar's daughter and an Irish orphan as your best man. Let the future come, Jason, and embrace the here and now. I bet if you were to ask Alexandra Gray if she'd have done anything differently, she'd have told you no."

Jason smiled at the wisdom of Katherine's words, but the tightness in his chest wouldn't ease. He'd thought he understood the world and his place in it, and had made reckless decisions, knowing that he'd be the only one to pay the price were he to miscalculate the risk, but he was a father now, and the thought of letting his daughter down terrified him. He wished he could change the world for her and make it a safer place, and a more welcoming place for a young woman. He wanted her to have dreams and the chance to pursue them. And despite his terror at getting it wrong, he wanted more children. Another daughter to love, or maybe a son to follow in his footsteps—or to forge his own path, to be a gentleman of the twentieth century.

Pushing his worries aside, Jason moved on top of Katherine and captured her mouth with his own, suddenly desperate for her. Perhaps they'd make another baby tonight, or maybe they'd just love each other as they had so many times since saying their vows. Katie was right, as usual. The future would come, whether he liked it or not, and he'd take it one day at a time and do everything in his power to keep those he loved safe.

Chapter 33

Saturday, September 19

Saturday dawned sunny and bright, with wispy clouds scuttling across a vivid blue sky, whipped along by the stiff breeze. Jason woke up ridiculously early, and instead of dawdling in bed, got up, washed and dressed, and went down to the kitchen, where Mrs. Dodson was already kneading dough for bread.

"You look like you have a hunger on you this morning," she remarked as Jason settled at the table. He didn't visit with Mrs. Dodson as often as he had when he'd been unmarried, but they still shared a cozy chat from time to time, especially when neither could get to sleep.

"Shall I make you some breakfast?" Mrs. Dodson asked.

"Please. And coffee."

Mrs. Dodson smiled. "As if I didn't know," she scoffed. "At the rate you guzzle the stuff, I have to keep sending Dodson out for more beans."

"Old habits die hard," Jason said. He'd learned to drink tea, but coffee would always be his beverage of choice.

"Just give me a moment to clean my hands, and I'll see you properly fed," Mrs. Dodson said, smiling at Jason affectionately.

Once Jason had his fill of eggs, bacon, and buttered bread, he set off on foot toward Scotland Yard. It was brisk outside, but he enjoyed the walk, the pleasant weather clearing away the last of his worries. He smiled at the memory of Katie's ardor last night. Whatever happened in the future, he was a lucky man, and he knew it.

Daniel was already there when Jason arrived, pacing the interview room like a caged beast.

"I should have gone to bring him in myself," he said as soon as he saw Jason. "I hope Meadows doesn't bungle the job."

"Sergeant Meadows is perfectly capable of bringing a suspect in," Jason reassured him. "And he's got Constable Napier with him, doesn't he?"

"He does," Daniel conceded.

"Then they should be here soon."

When Ezra Hall was shown into the interview room, he looked pale and frightened, the heavy handcuffs out of place on his elegant wrists. His gaze, when he looked from Daniel to Jason, reflected his panic.

"Inspector, I don't understand," he cried. "What have I done? If you wished to speak to me, all you had to do was ask, and I would have gladly come in of my own free will. There was no need for the cuffs and the police wagon. The whole street watched as I was marched out of my house like a criminal."

"Please, take a seat, Mr. Hall," Daniel said, his earlier anxiety replaced by a chilling calm. He had his man, and now he could take his time about letting Ezra Hall hang himself.

"This is all a misunderstanding," Ezra exclaimed as he dropped into a seat. "I didn't kill Alex, if that's the reason you brought me here."

"Mr. Hall, I advise you to be honest with us. It will go easier for you if you simply tell us the truth."

"Dr. Redmond," Ezra pleaded. "Surely you don't think I'm guilty of murder."

"Mr. Hall, some evidence has come to light that implicates you in the death of Alexandra Gray. Please, answer Inspector

Haze's questions truthfully," Jason said as he settled at the table next to Daniel.

The fight seemed to go out of Hall, and his shoulders slumped, his cuffed hands dangling between his thighs. "Ask whatever you will, Inspector," he said. "I have nothing to hide."

"I'm glad to hear that," Daniel replied. "Let's start from the beginning, then, shall we? You told me that you and Alex Gray had never spent time alone together. Do you stand by that statement?"

Ezra Hall looked like a cornered animal. "I do not," he muttered.

"Tell me about your assignations," Daniel invited. "Were you involved in a romantic relationship?"

"God, no," Ezra exclaimed. "I didn't know Alex was a woman. I swear."

"You never suspected?" Jason asked, watching Ezra for any hint of deception.

Ezra shook his head. He looked miserable. "I thought perhaps he was younger than he pretended to be, but I never imagined he was the wrong sex altogether. I suppose now that I know, I realize I should have guessed at the truth, but, at the time, I simply accepted what I was told, much like everyone else."

"Then what were you two doing together?" Daniel asked.

"We were studying."

Daniel scoffed. "Really, Mr. Hall. I thought we were going to be honest with each other."

Daniel paused when he noticed a change in Jason's expression. Jason fixed Ezra with an intense stare, amazed it had taken him this long to figure it out.

"You were practicing your surgical skills on fresh corpses," Jason said.

Ezra's chest deflated like a pierced balloon. He nodded, his gaze sliding away from the two men and going to his cuffed wrists. "Alex felt that we'd never become better-than-average surgeons if we didn't practice. Watching surgeries is all well and good, but we needed hands-on experience to improve our technique, and we get so little time with a cadaver when there are ten other students waiting their turn."

"Did you dig up the cadavers yourselves?" Daniel asked. He was doing his best to hide his shock and obvious disappointment at not having figured out the connection between the secret meetings and the surgical tools Alex and Ezra had acquired.

"No."

"So, what was the arrangement?" Jason inquired. He couldn't help but wonder if any of the other students were in on the scheme or had an arrangement of their own, students like Aubrey Dixon, who worked hard to get ahead of the herd.

"Alex had some money that was left to her by her aunt. She wanted to spend it on things that mattered, so we bribed the Ludlows to exhume freshly buried corpses for us. We didn't want just anyone, though. We were particularly interested in young people who may have been ill so that we could see the effects of the illness on the body. Alex and I studied the obituaries and chose particular individuals," Ezra Hall admitted. "When there was a potentially interesting case, we'd send a message to Harry Ludlow, and he'd have the corpse ready for us when we arrived. Once we were finished, the Ludlows would rebury the corpse, and no one was the wiser."

"I presume it was the Ludlows that unlocked the gates for you?" Daniel asked.

Ezra nodded. "They have a key for when they need to enter the cemetery for those early morning burials."

"And where did you perform these autopsies?" Jason asked. He was horrified and impressed in equal measure and fairly certain he already knew the answer to his question.

"In the Ashford vault."

"How did you get in?" Daniel asked. "There were no signs of a break-in."

"I have a key," Ezra said, still not meeting anyone's gaze. "We used one of the empty shelves as a slab and even installed a hook in the ceiling to hang a lantern. We kept all our instruments and supplies in a wooden crate inside the vault so we wouldn't need to bring anything or give ourselves away in any way. If anyone saw us at the cemetery in the middle of the night, they'd simply think we were there for a lark, acting like the foolish young men we were." He sighed heavily.

"It wasn't ideal, but it was private, and we didn't have to move the corpse out of the cemetery. We always checked to make sure a member of the Ashford family hadn't died and we were safe to keep using the vault. When the viscount passed, we cleared out all our supplies, since he'd be buried in a few days."

"And it was just the two of you this whole time?" Jason asked.

"Yes. Alex broached the subject when we were at the King's Arms one evening, just after Christmas, but no one took her seriously, so she didn't bring it up again."

"But you knew she was serious?"

"I thought she was testing the waters. Man or woman, Alex was the most ambitious, driven person I'd ever met. To be honest, I was in awe of her and thought I could learn a thing or two from someone who was so focused on achieving their goal. She inspired me to be better, to work harder. I didn't want to drink myself into an early grave like my father, having achieved next to nothing in my lifetime."

"And what about Edward Gray?" Jason asked. "Did he know what his sister was up to?"

"I think he suspected, but he wanted no part of it. Edward chose surgery because of Alex, not the other way around," Ezra said. "He is not like his sister. Edward has no fear of mediocrity. His goal is to earn enough to afford a comfortable existence and have enough left over to spend a few weeks at the seaside every summer and enjoy a pint with friends after a day spent at the hospital. He never wanted the position with Hiram Bosworth. He didn't think he was up to the challenge and didn't care to make a fool of himself."

"Did Edward resent his sister's brilliance?"

"He was proud of her. They were never in competition with each other, not that I saw. They were the best of friends and the closest confidants."

"So why did you kill Alex Gray?" Daniel asked. He wasn't interested in Edward Gray, since the man had an alibi for the night of the murder. Daniel wanted to get his ducks in a row before Superintendent Ransome arrived at Scotland Yard, if he hadn't already. "Did you two have a disagreement? Did you find out she was really a woman and making a fool out of you?"

"I didn't kill her," Ezra cried. "Alex and I were friends. We were kindred spirits, but we were never lovers, nor did I think she was deceiving me. We simply wanted to be better surgeons and had the courage, or the stupidity, to do something about that."

"Mr. Hall, Alexandra Gray bought the instruments you'd need and bribed the Ludlows, so I assume your contribution to the scheme was a place where you could work in secret. How did you get a key to the Ashford vault?" Daniel asked. "That's not the sort of thing that would just fall into your hands by accident."

"I borrowed it," Ezra mumbled.

"From whom?"

Daniel's earlier calm had been replaced with a quiet urgency. He wanted answers, and Ezra Hall was doling out the information in bite-sized increments and still denying that he'd killed Alexandra Gray, perhaps hoping to talk his way out of an arrest. Daniel wanted a confession, but Ezra was in no hurry to admit to the crime.

"From Rhona Christie," Ezra said at last, hanging his head in defeat. Whatever he felt for Rhona Christie, it was clear he hadn't wanted to implicate her in this mess he'd created for himself, knowing Rhona wouldn't thank him for admitting to her part in the setup.

"And how did Rhona Christie come by it?" Daniel demanded, taken aback by Ezra's answer.

"Rhona worked as a parlormaid for the Ashfords before she married Todd Christie. She pocketed the key when they started courting."

"Why?" Jason asked. "What did she intend to do with it?" If Rhona's daughter had been eight at the time of her death, the woman would have been married for at least that long, so she must have had plans for the vault long before Ezra began his studies. Ezra was around twenty-five, so he would have been only sixteen or seventeen at the time.

"Todd was involved in smuggling. Had been since before they met. The vault was the perfect place to hide smuggled goods until they were ready to be moved," Ezra explained. "Todd could no longer use the vault after his accident, but Rhona held on to the key. It's not as if she could simply return it. She told me about Todd's dealings years ago, when she started working for me and we became close." Ezra's cheeks turned a mottled red, as if admitting to sexual relations with a woman could still embarrass him after the conversation they'd been having for the past half hour.

"When Alex and I began to talk seriously about going ahead with our plan, I thought that the vault would be the perfect place to do our work. I asked Rhona for the key, and she gave it to me."

"You are a regular crime ring, aren't you, Mr. Hall?" Daniel asked. "A thief, a smuggler, and a body snatcher."

"It wasn't like that," Ezra retorted. "We weren't hurting anyone. These people were already dead. They'd be eaten by worms within weeks, but we were able to learn from their deaths, and to improve our skills. We would save lives."

"I don't think you'll be saving anyone's life, Mr. Hall," Daniel said. "If anything, you can make a provision to donate your body to science after you hang for the murder of Alexandra Gray."

"I didn't kill her," Ezra Hall wailed. "I don't know who did. The last time Alex and I were at Highgate was a week before she was murdered."

"And what did you do that night?" Jason asked.

"We performed a postmortem, as usual, but we got into an argument because we disagreed about the cause of death. There were no visible signs of illness. Life had simply been snuffed out for no apparent reason."

"Did Alex Gray believe she had figured out the cause of death?"

"She thought it might have been an aneurism, but there was no evidence of that."

"Were you meant to meet Alex Gray at Highgate the night of the murder?" Daniel asked.

"No. We knew the viscount would be entombed in the morning, so we stayed away."

"Did you intend to return to your activities after the funeral?" Jason asked. "Or were you planning to autopsy the viscount?"

Ezra had the decency to look guilty. "Alex heard that the viscount had died of a myocardial infarction and wanted to study his heart. But once the viscount was laid to rest, there'd be no more empty shelves, so we'd need a table or something to work on. I told Alex that perhaps we should stop. We'd dissected a dozen cadavers since we began. It was enough to hone our skills."

"Was Alex angry with you?" Daniel asked.

"She was, and we argued. I told her I'd give her the key if she found another partner, so she could have continued if she wished."

"Did she threaten you with exposure, Mr. Hall, because she wasn't ready to give up your little project?"

"She was disappointed and upset, but she didn't threaten me. She begged me to continue. She was addicted to surgery. She couldn't simply stop. She needed to be great."

"Greater than you would ever be?" Daniel taunted.

"Yes, she would have been a much better surgeon. I didn't have her drive, or her ruthlessness, to be honest. And speaking of ruthlessness, why would I go through the trouble of poisoning her, then hanging her in the vault? What would that accomplish other than bring attention to the fact that we'd been using the vault? Alex's murder was a statement, an act of revenge. I held no grudge against her."

"Were you not upset that she might get a place with Hiram Bosworth?"

"I was never truly in the running, Inspector, so no, I wasn't upset. There are other renowned surgeons and plenty of hospitals. There's enough work for everyone."

"Mr. Hall, where were you the night Alexandra Gray was murdered?" Daniel demanded.

"I was at home. In bed. With Rhona. I slept through the night and woke at six. Rhona was still there. She can vouch for me."

"Did you wake at all during the night?" Jason asked.

"No. Why?"

"Do you normally wake?"

"I'm always thirsty, so I leave a glass of water by my bed. I usually wake at least once," Ezra Hall replied. He seemed surprised by the question.

"Does Rhona Christie give her husband any medication?" Jason asked.

"She gives him laudanum before bed. It helps him sleep. Otherwise, he moans and groans all night. He's broken, in both mind and body." Ezra stared at Jason, a glimmer of understanding igniting in his eyes. "You don't think…"

"It's a possibility," Jason replied.

"But why would Rhona drug me?" Ezra asked. He seemed confused, but there was something in his eyes that to Jason looked too much like guilt.

He turned to Daniel. "We need to speak to Rhona Christie."

"Agreed. Constable Napier," Daniel called out. "Please take Mr. Hall to the cells."

"But Inspector," Ezra Hall protested. "I'm innocent."

"That remains to be seen, Mr. Hall," Daniel replied absentmindedly.

Chapter 34

"You think Rhona Christie did it," Daniel said as soon as Ezra Hall was taken down to the cells.

"According to Ezra Hall, Rhona Christie had intentionally taken the key to the vault from the Ashford residence to assist her future husband with his illegal activities and was giving Todd Christie laudanum to help him sleep. Hall might be trying to implicate her to mitigate his own guilt, but if he's not, would it be such a stretch to imagine that she'd given him some laudanum as well and slipped out during the night, setting him up as her alibi should she need it when he foolishly believes she's his alibi instead?" Jason asked. The theory had been forming in his mind over the past few minutes, but he needed to discuss it with Daniel to see if the facts fit the idea that was only just beginning to crystalize.

"Why would Rhona Christie want to kill Alexandra Gray?" Daniel asked. "As far as we know, the two had never met, while Ezra Hall had been meeting Alexandra Gray at Highgate for months and performing illegal postmortems in the dead of night. Had Alexandra threatened to grass on him, he'd be expelled by the Royal College of Surgeons and would never practice surgery in England, at least not lawfully."

Jason shook his head in disagreement. "Why would Alexandra Gray betray Ezra? She had as much, if not more, to lose if their activities ever came to light," he argued. "And just because Rhona and Alexandra never met doesn't mean Rhona Christie had never seen her. Rhona was close to Ezra and knew about his activities, having been the one to give him the key to the vault. She might have been curious about Alex Gray and found an opportunity to size him up, to perhaps see how much influence Alex Gray had on Ezra," Jason speculated, the words coming faster now.

"Ezra Hall might not have suspected that Alex Gray was a woman, but maybe Rhona did and felt threatened by her. Todd

Christie is clearly not long for this world, especially if Rhona Christie is capable of murder. Perhaps, despite what she told you, she had hopes of marrying Hall and embarking on a new life, and since she had recently lost her only child, she might have felt that there was nothing holding her back from moving forward with her plans."

"The death of Alexandra Gray would not ensure that Ezra would change his mind about marriage," Daniel pointed out.

"No, but if Rhona's word that Ezra was with her on the night of the murder was the only thing standing between Ezra and the hangman's noose, he would feel obligated to her and eager to keep her sweet. If Ezra hadn't told us where he got the key, we'd have nothing to connect Rhona to the crime," Jason said. "Therefore, we'd never have cause to suspect her."

"So, you think Rhona sent a message to Alexandra Gray pretending to be Ezra and asking to meet at the vault and then poisoned her and strung her up?"

"Why not? Staging the scene would ensure that the victim had a postmortem, which would reveal her secret. An act of both jealousy and revenge. It fits, Daniel."

"Yes, I suppose it does, but I'm not convinced. Ezra Hall claims he had no idea Alexandra Gray was a woman. He wasn't in love with her. So why would Rhona Christie feel so threatened, especially when Alex Gray's only ambition was to be an exemplary surgeon? She would not give up her plans for the love of a man."

"Maybe not, but Rhona didn't know that. She only knew that she might lose Ezra to another woman if she didn't do something to preempt it. Maybe she was afraid Alex would confide in Ezra, and then his feelings toward her would change."

"I think we'd best bring her in before she makes a run for it. Once she finds out Ezra has been arrested, she might flee the city," Daniel said, making to rise to his feet.

"Good God!" Jason exclaimed, bringing his hands down on the table for punctuation. "I can't believe this didn't occur to me right away!"

"What are you talking about?" Daniel demanded, dropping back into his chair.

Jason ran his hands through his hair, furious with himself for not seeing the other possibility sooner. He'd been so fixated on Ezra's reasons for resenting Alexandra that the magnitude of what he was admitting to had been lost in speculation and questions meant to make him admit that he'd killed Alexandra Gray.

Perhaps Jason was completely off the mark, but this felt right, his conviction mounting as he considered the facts that had now rearranged themselves in his mind and fit into a totally different pattern, one that explained everything to his satisfaction.

"Daniel, there might be another explanation," Jason said, his entire being focused on what needed to be done. "The murder of Alexandra Gray might have had nothing whatsoever to do with romantic jealousy."

"What, then?"

"Betrayal of the worst kind, and the reason Alex and Ezra had fallen out and argued the night John Mumford saw them together at Highgate," Jason said. "Daniel, do you require an exhumation order to open a grave?"

"Yes. Who do you want to exhume?" Daniel asked urgently, still lost since Jason had failed to verbalize his suspicions.

"Veronica Christie."

Chapter 35

Having dispatched Sergeant Meadows and Constable Napier to bring Rhona Christie in for questioning, Daniel turned his attention to obtaining an exhumation order. John Ransome had just arrived, so Daniel knocked on his door and stated his request without bothering to sit down or lay out the facts.

"Absolutely not," Ransome replied. "Do you know what it costs to exhume a corpse, Haze? No? Well, allow me to illuminate you. More than it costs to bury one, and then the diggers must be paid to rebury the said corpse once again. And you would need an exhumation order signed by a judge. And it being a Saturday, you will not find a reputable judge anywhere near his chambers. They don't work as hard as we do, or so I hear."

"But, sir," Daniel protested, frustrated by Ransome's lack of cooperation.

John Ransome leaned back and studied Daniel, his dark gaze thoughtful. "There is another way," he said at last.

"Oh?"

"Sit down, Haze. You look like you need to take a moment."

Daniel swallowed back his anger, took a seat, and heard John Ransome out. He hated to admit it, but the man was correct on all counts, and his approach would be cheaper and probably as effective.

By the time Daniel and Jason arrived at Highgate Cemetery, it was nearly noon, but the Ludlows weren't difficult to find. Since there was no funeral in progress, they were in their shed, playing cards instead of directing their efforts toward maintaining the cemetery grounds.

"Good afternoon, lads," Daniel said cheerfully.

"Good afternoon, Inspector," the brothers replied, their faces showing degrees of wariness. "What can we do for ye?" Harry Ludlow asked.

"You can grab your shovels and come with me," Daniel replied. He produced an exhumation order signed by John Ransome and showed it to Harry.

"Cor," Harry replied, staring at the paper and scratching his head.

Daniel realized that Harry was likely illiterate and read the order out to him, watching the expression on his face all the while.

"Ye sure ye want us to do that, guv?" Harry Ludlow asked, his reluctance obvious. It was a warm day and digging up six feet of earth was a lot less pleasurable than playing cards in the cool shed and chugging gin from the dusty bottle that stood in the middle of the table. Evidently, cups were optional.

"Yes, I am. Unless you can tell me what I need to know— then there'll be no need to disturb the child's remains unnecessarily."

Harry nodded, knowing he was beaten, while his brothers looked on in mute belligerence, realizing all too well what Harry's admission would mean to them and their future prospects as employees of the London Cemetery Company.

"We dug 'er up 'bout a fortnight ago," Harry admitted grudgingly.

"Why?" Daniel asked, even though he thought he already knew the answer thanks to Jason's quick thinking.

"Because we was paid to," Harry replied.

"By whom?" Jason asked. His voice was tight with anger, but he kept his tone even.

"Mr. Gray, guv. 'E paid us good and proper to bring 'er up," Harry Ludlow said, confirming Jason's suspicions and finally pinpointing the true motive for the murder of Alexandra Gray.

"Still want us to do it, guv?" Harry asked.

"Let's hold off for now," Daniel replied.

John Ransome had been correct in assuming that the Ludlows wouldn't know an order signed by a judge from a sheet of paper signed by the superintendent and would buckle under the pressure, realizing full well the jig was up. There was no immediate need to exhume the body of Veronica Christie if they had a statement from the Ludlows admitting to the desecration of her grave on the orders of Alexander Gray.

Daniel pulled out the folded sheet of paper he'd prepared and read the charge before setting the document before Harry Ludlow. "Sign here to show you understand and admit to performing an illegal exhumation of the body of Veronica Christie."

"I'll lose me job, guv," Harry moaned, but Daniel jabbed his finger at the empty space before the lines of writing.

"You'll lose a lot more than your job if you don't sign," Daniel replied sternly.

Harry Ludlow blessed him with an evil stare and made his cross on the paper. He glanced at his brothers, presumably conveying to them that he'd take the fall and they could deny all knowledge—not that anyone would believe that, but Daniel wasn't inclined to deal with the Ludlows at the moment. He would present their employers with the document once he was finished with Rhona Christie and allow them to deal with the gravediggers however they saw fit.

Daniel wished he could threaten the men with execution or deportation to Australia, but graverobbing was considered a misdemeanor under common law and was usually punishable by either a monetary fine or insignificant jail time, which was why

Superintendent Ransome had been reluctant to waste funds on an exhumation or call in valuable favors by asking a judge to sign the order on such short notice. He saw it as a waste of resources, and given the circumstances, he was right. The Ludlows had caved quickly enough.

They certainly weren't the first or the last men to get caught graverobbing and would likely get off with a much lighter sentence than they should. The authorities often turned a blind eye on resurrection men, as the body snatchers were known, simply because they saw the benefits of providing the medical schools with fresh corpses. As far as the justice system was concerned, the desecration of the graves and autopsying of the recently deceased was a necessary evil if the medical profession were to make strides and save the lives of those who might otherwise perish

Those who could afford it buried their dead in iron coffins or took turns watching over the grave for at least a week after the burial, but Rhona Christie had clearly not taken any precautions, believing her child to be safe from her lover's scalpel. She had miscalculated both Ezra's decency and Alex Gray's willingness to be dissuaded from passing on such a golden opportunity.

Daniel tucked the signed paper and the fake exhumation order into his breast pocket and followed Jason out the door. He hoped Rhona Christie had not availed herself of the opportunity to escape, but even if she had, she couldn't have gone far. Her days of freedom were numbered.

Chapter 36

Rhona Christie was awaiting their pleasure in the interview room where her lover had been questioned only a few hours before. She sat still as a statue, her stare fixed on the tiny window, her hands clasped in her lap, and her shoulders rigid with tension. When Sergeant Meadows and Constable Napier had arrived at her home, she had been tending to her husband, blissfully unaware that Ezra Hall had been taken into custody that morning, not having spent the night with him.

"Good afternoon, Mrs. Christie," Daniel said as he and Jason took seats opposite her.

The woman inclined her head in acknowledgement but didn't reply.

"We'd like to talk to you about the murder of Alexandra Gray," Daniel continued.

"I don't know anything about it, Inspector," Rhona said, her voice steely.

"I think you do," Daniel countered. "In fact, I have rather a good idea what happened. Shall I tell you?"

"If you wish."

Daniel nodded. He didn't expect her to admit to anything at the start. She was a clever woman who would deny all culpability until the very last moment, but he was fairly sure he had her. The papers in his pocket would see to that.

"You were employed by the Ashford family before marrying Todd Christie. While there, you stole a key to the vault at the behest of your lover. He was involved in smuggling and fencing of stolen goods and used the vault as a hiding place for his loot. Quite possibly to hide the goods he'd stolen from his partners," Daniel added. "Once he thought it safe, he fenced the items and made a tidy little bundle for himself. You were comfortably off before the accident that robbed your husband of his vitality and wits."

Rhona Christie remained silent, so Daniel continued. "Forced to char for your neighbors once the money ran out, you became close with Ezra Hall, who talked to you of his studies and plans for the future. You gave him the key to the vault, since he needed a place to perform secret postmortems with his friend, Alex Gray, and you had no use for it now that your husband was incapacitated."

"Giving Ezra a key is not a crime," Rhona replied, roused out of her sulky silence by Daniel's narrative.

"Not in itself, but if the key is stolen and allows the new owner to trespass on private property, it is."

Rhona shrugged, as if that part had nothing to do with her. "Is that all you got?" she asked calmly. "If it is, then you may as well let me go. I didn't finish feeding Todd and he'll be hungry."

"I'm not quite finished," Daniel replied, impressed with her feigned indifference. She was as cool as a freshly picked cucumber. "Ezra Hall and Alex Gray had an arrangement with the Highgate Cemetery gravediggers. The Ludlows would dig up newly buried corpses and bring them to the vault for Ezra and Alex to dissect. The gravediggers would then rebury the corpses by morning, so no one ever suspected a thing, least of all the families of the deceased. Everyone got what they wanted. You got Ezra, Ezra and Alex got to practice their surgical skills, and the Ludlows made a handsome profit."

"Until Veronica died," Jason said softly.

At the mention of her daughter's name, Rhona's eyes filled with tears, but she remained silent, suppressing the outburst Daniel had hoped for. So he pressed on.

"You weren't bothered by the desecrations of the graves. What Ezra and Alex did had nothing to do with you. But then you learned that Veronica's body had been exhumed and a postmortem had been performed on your child."

Daniel took out the folded sheets of paper. "What I have here is a statement signed by Harry Ludlow that confirms that the Ludlows exhumed Veronica's body for the purpose of an illegal autopsy. I also have an exhumation order that would allow me to dig up Veronica's remains to serve as proof that a postmortem had been performed."

Rhona's eyes blazed with fury and unspeakable pain. "Don't you dare!" she screeched. "Don't you dare disturb her resting place again. Leave her be, you hear?"

"Then tell me what happened," Daniel pressed. He hated to admit it, but he felt sympathy for Rhona Christie. Any parent would under the circumstances.

"It was him. Alex Gray. Alexandra, or whatever her name was," she spat out. "Ezra wouldn't do it. He told me so. He understood what it would do to me, but he…she wouldn't be deterred. She wanted to know what killed my girl. To her, Veronica was nothing more than an intricate puzzle, a way to benefit and hone her skills, but to me, she was everything. She was my reason for being, my beautiful girl. I'd lost three babies before her. All dead at birth. I thought I'd never have a living child, and then Veronica came along, and everything changed. I changed," Rhona whispered.

"Veronica was the only person I ever truly loved, and then she was taken from me without any warning or explanation. One moment she was warm and alive and smiling at me, and then she was cold and stiff, her life snuffed out before it had even begun. Why?" Rhona cried. "Why was she taken from me? I'd done everything right. I'd taken such good care of her," she wailed, looking to Jason. "You're a doctor. Tell me why she died."

"I don't know, Mrs. Christie. She might have had a clot in her blood, or perhaps she had some congenital condition she'd been born with that you knew nothing about. I'm sure it was nothing you had done. She died knowing she was loved," Jason added, too kind not to try softening the truth.

"As if that makes any difference," Rhona cried. "I couldn't even protect her from the likes of Alex Gray. I should have slept at the cemetery next to her grave. I should have known," she howled.

Rhona's chest heaved with emotion, and she balled her hands into fists, wincing when her nails dug into her palms, but she likely needed to feel the pain in order to regain control. She drew in a shaky breath and went quiet, staring at the scarred wooden table before her.

"So, Alexandra performed the autopsy on Veronica by herself?" Jason asked.

Rhona nodded, then raised her eyes to meet Jason's gaze. "She butchered my child and stitched her back together. Like that Frankenstein monster Ezra told me about. Well, I couldn't let that go unavenged. If she was going to profit off my grief and mutilate my baby, she was going to get the same treatment."

"So you poisoned her?" Daniel asked.

Rhona Christie nodded. She had nothing left to lose, and it was clear she felt no remorse for what she'd done. Daniel couldn't say he blamed her. He'd feel a murderous rage if Felix's remains had been exhumed and desecrated. Or Sarah's, his mind added unhelpfully. At least neither was buried in London, where there was a brisk trade in dead bodies. They were safely sleeping in the graveyard at St. Catherine's in Birch Hill, Daniel reminded himself, and turned his attention back to the broken woman before him.

"How did you do it, Rhona?" Daniel asked softly. He wanted nothing less than a full confession.

"It wasn't hard," Rhona said. All the emotion had gone out of her voice, and now it was flat and even, her gaze fixed on something just beyond Daniel's right shoulder. She sighed and continued.

"Ezra often left notes for me on the kitchen table. They'd say, 'Come tonight' or 'Meet me this evening.' I kept them all. I knew he didn't love me or have any plans for a future together, but he was the only thing that kept me tethered to this world after Veronica died. He was the only person who held me close and made me feel like my life was still worth something. If not for him, I might have taken all of Todd's laudanum myself and ended it all."

Daniel ignored the kick to the gut he experienced at the mention of suicide by laudanum and nodded for Rhona to continue.

"I knew of their arrangement, had known all along, so I sent one of the notes written by Ezra to Alex Gray's lodgings, then sent another note to the Ludlows so they'd know to open the gate. They just pretend they can't read, you know," she said, giving Daniel a knowing look. She'd noticed the X in place of the signature. "They like to play dumb when it suits their purpose."

Daniel tried to hide his surprise. He wondered if Harry Ludlow would deny signing the statement, but then, it didn't really matter at this point. Rhona was talking, and Daniel was sure Ezra would as well, now that the truth was out in the open.

"Please, go on," Daniel said, realizing that Rhona had stopped speaking.

"I knew he'd…she'd come," she corrected herself. "And sure enough, there Alex was, waiting impatiently by the vault when I got there, ready to carve up someone else's loved one." Rhona grinned slyly. "I told her Ezra was running late and had sent me to tell her. I had the key I'd taken from Ezra, and we went in."

"Are you telling me that Ezra Hall wasn't privy to your plans?" Daniel asked.

"Ezra knew nothing. I slipped a few drops of laudanum into his wine at supper, so he slept through the night, and I was there when he woke." She smiled wryly. "Ezra is a decent man, Inspector. He would never intentionally hurt anyone. And he didn't want to hurt me. He'd argued bitterly with Alex Gray and thought he'd made his point, but she wouldn't listen. She'd gone behind his back and performed the postmortem anyway."

"How did you know that Alex Gray had performed an autopsy on Veronica?" Jason asked.

"I visit the grave every day. It wasn't difficult to see it had been disturbed, and the lilies had been tossed aside. The Ludlows never thought to put them back after they reburied the body. They were probably drunk," Rhona said with obvious disgust.

"What happened once you and Alexandra Gray entered the vault?" Daniel asked, fascinated with the woman's account. She had planned it all very carefully and would have got away with it had Ezra not mentioned that she'd worked for the Viscount of Ashford and had taken the key.

"I offered her a drink from my flask. It was chilly that night, and even colder inside the vault. She took it. She had no reason to suspect me, since she assumed I knew nothing of what she'd done. When she handed the flask back to me, I told her that she would pay with her life for disturbing Veronica and cutting her up like an animal carcass. Her eyes opened wide, and she looked terrified," Rhona said, obviously relishing the memory of her moment of triumph.

"She understood that I had just killed her. She opened her mouth to speak, but it was too late for conversation. She grabbed at her stomach. Her eyes were huge, pupils dilated, and she went all clammy and pale," Rhona said, now matter-of-fact. "I thought she'd be sick, and I'd have to clean up her puke, but she didn't have the time. I made sure there was enough wolfsbane in that brandy to fell a horse."

"So, she died almost instantly?" Jason asked.

"Unfortunately," Rhona replied. "I would have liked her to suffer a little bit longer, just to have the time to reflect on what she'd done and what it had cost her. But the poison acted quickly, and she just dropped like a sack of turnips."

"Where did you get the wolfsbane?"

"It's not hard to find if you know what you're looking for."

"And then you strung her up, knowing she'd be discovered the next day when the viscount would be laid to rest in the vault," Daniel concluded.

"I did. I knew a postmortem would be performed and she'd suffer the same fate as my girl. She'd go to her maker crudely sewn together, like Frankenstein's monster."

Daniel ignored Jason's hurt expression at the suggestion that his work was crude and focused on Rhona instead.

"It brought me peace to know that her last thoughts were of my Veronica and the sin she'd committed against her. And me."

Jason looked at Rhona Christie with ill-disguised pity. "You know you'll hang for this, Mrs. Christie," he said softly.

She lifted her chin defiantly and looked him in the eye. "What does it matter if I hang? Who'll care? My husband's as good as dead. My beloved child is gone. And Ezra was only using me to satisfy his lust without having to pay for a whore. I've got nothing left to live for, so I might as well die and lie next to the one I love. I only hope my own body won't be butchered in the same manner, but I suppose it would be cruel justice if it were."

"I'm sorry, Mrs. Christie," Daniel said. "What happened to your daughter was wrong. I wish you would have reported it to the authorities rather than taking measures into your own hands."

"And what would you have done, *Inspector*?" she asked, spitting out his title like a mouthful of bile. "You'd have arrested me for theft and let that fiend go free when she would have denied all knowledge. She duped you all and would have continued to do so. If she thought you'd arrest her, she'd have simply dropped her disguise, and Alex Gray would disappear until it was safe for him to come out again. Perhaps he'd show up in Edinburgh and use his credentials to get a position there," Rhona said bitterly. "She was too smart for the lot of you, but not for me. I got justice in the end."

"Rhona Christie, I hereby charge you with the murder of Alexandra Gray," Daniel said. "You will be taken to Newgate Prison, where you will await trial. I will send someone to collect your husband and bring him to the nearest hospital," Daniel promised.

Rhona gave him an incredulous look. There was nothing a hospital could do for Todd Christie, and he would most likely be turned away, the bed and resources needed for someone who was in need of urgent medical care rather than round-the-clock nursing. What Todd Christie needed was a private nurse, but since Rhona couldn't afford to pay for one, he wouldn't survive on his own for long.

"Don't worry about Todd, Inspector," Rhona said, a sad half smile forming on her lips. I knew how this might end when I saw them come for Ezra this morning. I took care of Todd. I would appreciate it if you would see him decently buried though. Or do you think I should donate his body to science?" Her tone was flippant, but Daniel could see the naked pain in her eyes. Rhona had suspected she wouldn't be coming back and had done her husband one last kindness, killing him quickly rather than leaving him to waste away as he lay dying in his own waste, since there was no one left to care for him.

"You have my word, Mrs. Christie," Daniel said. "Your husband will be buried next to Veronica."

There didn't seem to be anything left to say, so he stood and opened the door. Constable Napier was waiting patiently outside in the corridor. "Take Mrs. Christie down to the cells, Constable, and arrange for her to be transported to Newgate. And I'd like to see Mr. Hall, but after luncheon," Daniel added when his stomach growled loudly.

Daniel returned to the interview room and sank into the seat, suddenly very tired. "I feel sorry for her," he said. "I know she murdered Alexandra Gray in cold blood, but I can understand how she felt."

"So can I," Jason replied. "I'm a man of science, and I understand the value of studying the signs various diseases leave on the body, but I wouldn't want someone I love to be dissected in the middle of the night in a deserted cemetery. It would feel like a terrible violation."

"Now that she has confessed, she will hang for certain," Daniel replied. "Lucky for her, public executions have just been outlawed. At least she'll die in private, with dignity."

"I'm not sure that will make much difference to her," Jason replied. "Perhaps she would prefer to die publicly, to bring attention to what was done to her daughter, and by extension, to her as a mother. There must be a better way for students to learn."

"There won't be until people start donating their loved ones' remains to science," Daniel replied. "I can't see myself doing it. Can you?"

"As a surgeon, I can. As a husband and father, I can't fathom the thought," Jason admitted.

"You know, I haven't visited Sarah's grave," Daniel confessed. "I simply couldn't bring myself to imagine her lying there, beneath the earth, in that wooden box, but the idea of her body being desecrated fills me with rage, even though I know she can no longer feel anything."

Daniel pushed to his feet. "What do you say we get something to eat? Then I'm going to deal with Ezra Hall and inform the London Cemetery Company in person of what their employees have been up to. I bet the Ludlows had a nice sideline digging up corpses to sell. I doubt Hall and Gray were their only clients."

"You're probably right," Jason agreed. "It might be a good practice for medical schools to offer to buy corpses directly from the families. It would benefit both the loved ones of the deceased and the schools, but it would be a great expense that the schools wouldn't want to incur."

"Do you think many families would sell their dead?" Daniel asked, horrified by the prospect.

"I think if they were assured that the deceased would be treated with respect and then properly buried, they might. For those who are very poor, the money could go to pay for a headstone or other necessities. Besides, some individuals would relish the idea of promoting scientific discovery."

"Maybe in America," Daniel muttered. He couldn't see Godfearing English folk selling their dead, but although Jason's ideas were often radical, in his opinion, they had merit and might someday come to pass.

They left the interview room and then walked out into the balmy September afternoon, heading toward the nearest chophouse.

Chapter 37

Feeling pleasantly full after a plate of roast beef, potatoes, and peas, and two tankards of stout, Daniel returned to Scotland Yard to complete the day's business. Jason had gone home, and Daniel looked forward to going home as well. He felt unexpectedly drained and desperate to see Charlotte after learning of Veronica Christie's fate.

"Constable, please bring Ezra Hall to the interview room," Daniel said to Constable Napier, who'd come out to greet him.

Ezra Hall looked ashen when he was brought in, his eyes filled with the kind of fear Daniel saw in men who were condemned to die.

"I didn't know," he said as soon as he sat down across from Daniel. "I had no idea it was Rhona."

Daniel supposed their cells were close enough for Ezra Hall and Rhona Christie to have traded news of the day's events, but it didn't matter if Ezra knew what had transpired. Rhona's confession wouldn't mitigate his own crime.

"Mr. Hall, you might not be guilty of murder, a certainty you should thank Mrs. Christie for, since she made sure to absolve you in her statement, but you have still committed a crime. You have trespassed on private property, have paid to acquire illegally obtained corpses, and have performed postmortems without the express permission of the deceased's families. You will be sent to Newgate Prison along with Mrs. Christie, where you will await trial."

"What is the sentence for my crimes?" Ezra asked, looking desperate and terrified.

"Most likely you will have to pay a fine and possibly serve a custodial sentence, but I must warn you that your future as a surgeon is most likely at an end. I don't know what the regulations are regarding bodysnatching and performing illegal autopsies, but I highly doubt the RCS will keep you on or allow you to qualify now that you will have a criminal record."

Ezra's dark eyes filled with tears. "Inspector Haze, please, is there any other way I can atone for what I've done? Surgery is my life's work. Please, don't take that away from me."

Daniel sighed, exhausted by all the emotion he'd had to witness on this day. "You made a conscious decision, knowing what the consequences would be if you were discovered. I suggest you use your time in prison to figure out what you're going to do with the rest of your life. At least you will have a life, unlike Rhona Christie."

"Will she hang?" Ezra asked, realizing, possibly for the first time, the ramifications of what Rhona had done.

"Yes, Mr. Hall. She will hang."

Ezra hung his head and grabbed it with his hands, which were no longer cuffed. "Dear God," he whispered.

"Constable," Daniel called.

"Inspector, can I ask a favor of you?" Ezra asked as Constable Napier took him by the arm to escort him back to the cells.

"You can ask, but I don't know that I will be able to grant it."

"Please, can you make sure Rhona is buried next to Veronica? It will mean the world to her. I will gladly pay for the burial. I have some savings put by."

Daniel nodded. "I'll see what I can do, Mr. Hall."

Daniel watched as Constable Napier led Ezra Hall away. His life wasn't over, but by the time his ordeal was over, he'd be starting from scratch, with nothing to fall back on save the money he had left after paying for Rhona's burial.

It was a sad and unexpected end to several young lives, but Daniel didn't want to think about Alexandra Gray, Rhona Christie, or Ezra Hall anymore today. He'd report to John Ransome, then go home and spend what was left of the day with Charlotte. And Miss Grainger, he thought happily.

The visit to the London Cemetery Company would have to wait until tomorrow, as would a meeting with Edward Gray. Daniel briefly wondered if Edward would continue with his chosen profession or give it up now that he didn't have his sister to spur him on, but Edward's future had nothing to do with him.

Daniel left the interview room and headed down the corridor to John Ransome's office, ready to eat humble pie and inform Ransome that he'd been right about the exhumation order. At least he had two arrests to show for his pains. All in all, this had been a good day.

Epilogue

December 1868

Daniel handed Charlotte the shiny bauble and guided her tiny fingers toward the branch of the fir tree. She beamed with satisfaction as they strung the ornament onto the branch and stood back to admire it as it glowed in the light reflected from the drawing room gas lamps.

"Pretty," Charlotte said.

"It is beautiful," Miss Grainger agreed. "My parents never put up a tree for Christmas when I was growing up. My father said it was a pagan ritual."

"All traditions come from somewhere," Daniel replied. "Sarah's father used to buy her a new ornament every year. Most of these were purchased by him," he added, glancing toward the still-full box.

"Will you continue the tradition with Charlotte?" Miss Grainger asked.

"I hadn't considered it, but I think I will," Daniel replied. "What do you say you and I go and buy a new bauble today, Charlotte?"

The little girl's eyes lit up, and she nodded vigorously. "Angel," she said. "I want an angel."

"All right. We will buy a beautiful angel," Daniel promised. "You can pick it out yourself."

He was just about to suggest taking a walk afterward when there was a loud knock on the door. Miss Grainger reached out and took Charlotte from Daniel.

"Something tells me we won't be shopping for Christmas ornaments today," she said with a wistful smile.

"Something tells me you're right," Daniel replied as Grace escorted Constable Collins into the drawing room.

"I'm sorry to bother you at home, sir, but you're needed." He stole a peek at Miss Grainger and lowered his voice, perhaps in the hope that she was hard of hearing. "A body's been found. Stabbed through with a pitchfork. The prongs went all the way to the other side, guv. Pinned the poor sod to the wall."

"Is he a farmer, then?" Daniel asked as he turned toward the door, wishing fervently that he could have spent the day with Charlotte and Miss Grainger instead of looking at a dead body. And why was he being summoned if the murder had taken place on a farm? Anything outside of London wasn't his jurisdiction. Whoever had found the victim should have summoned the local constable.

"No, sir. It's the Earl of Granville. Killed at his country pile in Sussex."

"Sussex?" Daniel echoed, incredulous. "Why on earth is the case not being handled by the Brighton Borough Police then? Sussex is their patch, after all."

"Personal friend of Her Majesty, or so I've heard," Constable Collins said, puffing out his chest with importance, as if the victim's association with the queen somehow reflected on him. "The Palace will want this investigated by Scotland Yard."

"Indeed?" Daniel said irritably.

He could see Charlotte's little face out of the corner of his eye, her lips quivering as she tried to hold back tears of disappointment. Miss Grainger followed the direction of his gaze and scooped Charlotte up, whisking her from the room before more gory details of the murder were revealed. Daniel heard the child's wail of protest as he returned his attention to the constable.

"And was the earl stabbed with a pitchfork *inside* the house?" Daniel asked, incredulous that such a thing could happen to a personal friend of the queen.

"No, sir. He was found in the stables by one of the grooms."

Daniel sighed and headed for the door. There was no way around this. He'd have to go to Sussex. Today.

"Has Jason Redmond been informed?" Daniel asked as he accepted his coat, hat, and gloves from Grace, who rightly assumed that the arrival of a constable on their doorstep meant that her employer would be going out.

"Constable Napier went to fetch him, sir. With any luck, they'll meet us there."

"And the police photographer?"

"On his way, although I expect there'll be a gag order on this one, the victim being such an important personage."

"We still require photographs of the crime scene," Daniel said irritably as he followed Constable Collins to the police wagon.

"Not my decision, sir. I've been tasked with getting your good self there, and that's what I mean to do," Constable Collins said as he climbed up onto the bench and waited for Daniel to take a seat next to him. Daniel sighed and huddled deeper into his coat. This was going to be a long and frigid ride.

"Let's go, then, Constable. The earl awaits."

The End

Please turn the page after the Notes for an excerpt from

Murder in the Mews

A Redmond and Haze Mystery Book 10

Notes

I hope you've enjoyed this installment of the Redmond and Haze mysteries and will check out future books. Reviews on Amazon and Goodreads are much appreciated.

I'd love to hear your thoughts and suggestions. I can be found at

irina.shapiro@yahoo.com, www.irinashapiroauthor.com,

or https://www.facebook.com/IrinaShapiro2/.

If you would like to join my Victorian mysteries mailing list, please use this link.

https://landing.mailerlite.com/webforms/landing/u9d9o2

An Excerpt from Murder in the Mews,

A Redmond and Haze Mystery Book 10

Prologue

Thomas Grady left by the servants' entrance and headed toward the stable block, his breath escaping in great vaporous puffs as he hurried across the snow-covered yard. It was still pitch-dark, sunrise two hours off, and colder than a witch's tit, the moon hovering above the dark outline of the trees as if it were the middle of the night. *To some people, it may as well be*, Thomas thought angrily. The family would remain abed for hours yet, warm and snug under their eiderdowns, with fires blazing through the long hours of darkness to keep them comfortable, a far cry from his freezing room in the attics. He might have snatched another half hour of sleep had the earl not entrusted him with the well-being of the new filly.

The Arabian was as skittish as a teetotaling virgin and about as likely to show him any affection. That damn horse had cost more than Thomas would earn in a lifetime, but such was life. Some were born to inherit great wealth, others to shovel shit until they either retired from a life of service with a little something put by or wound up in a workhouse, where the only thing they had left to look forward to was the tender embrace of the pauper's grave.

Thomas's boots left deep footprints in the fresh snow, and the cold seeped through the worn soles, reminding him that he'd have no choice but to spend his wages on a new pair. He peered at the low brick building, suddenly noticing that the door was not only unlatched but partially open. His heart sank. The earl would have his guts for garters if the Arabian had escaped.

Thomas rushed toward the stable and burst through the door, his gaze leaping to the Arabian's stall. The horse was there, as were the grays, but their restless snuffling, along with the awful smell emanating from the other side of the building, immediately put Thomas on his guard as he looked around for the source of the stench. He cried out in horror when he spotted the earl, the man's ashen face illuminated by the feeble moonlight streaming through the narrow window set high in the wall.

Thomas edged closer until he could see around the partition. It was clear the earl was dead. His head had lolled to the side, and his torso was caked with dried blood, a pitchfork sticking out of his belly as if he were a Sunday roast. The straw-covered floor was smeared with congealed blood. The earl's gaze appeared to shift, and Thomas rushed forward, thinking the man might still be alive. But as he drew closer, he realized that the man's eyeballs were shiny with frost, the ice simply reflecting the silvery moonlight.

Heaving with fear and disgust, his mouth filling with bile and his empty stomach threatening to turn itself inside out, Thomas erupted out of the stables and ran back the way he'd come, puffing like a locomotive as he exploded into the warm servants' hall and sprinted toward the butler's pantry.

"What's the matter with you, boy?" Mr. Simonds exclaimed, ready to subject Thomas to a tongue-lashing, but Thomas was in no mood for the well-deserved reprimand.

"It's his lordship," he cried, tears running down his chilled cheeks. "He's been murdered."

Chapter 1

Wednesday, December 23, 1868

The morning was bitterly cold, the ground covered with a thin layer of snow that crunched beneath the wheels of the carriage. Jason Redmond stared out the window, enjoying the drive despite the macabre reason for this foray into Surrey. The frosty fields sparkled in the weak winter sunshine, and the bare branches formed an intricate latticework against the pale blue sky, the crows that dotted the landscape like charcoal smudges on a nearly finished canvas. They'd passed several neat cottages, ribbons of smoke curling from stone chimneys and the lowing of cows in the barn carrying on the wind.

As Jason surveyed the peaceful scene, he wondered why it was that people never got tired of killing each other. Surely most grievances that led to murder were not that serious, the sort of conflicts that could be peacefully resolved should the injured party consider diplomacy rather than violence. The more pressing question, however, was why he'd been summoned to a sleepy village that lay more than twenty-five miles from London. According to Constable Napier, who'd been dozing for the past half hour, his helmet in his lap and his head resting against the side of the carriage, Surrey had its own police service that was headed by a well-respected and experienced chief constable and was based in Guilford, but surely there was a parish constable who could have taken charge until reinforcements arrived.

The answer to Jason's question materialized a short while later as the peaked roof of Langley Hall came into view. The palatial house sat proudly amid acres of lawn and parkland and could be accessed only via the mile-long lane, which culminated in a circular driveway that wound its way around a marble fountain worthy of a Roman piazza. Built in the Palladian style, the house boasted a triangular portico supported by six massive columns that was reminiscent of an ancient temple. Romanesque statues gazed down their prominent noses from the roof, and massive urns flanked the steps that led to the front door. The victim was too wealthy and influential for the handling of his killing to be left to the local police.

The splendor of the house and grounds made the method of the murder seem incongruous. What sort of individual skewered the lord of the manor with a pitchfork, and what had tipped him or her over the edge? Jason could conceive of a few reasons someone would resort to such savagery, but now wasn't the time to analyze the mindset of the killer. A boxy police wagon, a blight on an otherwise picture-perfect scene, was parked at the top of the drive, awaiting the victim's earthly remains, which Jason was here to examine.

Jason grabbed the medical bag he'd brought just in case, thanked Joe for getting him to his destination without getting lost, and alighted from the carriage, followed by the bleary-eyed constable. Joe would seek shelter from the cold in the servants' hall until it was time to leave, and Jason hoped they'd be gracious to an outsider.

"Good morning, my lord," Constable Collins called out as he came around the side of the house. "This way, if you please."

"Good morning, Constable," Jason said. "Is Inspector Haze here?"

"Indeed, he is, sir. Just getting acquainted with the dead cove," the constable answered flippantly.

Jason didn't approve of making jokes at the expense of the deceased, but everyone dealt with violent death differently, and some people, especially someone as young as the constable, needed a way to come to terms with the carnage they so often faced.

Jason's boots crunched on the snow as he followed the constable to the stable block located a good way behind the stately mansion. He wished he'd have listened to Katie and worn woolen socks. His feet were growing numb with cold. Jason hunched his shoulders against a sudden gust of wind and grabbed his top hat, which was about to fly off his head.

"It's a cold one," Constable Collins observed as they trudged toward the stables, Constable Napier lagging a few steps behind in order to right the helmet that slid into his eyes with every blast of wind. Jason couldn't conceive of less practical headgear for policemen, who often had to run to apprehend a suspect, but kept that opinion to himself.

"Have you seen the victim?" he asked instead.

"Oh, aye," the young constable replied. "It's not a pretty sight."

"It rarely is."

Jason couldn't help but smile as Inspector Daniel Haze emerged from the stables, his cheeks ruddy with cold and his glasses reflecting the ray of sunshine that broke through the clouds and illuminated Daniel in a heavenly halo. He wore his usual bowler hat, but today, he sported a red and green tartan muffler, which Jason could just bet was a birthday present from a certain someone they never discussed openly.

"Jason," Daniel said, his pleasure at seeing Jason obvious. "Thank you for coming. I do hope the superintendent's message didn't interfere with your hospital commitments."

Jason had been volunteering at St. George's Hospital since moving to London in the spring, but although he had been repeatedly asked to join the staff full-time and had been offered a wage due an experienced surgeon, he preferred to both operate and teach on a volunteer basis, a decision that allowed him to determine which patients he chose to help and which surgeries he was willing to open to the medical students. He liked the flexibility of the arrangement and the satisfaction of being able to help those in need without the suffocating restrictions of the bureaucracy that dominated every medical institution. He often took on cases other surgeons elected to pass on, deeming the effort either futile, since the chances of survival were minimal, or unnecessary.

"I had an operation scheduled for this afternoon, but Mr. Harris was kind enough to offer to perform the procedure in my stead," Jason replied.

Daniel's brows furrowed and his nose wrinkled with obvious disgust. "Is he not the one who walks around in a soiled apron and adds a notch to the handle of his blood-spattered saw for every limb he amputates?"

"He is," Jason replied curtly.

Jason was forever advocating the benefits of cleaning the surgical instruments and washing hands before and after an operation but most of his British counterparts either laughed at him outright or attributed his eccentricity to being American and simply ignored him. They believed the key to survival was the timing of the surgery rather than the method. It was said that certain surgeons could amputate a limb in as little as thirty seconds, hacking through the bone as if it were a hunk of firewood.

Jason supposed speed was imperative in situations where the unfortunate patient was conscious, but with the use of ether, the operating surgeon could afford to take his time and try to minimize the damage to the remainder of the limb as well as the possibility of infection.

"I expect the operating theater will be full," Jason mused. "The students admire Mr. Harris's decisiveness and strive to copy his technique. They don't much care if postoperative infection kills half his patients."

"Surely, who lives and who dies is not entirely up to the surgeon," Daniel said. "Unless the individual dies by suicide, the outcome is determined by divine will."

"I'm not so sure about that," Jason replied bitterly. In his opinion, the most basic of hygienic practices would go a long way toward saving more patients, but no one at St. George's paid much attention to his opinion on the subject.

Daniel seemed poised to disagree but changed his mind, since this was neither the time nor the place to engage in a discussion on the role of science versus the will of God, when a fresh corpse awaited their attention.

"Let's see our man," Jason said.

Daniel led Jason into the stables and toward the back. Several horses, one of them a snowy white beauty, occupied the stalls on the right side, their restlessness and loud snorting evidence of their distress. The sooner the victim was removed, the better for the poor animals that were clearly agitated by the comings and goings and the reek of the blood that accosted Jason's senses the moment he entered the building.

Despite the brightness of the day, the interior was dim, which explained the oil lamps strategically positioned to illuminate the crime scene.

Jason let out a low whistle when he saw the body slouched against the wooden partition separating two stalls. The tines of the pitchfork had been driven in so deep as to securely affix the victim to the wood. The man had to be nearing forty and had shaggy dark-blond hair and a long, thin face that was frozen in the serene expression of a Biblical saint. Saint Sebastian, who'd been tied to a post and shot with arrows, sprang to mind, but this was no Bible lesson, this man no Christian martyr.

Setting down his Gladstone bag on a bale of straw, Jason approached the victim and studied him closely, noting the thin layer of frost on his skin and the blood on his clothing and hands. He must have touched his perforated abdomen either in shock or in an effort to free himself, perhaps believing there was still a chance of survival.

"Has the victim been positively identified?" Jason asked.

"Yes. This is Damian Langley, the Earl of Granville, close friend and advisor to Her Majesty the Queen." Daniel looked so tense as he made this pronouncement, if his spine grew any stiffer,

Jason thought it just might crack. "There's much at stake, Jason," Daniel added.

"I understand. Has Mr. Gillespie taken photographs of the crime scene?"

Daniel shook his head. "He hasn't been sent for. Superintendent Ransome wants this one kept quiet until we know more of what happened here."

"To have a photographic record of the crime scene would have been helpful," Jason replied.

"I agree, but I can't go against Ransome on this."

Jason nodded, then turned to the two constables hovering in the doorway. "You may take him down."

Worried the constables might inflict postmortem injuries that would cloud the results of the autopsy, Jason grabbed onto the pitchfork and pulled, extracting the murder weapon from the body. The mortal remains of the earl, now freed from the partition, slid sideways, falling onto the bloodstained straw at their feet.

"Take this too," Jason told Constable Napier as he handed him the pitchfork.

"Can you perform the postmortem right away?" Daniel asked. He stepped aside to allow the constables to lift the body onto a canvas stretcher, then placed the bloodied pitchfork atop the corpse, lest the constables forget to take it.

Jason shook his head. "He needs to thaw."

"Are you suggesting—" Daniel sputtered.

"The corpse is partially frozen," Jason replied.

"How long will he take to defrost? The countess is beside herself, and Ransome will be breathing down my neck like an enraged bull as soon as I return to the Yard, demanding answers I don't have."

"I understand that, but I can hardly perform an autopsy on frost-hardened remains, and the body is not likely to thaw on the way. It's too cold. I suggest we interview the countess and the staff, then find an establishment where we can get something to eat. By the time we return to London, the earl should be ready, if the body is kept upstairs in one of the warmer parts of the building," Jason said as he reached for his bag. "Oh, and please instruct the constables not to leave the earl too near the hearth," he added, worried the constables might think that slowly roasting the corpse might speed up the process.

"Yes, of course," Daniel said, nodding in agreement. "I've already taken a statement from the groom who found the body."

"What did he say?"

"Nothing that can be of any use in finding the killer. Tom Grady arrived at the stables well before dawn, as usual, to check on the horses. His lordship was very fond of his grays, apparently, and the white horse is a new acquisition, a Christmas gift for his daughter. The groom came upon his employer, correctly assumed that he was beyond earthly help, and ran back to the house to inform the butler, Mr. Simonds. The butler had the presence of mind to dispatch a rider to Scotland Yard once he ascertained there was no need to summon the family physician and to keep the matter quiet in order to prevent gawkers from contaminating the crime scene."

"Clever man," Jason said as they saw off the earl's remains and headed toward the grandiose entrance Jason had passed earlier.

"He is that," Daniel agreed. "Ex-military. Seems he and the earl go back a long way."

"Have you interviewed him?"

"Very briefly. I thought it was more important to keep the murder scene intact until you arrived."

"And the family?"

"Safely indoors."

"Were there any footprints when you arrived?" Jason asked.

"Yes, but they belong to the two people who were first on the scene, Grady and Simonds. Grady is certain he did not see any footprints in the freshly fallen snow."

"Which means the earl was murdered before it began to snow," Jason mused. "That's good to know, since it will be difficult to determine the exact time of death. What time did the groom leave the stables last night?"

"Six. He went up to the house to clean up for supper and then headed to bed around ten."

"Is there just the one groom?" Jason asked. In a house this size, he'd expect an army of employees.

"No, but the second man wasn't needed and left an hour before, since he'd been feeling unwell. The earl and his family only came to the house for the Christmas holiday and were due to leave after Boxing Day. They did not bring the entire staff, only the individuals they needed for the duration. The Langleys reside in Park Lane for most of the year."

"Will you permit them to leave if they wish?" Jason asked.

"I don't see any reason to keep them here, and it will make it easier for us to investigate from a geographical perspective."

"Yes, I agree."

"Jason, would you say he died quickly?" Daniel inquired as he used the ornate knocker to announce their presence.

"I hope so," Jason said. "For his sake."

In truth, given the amount of blood on the victim's hands and the floor, Jason thought the earl had remained conscious long enough to experience not only great pain but terrible fear as the realization that he was about to die dawned on him. He may have suffered for as long as an hour before passing out due to blood loss, but Jason didn't want to commit to any answers before he had a chance to open up the body and base his suppositions on scientific evidence rather than guesswork. He unwittingly squared his shoulders as the bolt was drawn back and the door opened. A new investigation was about to begin in earnest.

Chapter 2

Simonds had to be in his late forties or early fifties. His hair, which was snow-white and contrasted sharply with his deeply tanned skin, made his exact age difficult to gauge. He had a wary dark gaze and a posture so erect, he might have had a length of rail track for a spine. His suit was neatly pressed, and his shoes shone with polish. Whether the death of his master had rattled him was impossible to tell, since on the outside, he was a pillar of decorum.

"Mr. Simonds, this is my associate, Lord Redmond. We would like to speak to the countess," Daniel announced as they surrendered their things to a maidservant hovering nearby.

"I'm afraid that's impossible," Simonds replied. "Her ladyship had suffered a nervous collapse on hearing that her husband is dead. The housekeeper, Mrs. Pike, administered smelling salts and then we helped her ladyship to her bed."

"I see," Daniel said. "Then we shall start with you, Mr. Simonds."

"Very well, Inspector. We can speak in the butler's pantry, if you have no objection."

"Are any other members of the family at home?" Jason asked.

"Only the children."

"And how old are the children?" Daniel asked.

"Lord Robert is eleven, and Lady Viola is sixteen."

"Have they been informed of their father's death?" Jason asked, hoping the children were not in shock.

"Not yet. We thought it best to wait until we had more information."

"Will they not ask after their father?" Daniel inquired as they followed the butler through the green baize door into the servants' domain.

"They don't expect him back for several days, so no."

"Where do they think he is?" Daniel asked once they were seated in the cane chairs that faced the butler's desk. Simonds took his place, his expression that of a schoolmaster facing his pupils.

"His lordship left early Monday morning to visit his aunt in Hastings. She's quite elderly, and he pays her a visit once a month. He was expected back tomorrow," Simonds added. "In time for Christmas Eve dinner."

"Did anyone know the earl had returned early?" Jason asked.

"No. He did not come to the house, nor is his brougham here."

"But the horses are," Daniel pointed out. "We saw them in the stables."

"The family had arrived in two separate conveyances, Inspector. His lordship took the grays to Hastings, as was his habit."

"And the family was meant to return to London after Boxing Day?" Daniel asked.

"They were. The countess detests the country and wished to return as soon as possible.

Daniel nodded and flipped his notebook open to a clean page. He imagined that after the brutal death of her husband she wouldn't be too fond of Christmas either. Christmas had certainly lost its magic after the death of Sarah, but now wasn't the time to dwell on his personal feelings. "Mr. Simonds, did the earl have any enemies that you know of?" Daniel asked instead.

"I wouldn't know, sir," Mr. Simonds replied. "He never discussed his private business with me."

"It was my impression that you served together," Jason said, recalling Daniel's earlier comment.

"We did. Saw action during the Indian Rebellion of fifty-seven. I was his lordship's batman until he sold his commission in fifty-nine."

Jason wasn't sure what a batman's role was, but it didn't sound an enviable position based on the title alone.

"You must have grown close," Daniel said, shifting his bulk in the flimsy chair and making it squeak in protest.

"Hardly," Simonds replied. "But the earl saw fit to reward me for my service."

"There must be a reason for such loyalty," Jason interjected.

Simonds's expression turned bashful. "It was my honor to assist his lordship in his greatest hour of need."

"Meaning?" Daniel demanded.

"I saved his life," Simonds said, his gaze sliding away in obvious embarrassment. "I carried him to safety when a shed used for storing munitions was blown up while he was inside. The injury I suffered eventually led to my discharge from the army."

"Was the earl injured?" Jason asked.

"His lordship had suffered a head wound and minor burns when he was thrown by the blast."

"And you?"

"I suffered burns to my back and arms," Simonds replied quietly. "Spent months in hospital."

Daniel jotted that down and looked back up, evidently ready to move on to an alternative line of questioning. "Were the earl and his wife happily married?"

"Are you suggesting that the countess did that to him?" the butler asked, his shapely brows lifting in astonishment.

"Not personally, but perhaps there was an interested party," Daniel suggested.

"You mean a jealous lover?"

"I do."

"I can assure you there isn't."

"How can you be so certain?" Jason asked.

"Her ladyship is—was a devoted wife. You won't find anyone who'll tell you different."

Daniel nodded. "I'd like to speak to the countess's lady's maid. May we interview her in here?"

"Of course. I will send Adams in."

Simonds hoisted himself to his feet, his distaste for Daniel's line of questioning blatant in the pursing of his lips and the angry sidelong glance the butler directed at him as he left the room.

"You think the earl was killed by a jealous lover?" Jason asked once they were alone.

"I think it was a crime of passion," Daniel replied. "Whoever killed the earl did so on the spur of the moment, with whatever he had to hand. The brutality of the attack speaks of murderous fury."

"I agree with you there," Jason remarked. "This was not planned, unless the murderer wanted it to look like a spontaneous attack."

"Could this have been done by a woman, do you think?"

"It would have taken a great deal of strength to drive the pitchfork so far in as to nail the victim to the wall. I suppose a strong, angry woman might have managed it, but just now, I'm leaning toward a male killer."

"As am I," Daniel agreed.

They paused in their speculation when a young woman of about twenty-five entered the room. She had shiny chestnut hair, parted in the middle and tightly pulled back beneath a lace cap, and a hazel gaze that passed over the two men before she lowered her gaze.

"I'm her ladyship's lady's maid," she announced.

"Have a seat, Miss Adams."

The maid looked utterly scandalized at taking the butler's seat, so Daniel moved behind the desk, offering her the guest chair.

"What is your full name?" he asked.

"Leanne Adams, sir."

"And how long have you been with the countess?"

"These three years, sir."

"Where were you employed before?"

"With Lady Benton, sir. She had me trained up as a lady's maid. She passed," Miss Adams added.

"When was the last time you saw the earl?"

"Just before he left for Hastings, sir. He came in to say goodbye to her ladyship. I was in the room."

"Did your mistress ever complain about her husband to you?" Upon seeing the maid's closed expression, Daniel hastened to warn, "If you lie to me, you can be charged with obstructing an investigation. Anything you tell me will be kept in confidence," he promised, understanding only too well that the young woman would be in fear of losing her position if she revealed anything unflattering about her mistress.

"No, sir. Their lordships were devoted to each other. A well-suited couple if ever I saw one."

"Did your mistress keep secrets from her husband?"

"What sort of secrets, Inspector?"

"Did she perhaps have an admirer?" Daniel clarified.

"She was admired by many, but not in the way you're suggesting."

Daniel turned to Jason, silently encouraging him to ask his own questions, since he seemed to have exhausted his own line of inquiry.

"Miss Adams, did the earl and his wife engage in marital relations regularly?" Jason asked.

Adams colored and averted her gaze. "Yes, sir. His lordship came to my lady's bedroom twice a week."

"And did the countess welcome his visits?"

"Why, yes, sir. She was hoping for another child."

"Did she tell you that?"

"She did. She would have liked to have another son."

"A spare?" Jason asked.

The maid nodded. "Lord Robert is hale, but things happen, don't they?"

"Indeed, they do," Daniel agreed. "Lord Robert is now an eleven-year-old earl."

Miss Adams looked momentarily shocked, as though she hadn't realized the boy had inherited the earldom the moment his father breathed his last, although as the son of an earl he probably held a courtesy title. "The poor mite," Miss Adams muttered. "What a responsibility to care for his mother and sister at such a young age."

"Did the earl have any siblings?" Jason asked. "Perhaps someone who can guide Lord Robert until he's of age."

"No, sir. His lordship was an only child." Miss Adams leveled a questioning look at Daniel, clearly hoping to be excused. "I need to check on my mistress, sir," she said when Daniel failed to dismiss her. "May I go?"

"Yes. Please send down the earl's valet."

"He's not here, sir. He'd gone off with his lordship."

Daniel nodded. "You may go, Miss Adams. Please send for me if you think of anything pertinent."

"I will, sir."

"It seems that neither the coachman nor the valet have returned. Might they have had a hand in the murder?" Daniel asked, his expression thoughtful.

"I think we need to discover where they are in order to answer that," Jason replied.

"I think that's me off to Hastings tomorrow," Daniel said as he heaved himself to his feet. "Perhaps they're still at the aunt's house. I'll get the address from Simonds."

Mr. Simonds seemed to have forgotten his earlier pique when they found him in the servants' hall, enjoying a cup of tea. Jason's coachman, Joe Marin, silently sipped his own brew, an empty plate before him.

"Mr. Simonds, I will need the name and address for the earl's aunt. And is there a place near here where we can get coffee or a spot of lunch before we head back to London?" Daniel inquired. He'd obviously noted the time on the clock mounted on the wall.

"I will write down the address for you," the butler said as he pushed to his feet. "Cook will be happy to make you coffee and sandwiches," he offered.

"That would be most kind," Jason replied.

"I will have the refreshments sent to the drawing room," Simonds announced, glancing toward Jason surreptitiously. He was probably still trying to figure out Jason's role in the investigation and how his American accent tied in with a British title, but being a well-trained butler, he knew that to offer him refreshments in the servants' hall would not reflect well on the family.

"There's really no need. We'll take our coffee right here, if that's all right, and then we'll be on our way," Jason said, not wishing to waste time repairing to the other side of the house and waiting for the refreshments to be brought when the servants' hall was a stone's throw from the kitchen. Daniel seemed taken aback by Jason's response but didn't bother to argue.

Jason didn't usually eat before performing a postmortem, but if he didn't have lunch, he would suffer a dip in his blood sugar levels and experience a bout of dizziness and weakness. Despite all the recent medical advancements, there was no cure or treatment for hypoglycemia, so Jason had been compelled to figure out for himself how to manage the condition. He found that eating at regular intervals, partaking of a protein with every meal, and monitoring his sugar intake helped to manage the episodes.

"May we return to London tomorrow, if that is her ladyship's wish?" Mr. Simonds asked once he'd instructed one of the kitchen maids to ask Cook for coffee and sandwiches.

"You may," Daniel replied. "Please notify me as soon as you arrive. I will no doubt have more questions, and I intend to speak to the countess as soon as she feels up to it."

Simonds left to write down the address, and Joe sprang to his feet. "I'll fetch the carriage round, shall I?" he muttered, and headed for the door without waiting for an answer.

Jason and Daniel settled at the long oak table, mindful that they'd have to finish before the staff came down for their midday meal. Jason inhaled deeply as the smell of freshly brewed coffee wafted from the kitchen, followed by a maid with a silver pot and a plate of sandwiches. She made sure they had everything they needed before leaving them on their own, but as if by silent agreement, neither man mentioned the case, instead speaking of trivialities and gauging what time they would arrive back in London if the weather held.

Since the constables had taken the body and the police wagon, Daniel would travel back to London with Jason, which would give them an opportunity to speak privately. There was nothing more to learn at Langley Hall just then, and a partially thawed corpse awaited them in London.

Chapter 3

By the time they returned to London, Jason concluded that the earl, who'd been left to thaw in the middle of a back corridor, was as ready as he'd ever be, and asked for the body to be moved to the mortuary so that he could begin the postmortem. He hoped to finish by six o'clock, which would give him enough time to get home, clean up, and dress for dinner. Katherine had invited a new acquaintance and her husband to dine and would be upset if Jason failed to join them. Jason wasn't really in the mood to socialize, given the day's events, but Katherine so rarely asked anything of him, he wouldn't want to disappoint her or put her in an awkward position.

Jason removed his coat and hat, tossed his scarf and gloves onto a small table next to his medical bag, then donned a leather apron and the linen cap he used to keep the hair out of his face while working. Once ready, he fixed his attention on the victim, whose skin was still icy to the touch and unpleasantly damp. Jason began by checking the man's pockets, which yielded a few coins, a train schedule, an inexpensive watch, which was scratched and dented, and a hardboiled sweet. An odd assortment of items, but he supposed there was no accounting for what people stuffed in their pockets. Once all the items had been examined and placed in a cardboard box, Jason began to undress the corpse.

Much like the contents of the pockets, the garments didn't fit with what he knew of the man, which was that he was not only wealthy but highly influential and widely respected. Jason had seen a photograph of the earl in *The Times* several months ago, the man meticulous in his appearance—his clothes immaculate, his face cleanly shaven, and his hair neatly trimmed and gleaming with oil. The clothing he wore at present was inexpensive, the workmanship second-rate. The shoes were scuffed, the soles nearly worn through, and the earl's cravat was yellowed from repeated washing and threadbare with age. The shirt was neither very clean nor starched. Constable Napier had brought the earl's coat and hat, which were also rather shabby, but there was no walking stick or gloves, items that the earl would be sure to carry.

Jason carefully folded the clothes and set them aside, then took some time to examine the body's exterior before commencing with the postmortem. The man's skin was pallid. Not surprising in the winter months, but the earl looked borderline malnourished, his ribs clearly visible and his hip bones jutting out from a narrow waist. The nails were bitten to the quick, and his hair was greasy and lank, his lean cheeks coated with thick stubble a shade darker than the follicles on his head.

Whatever the earl had been up to the last few days, he hadn't been living in luxury, and given his unkept state and clothes, he might have been mistaken for a tramp. Jason's gaze slid toward the man's belly. There were three distinct holes where the pitchfork had entered the body and bruising where the base of the implement had met the skin. The earl's lower stomach and pelvic area were covered in blood as well as a yellowish-brown substance that smelled strongly of excrement. Since there hadn't been a great deal of blood at the scene, Jason concluded that most of the bleeding was internal. The gastrointestinal tract had been perforated, the contents leaking into the abdominal cavity and oozing from the wounds. Turning the earl over, Jason fixed his attention on the exit wounds. As with the stomach, there was some bleeding, but it hadn't been significant.

Jason rolled the body onto its back and reached for a scalpel, making a Y-shaped incision in the earl's chest. Three hours later, he tied off the thread he'd used to close up the corpse and pulled a sheet over the dead man, ready to make his report to Daniel and Superintendent Ransome, who'd wish to be present.

Printed in Great Britain
by Amazon